BLACK SHUCK

THE DEVIL'S DOG

Piers Warren is a wildlife film-maker and author living in rural Norfolk. He has walked the African plains with Maasai Warriors, tracked tigers in India on elephant-back, explored the Amazon rainforest, swum with sharks, trekked across Tanzanian deserts on a camel and filmed cheetahs hunting in Kenya. But his favourite place is the North Norfolk coast, where he spends his time capturing the flora and fauna on film … and looking for pawprints in the sand.

BLACK SHUCK
THE DEVIL'S DOG

Piers Warren

Published by

Wildeye
United Kingdom

Email: info@wildeye.co.uk
Websites: www.black-shuck.co.uk
www.wildeye.co.uk/publishing

First published 2011

ISBN 978-1-905843-01-5

Many thanks to:
Roland Clare for copy-editing
Ben Waddams for cover artwork (www.waddams.webs.com)
Joan Deitch, Helen Franklin, Leanne Thomas and
especially Tania Cheslaw (www.in-scribe.co.uk)
for advice throughout

The tempest is coming
To end all we know
We must batten down hatches
And reap what we sow.
A terror filled scream
Then He takes flight
But will he appear to you
This moonless night?
Pray that he won't
That Mad Shuck will abate
Because Lucifer's his master
And they're both filled with hate.
Heed well these words
I caution you please
Because He is after me
Will drag me to my knees.
I doubted his existence
I cursed what they did say
But now old Shuck
is making me pay.

Anon. 165

PROLOGUE

Thomas Grimes cursed and spat as the salt spray lashed his face yet again. Laden with linen from Flanders, he was starting to doubt if his boat would make it home this time. Truth be told, there was far too much on board that night, but Thomas was a greedy sort, and ditching some of his valuable cargo would be a last resort. In 1553, the year before, Thomas had sunk his small wooden vessel on a similar trip, but then he had been close enough to swim for shore, and had been lucky to recover his boat the next day. It had been found, washed up near the busy port of Blakeney, with surprisingly little damage.

But tonight the storm was altogether more ferocious. He knew he was not far from the Norfolk coast but he could see no lamps through the rain and spray. His dog, lying in the hull of the boat on a bale of linen, whined and shook and looked nervously into his master's eyes. He, too, knew this was no ordinary passage. Thomas was never seen without his hound by his side, on land or water. A dangerous looking beast with a thick, black, shaggy coat and hunched shoulders, he provided perfect protection for the cargo while Thomas bartered with tradesmen. The dog could be mighty fierce when called for, but, like all curs, was completely devoted to his master.

The boat caught a wave head-on and both dog and master were drenched. With water accumulating in the hull, the boat was now sitting lower in the sea and more waves washed over them. Thomas cursed again and strained to see anything: any sign of hope. He thought he saw a glimmer of a light in the distance and heaved the tiller over, only to have another wave crash over the side. It was no good, he would have to ditch some cargo. Swearing furiously at the God that sent such weather, he heaved a bale over the side, but, as he did so, the swell tipped the boat sharply and Thomas slipped over the side after it. The dog leapt to his feet barking in alarm. But Thomas was hanging on to the gunwale and, with great difficulty, managed to haul himself back in the boat. The dog started licking his face but Thomas pushed him away and grabbed for the tiller. The wind screamed, the rain beat harder, all seemed hopeless.

For a moment Thomas's thoughts went to his little cottage and the fire where they could have been warming their bones. Maybe it was time to give up this life of sea-trade. He had profited all right, but had nearly lost his life too many times now. And just as he decided this would indeed be his last trip… his wish came true. A huge wave hit the side of the boat and flipped it over. Thomas hit his head on the stern as it capsized and he blacked out immediately. The bales of linen quickly waterlogged and sank; the boat, with just the tip of the bow showing above the water, swirled in the waves. The dog was a strong swimmer and quickly found his master, floating, but face down. He grabbed the collar of his coat and swam, whimpering all the time.

Within ten minutes Thomas's lungs were waterlogged and his heart stopped beating. But the dog swam for a further half hour, trying to pull his master to safety, until exhaustion and the cold took their toll. His frantic paddling slowed and slowed until his head dropped. Thomas's body slowly spiralled down to the depths. The cur gave one last bay of anguish and then drank the cold sea, deep into his lungs.

The next morning the body of the dog was found washed up on the shore between Blakeney and Cley, and was buried on the beach.

Thomas Grimes was never found.

CHAPTER ONE

'Thank God,' breathed Harry Lambert as he slammed the car door and stretched his back after the two-hour drive from Newmarket. Geographically, at least, his troubles were behind him, for now. But the scream was still there, in his head. He took a deep lungful of salty air and held it in as long as he could, trying to calm his mind.

He surveyed the quay of Blakeney, as quaint a Norfolk coastal village as you could get, with its array of small boats resting on the low tide mud. He couldn't actually see the ocean from the quay but beyond the marsh there were many masts of larger boats, anchored in the natural harbour area. Locking the car, he walked along the quay, past the men selling tickets for boat trips to see the seals at Blakeney Point, and towards a couple of caravans selling mugs of tea and freshly-made sandwiches – local crab a speciality. Despite the autumn chill there were quite a few people about, including a row of old folks in their cars, lined up along the edge of the main creek, staring blankly at the mud banks as they munched their packed lunches. It was certainly peaceful, and that's what he needed more than anything else at the moment. Perhaps a week of relaxing and a little birdwatching would help exorcise his demons; help him make some sense of life.

His hunger demanded a sandwich right now, yet he decided to check into the B&B first. He approached one of the ticket-sellers.

'Can you tell me where High Street is?'

'Right behind you,' said the seal man, pointing to a narrow street that rose up an incline from the quay. 'On holiday are you?'

'Sort of,' murmured Harry.

'You'll have to fit in a seal trip while you're here then.' He passed Harry a leaflet. 'We do at least one trip every day and can guarantee you'll see hundreds of grey and common seals on the sands at the Point.'

'Thanks, I'll do that,' said Harry. 'I'm staying at Tern Cottage B&B – do you know it?'

'Just up High Street on the left – white cottage with a blue gate.'

Harry gave a thumbs-up of thanks and headed along the street. The blue gate did indeed have a 'Tern Cottage' nameplate fixed to it, so he stepped up to the door and gave a couple of knocks. Footsteps approached, the door swung open and there stood a homely-looking woman in her late fifties. She wiped flour from her hands on to her apron as she smiled questioningly.

'Hello, I'm Harry Lambert.'

'You found us all right then. I'm Linda Davies – call me Linda.' She offered her hand, which Harry shook. 'Come on in and I'll show you to your room. My husband Frank's not here at present but you'll meet him later. He's gone fishing, hoping to get a nice sea bass for our supper.' Harry followed Linda up the narrow stairs and into the first bedroom on the right. 'You're the only one staying here this week,' she continued. 'The other room's being redecorated – when my other half's here that is. Bathroom's opposite, towels are on the bed, dining room for breakfast is the first you come to downstairs. I'm just making bread for the morning so I'll be in the kitchen if you need anything.'

Linda bustled off down the stairs and Harry, despite not having brought in any of his things from the car, closed the door and sat down on the bed. For a moment he felt shockingly alone and wondered what on earth he was doing here. But the small room was cosy enough with its dark-green quilted bed, chest of drawers, pale green walls and paintings of boats and seabirds. Harry wasn't used to a single bed, but he had no use for anything else now. He moved to the window and, looking at an angle, could just about see the quay. He noticed that the tide was coming in quite fast along the creek, causing some of the previously grounded boats to bob about.

He crossed the landing to the bathroom and stared at his reflection in the mirror. Not long ago he had looked much younger than his forty years, but now he could see that recent events had aged him rapidly. His dark stubble was flecked with white, his short brown hair was greying in places and his eyes appeared sunken in shadowy hollows. He looked exhausted.

The sound of a seagull calling outside momentarily reminded him of long summer holidays in Cornwall when he was a boy. Happy holidays. To him then, life ahead had seemed full of possibilities and excitement. He wouldn't have wished the reality on anyone.

It was those days of exploring rock pools, catching crabs and watching gulls through an old pair of binoculars his grandfather had given him that had started his love for wildlife. He would happily spend all day outside, scrambling over the rocks and pretending he was shipwrecked on a distant island. Sometimes he would use the binoculars to watch the boats out at sea, as he bubbled with the imagined excitement of a voyage into the unknown. How magnificent it must be to look back to see your homeland disappearing into the distance as you steer for the empty horizon.

Harry had been only a teenager when his beloved grandfather had died, but he had inherited his old cine camera: a basic 8mm model but still in good working order. And it was using that camera to film the deer and foxes in his local wood that inspired him to seek a life as a wildlife film-maker. A degree in zoology followed and then a lucky break found him working as assistant cameraman to the experienced film-maker Doug Miller – making programmes for broadcast on ITV. This took him to Africa, India and South America – places he had dreamed of for so long. He earned little money but it was the best grounding in his trade he could have had. Then, at the age of twenty-nine, Harry met Mike Parsons, a fellow aspiring film-maker of the same age. They rapidly became best friends and business partners and spent the next decade making films, mostly for the BBC, specialising in the wildlife of the Amazon jungles. They formed what seemed an unshakeable bond – always helping each other out of scrapes – one strong when the other was weak. Along the way he had met and married the gorgeous Louise and set up home in an old country cottage in her birth-town of Newmarket. Life had been sweet. Up to that point.

Hunger pangs broke his reminiscing. He splashed cold water over his face and took a long drink from the tap, before trotting down the stairs and leaving Tern Cottage to head into the autumn sun. He bought a crab sandwich from one of the caravans and sat on the grass bank overlooking the quay, realising, as he relaxed slightly, how tense his body had become. These days his chest had become so tight with stress that even breathing was difficult sometimes – as if his lungs were smaller than they used to be.

From where he sat he could see several small groups of children bending over the side of the quay looking directly down as they dangled orange crab-lines into the water. Having finished his sandwich he walked down towards them for a closer look. The first group he came to – three girls and a boy – were gingerly pulling the line up from the water, some eight feet below. A small greenish crab was clinging to the bacon bait with one claw, but about halfway up the quay wall the crab let go and fell back, to the frustrated cries of the children.

The little boy turned to see Harry watching them and pointed to their bucket of water. 'Sixteen,' he boasted. Harry looked in the bucket and murmured approval at the sight of the crabs scuttling over each other and feeding on morsels of waterlogged bacon. Harry's attention was enjoyed fleetingly by the boy before he turned to help pull the next clawed victim from its home. Further down the quay another group had finished for the day and were slowly tipping out their bucket on to the slipway. Most of the crabs instinctively ran for the water's edge but one confused individual crawled towards the children at some speed, producing much squeaking and laughing as they leapt out of its way.

Harry could barely remember feeling as carefree.

He continued to his car, an ageing Land Rover Freelander, and pulled his holdall and coat from the back. It seemed odd to be travelling so lightly; usually the back of the vehicle was laden with heavy tripods and flight-cases filled with cameras and gadgets. Surely those days weren't behind him?

Back at Tern Cottage he unpacked his things: mainly clothes but also a few bird books and his binoculars. Not the pair his grandfather had given him, which were carefully stored at home, but a much-used pair of Opticrons that had travelled the world in his rucksack. He lay on the bed and let the weariness wash over him, sleep pulling at him like an ebbing tide until he drifted away to a place and time free of problems and pain. A time when Louise had held his hand and laughed.

They were walking in a wood: Louise was pulling him to her side tightly and Harry was feeling unbelievably happy. But then she broke free and ran ahead. She kept turning and laughing at him, daring him to catch her, but the harder he tried to run after her, the slower he seemed to go and the further away she ran. Then the scene started to change. Her laughter became more taunting and he realised she was not laughing with him but *at* him. Laughing at his helplessness, his weakness. Laughing at the pain she was causing him. And then he felt tree roots growing rapidly around his ankles, anchoring him to the spot. He strained and pulled, he had to get to her but he was held fast. Then to his right the forest seemed to be falling away until he was on the edge of a huge drop, and there was his friend and partner Mike – his face contorted – reaching out his hand to Harry while falling backwards over the edge in slow motion. Only Harry could save him now, but he was still held fast by the tree roots and there was no way he could reach Mike's grasping hand. Mike was in freefall now – his arms and legs flailing but so, so slowly. And then the scream started. Low and deep at first but becoming high and shrill as Mike fell, faster and faster.

CHAPTER TWO

As often happened, Harry woke at the moment of impact, his own shout reverberating round the small bedroom. He sat up slowly, his body feeling beaten up rather than rested, and smelled his own sweat. When the hell would this end?

It was getting dark already so Harry showered and changed, planning to find a local pub for an evening meal and a pint of beer. Maybe two or three. As he went down the stairs he could hear voices in the kitchen and knocked lightly on the door, pushing it open to see Linda stirring a pot on the stove, and a man who looked to be in his sixties sitting at the kitchen table.

'No need to knock, Harry, just treat the place as your own home,' said Linda. Then she nodded towards the man. 'This is my hubby Frank.'

Harry held out his hand and Frank Davies half stood up and shook it firmly. 'Pleased to meet you,' he said in a soft Norfolk accent. 'We heard you shouting upstairs a little earlier, I came up to see if you were all right but you were in the shower by then.'

Harry flushed. 'Ah, yes, sorry about that. I nodded off and had a bit of a nightmare. I must have shouted in my sleep.'

'Oh, you poor thing,' consoled Linda. 'Why don't you sit down and have a cup of tea, or even a glass of cider?'

'Actually I just came to tell you I was off out to a pub for supper, if you can recommend somewhere within walking distance?'

'There's several places in Blakeney that do good food, but as it happens Frank has come home with two lovely bass, so we were going to ask you if you wanted to join us for supper anyway.'

Harry nearly declined, thinking how he had been looking

forward to staring dolefully into a lonely pint in a strange pub. But the warmth of the kitchen and the friendliness of his hosts won him over. 'Okay, thanks, I will.'

'Right,' said Frank, rubbing his hands together and rising from his chair. 'I'm long overdue a cider. Care to join me, Harry?'

'I would, thanks.' Harry noticed how much like a classic fisherman Frank looked: white hair and beard, wearing a chunky ivory-coloured sweater over rough black trousers. While Frank poured two large glasses of cider, Linda opened the oven door to check progress and a fantastic smell of baking fish wafted out.

Frank passed a glass to Harry and raised his. 'Good health.'

'Cheers,' said Harry, taking a long sip. 'So, where is it you go fishing round here, Frank?'

'There's various spots I like, but the one I use most often is the beach at Cley – just a couple of miles down the road – good for mackerel and bass. You a fisherman, Harry?'

'I haven't since I was a boy. So you fish from a beach? I'd imagined you were out on a boat.'

'No – rod and line from a beach is successful enough – you'll find a group of us doing it most afternoons at Cley. Not that we talk to each other much mind you,' he chuckled. 'I used to be a crab fisherman for a living, with my own boat, but it's a hard life and I retired from that game a couple of years ago. Tell you what, if you fancy it you can join me tomorrow and have a go. It's a good place to spot some birds too.'

'That would be great,' said Harry. 'In fact I was hoping to do some birding while I was here: help me unwind.'

'We get birders come here from all over the world; most of our guests are birders. I can certainly show you some of the best places to go.' Frank took a long pull of cider and studied the haggard-looking new guest. 'So, what do you do for a living, Harry?'

'I'm a wildlife film-maker.' Harry hesitated, 'or maybe I should say I *was* a wildlife film-maker. I'm actually in a sort of recovery period after an accident.'

Linda pushed steaming plates of baked sea bass with a buttery sauce, broccoli and potatoes in front of them. As they tucked in,

Harry found himself unloading his troubles. Some of them.

He told them of his work with Mike and of their latest film about jungle birds of the Amazon. It was to have been a fifty-minute film for the BBC2 *Natural World* series and they had been filming on location for twelve months when the accident had happened. They were in a mountainous area of Ecuador filming the spectacular cock-of-the-rock, a pigeon-sized bird with stunning orange-red plumage and unique courtship displays. They had already filmed the males' displays on the ground and were now filming a group of females building their unusual clay nests on a vertical rock face. To get their camera to the level of the nests they had built a wooden platform high up in a tree, some fifteen metres from the rock face.

It was only their second day working from the platform. Harry was just attaching the camera to the tripod for the day's work while Mike was tightening the brackets holding the wooden planks to the scaffolding frame that made the platform. As it was twenty-five metres from the ground they both wore safety harnesses, but Mike had temporarily unclipped his in order to reach the outermost brackets.

As Harry was concentrating on the tripod he didn't see exactly what happened; he just heard Mike's shout, 'HARRY! I'M GOING, I'M GOING! GRAB MY HAND!'

For some reason Mike had manoeuvred himself to the outside edge of the platform and had lost his footing; one hand gripped the planked edge and was slipping fast, the other reached out towards Harry, fingers shaking in desperation. Harry hesitated for a fraction of a second. A fraction of a second that he would regret for the rest of his life. He hesitated because the expensive camera was not secured to the tripod and would fall if he let go. As the urgency of the situation kicked in he let the camera fall and dived for Mike's hand. That fraction of a second too late. He even fleetingly touched Mike's fingers before they disappeared. Harry scrambled frantically to the edge of the platform and looked down to see Mike plummeting, arms flailing. And that scream. That scream had stayed in his head ever since.

'NO!' yelled Harry, and saw to his horror that Mike was falling towards a stout horizontal branch below. Mike's head hit the branch with a sickening crack and whipped forwards over his chest, forcing him into a fast forward spin. The screaming stopped instantly. Then Harry lost sight of him as he disappeared into the foliage and undergrowth below. Absolute silence.

Harry scrambled down the tree as fast as he could, burning his hands on the rope in his haste. He quickly found Mike, lying at a grotesque angle over the buttress roots of the tree. He was unconscious but breathing, blood dribbling from the corner of his mouth. Harry was sure he must have broken his neck when his head had hit the branch, and by the look of his contorted limbs probably several other bones as well.

The next twenty hours were the most stressful of Harry's life. It took him an hour to run to the nearest village, punctuated by stops to vomit through shock and exertion. He didn't speak much Spanish but his hysterical gesticulations were enough for the villagers to know something tragic had happened. Six men from the village returned with him and quickly constructed a stretcher out of thin branches and vines. Carefully they lifted Mike's body aboard and then came an agonising five hours trek through the forest to the river. They had to go so slowly to avoid jogging Mike's injured neck and causing more damage. Then it was a two-hour paddle by canoe to the nearest town, and once there, an agonising wait for the ambulance followed by a long drive to a hospital in the regional centre. For six or seven hours Harry was beside himself with anxiety at the hospital while they scanned, tested and finally operated. Mike's neck had indeed been broken, but his skull had also been fractured badly, and the build-up of pressure on the long journey to hospital had done irreparable damage to his brain. He died in the operating theatre.

That had all been just one month ago. Since then Harry had been plagued with guilt for not having been there for Mike when he needed him most of all. He felt responsible. The bond had been broken.

As Harry got to the end of his story he realised that he hadn't meant to say so much. These poor people, whom he had only just met and who had been so welcoming, had suddenly been subjected to this dramatic tale. But they had gasped and looked shocked in all the right places. After the meal, Harry had been supplied with a large tumbler of whisky, and he staggered upstairs feeling shattered.

He cried into his pillow and twisted its fabric into his fist as he ached for Louise to hold him. To tell him that everything was going to be all right. Words he knew he would never hear again.

CHAPTER THREE

Harry spent the next morning wandering distractedly around Blakeney exploring the village and staring at the boats moored at the quay. He had always liked boats and realised he was window-shopping, wondering which boat would be the right one to take him away. When he was young he dreamt of heading towards adventure, now he just dreamed of heading away from disaster.

After another crab sandwich lunch he found Frank loading fishing rods and tackle into his rusty Ford Escort van, and they set off together down the coast road towards Cley. As they drove, Frank pointed out various places of interest: the famous delicatessen in the village where the road was so narrow they had to stop frequently to let other vehicles get though; the old smoke house, with kippers and other cured fish on display; the art galleries and the windmill: now a guest house. They soon popped out of the other end of the village and turned up the lane to the beach car park. Frank's voice was calming and Harry could feel himself relaxing in his company.

They parked beside the old coastguard station, which was now a café and second-hand bookshop, and Harry helped Frank unload the equipment and carry it over the shingle ridge to the edge of the beach. It was the first time Harry had seen the sea properly on this trip and he felt compelled to touch the water and taste the salt on his lips. For a few moments he gazed out to the horizon, imagining the vast expanse of dark North Sea between him and Norway. The shingle beach seemed to stretch endlessly to the west and east. There was a bleakness to it that matched Harry's state of mind.

As expected there was a line of other fishermen along the

beach: each standing alone, at least twenty yards from his neighbour. They needed the space to cast, but maybe they also needed the solitude. Some had large umbrellas set up next to their tackle boxes, but they all just stood, shrugged, staring out to sea, their rods supported on rests.

From his freezer, Frank had brought a couple of mackerel that he had caught previously, and he showed Harry how to cut them into strips to use as bait for bass. He assembled Harry's rod and watched him try a few casts, then moved a little further down the beach to set up his own rod. A few distant seabirds, probably terns, dived like arrows into the sea to catch tiny fish. Harry squinted at them – realising that in the excitement of going fishing he had forgotten to bring his binoculars. A cormorant, flying just above the surface of the sea with its neck outstretched, caught Harry's attention and he followed it with his gaze until it was a speck in the distance.

The sound of the surf on the shingle started to lull him into a daydream, and he jumped when Frank shouted across to him. 'Anything yet?'

'No, nothing.' Harry looked at the other dozen or so fishermen and there seemed a distinct lack of success. He wandered over to where Frank was standing next to his rod. 'How about you?'

'Nothing here, and from the look of these other boys we may be in for a quiet afternoon. Still, no matter – fresh air, sea and peace. What more could you want?'

Harry agreed, especially peace, that's what he wanted more than anything else.

'Are those terns I can see diving in the distance?'

'They are,' replied Frank. 'Hard to see from here but I'm pretty sure they'll be common terns. We get several species here but the common ones are usually the last to head south for the winter. Another week or two and they'll all be gone. In the summer they nest in their thousands at Blakeney Point. Mind you, there's even more to see in the winter as we get all the geese and waders flying in to overwinter from their breeding grounds up in the Arctic.'

'Can you get to Blakeney Point from here?'

'Just head west up the beach,' Frank nodded to the left. 'In fact if you want to get there on foot you have to start from here, cos this is the only access to the spit of shingle that takes you there. At the end it widens out into sandy areas where the seals lie out. It's a hard walk though: four miles on shingle and four miles back. You could take a seal boat but they don't often stop to let you off on the Point, and when they do it's not for long.'

'Actually I think a long walk is what I need. Maybe I'll do that tomorrow.'

As he spoke, a new arrival, laden with fishing rods, appeared over the shingle ridge followed closely by a large black dog, resembling a long-haired Alsatian. On seeing Frank the dog bounded over: they were obviously old friends and Frank received a good licking as he fussed the beast. On recognising Frank the owner also came over.

'Hello boy, what's biting today?'

'Not much, we haven't been here long but I haven't seen any action from any of the others yet. This is young Harry, who's staying at our place. Harry, this is Mack.'

'Real name's Jack actually,' said the newcomer, 'but everyone calls me Mack now.'

'On account of him winning every mackerel fishing competition we've held here,' chuckled Frank.

'So, Harry, you're a fisherman yourself?' asked Mack.

'Not really, but I'm learning from the master,' he nodded towards Frank.

'Ah well, Frank's the master all right. Now come away, Prince, leave the old bugger alone.'

'You never could control your Shuck,' laughed Frank as Mack and the dog moved on to find fishing space.

'Shuck? What does Shuck mean – is that Norfolk for dog?' asked Harry.

Frank laughed. 'Have you not heard of Black Shuck?' Harry shook his head. 'Black Shuck is our ghost dog. He's haunted Norfolk for hundreds of years; a huge shaggy beast with burning red eyes that roams around at night. Many say that if you see

Shuck either you or someone in your family will die soon afterwards. We all know about Shuck round here – he's been spotted around Blakeney and Cley more than anywhere else.'

'Have you ever seen him?'

'Not me, no, but I know people that have in years past, and there was a woman in the village who saw him just recently. Her husband died later that very same day. He was a decent bloke too – same age as me – I've had the odd pint with him in the King's Arms before now. An electrician he was, electrocuted in his own house.'

Frank was interrupted as his line took a bite. He grabbed the rod and Harry watched as he reeled it in and successfully landed a fine-looking bass. Further up the beach Mack gave them a thumbs-up. Harry looked at Prince, who was tossing pebbles in the air and catching them in his mouth as his tail wagged enthusiastically. It was starting to get dark. Harry shivered. After another ten minutes they decided to call it a day and packed the gear back in the van.

'I'll take you again if you like, in a couple of days or so – see if you have better luck next time.' Frank snapped his seat belt on and pulled away.

'Thanks, I'd like that.'

'Right, let's get this fish back to my lovely wife. This'll end up in the freezer mind you, even I don't fancy bass two days in a row. Talking of which: do you have a lovely wife back home?'

Harry hesitated. It was hard to explain how this simple question made him feel. 'Well, I do have a wife, but she's not back home and I'm not sure I'd describe her as lovely any more. She's beautiful all right, but not the lovely woman I thought I'd married.'

'Oh, lad,' Frank patted Harry's arm. 'It seemed you'd had your fair share of troubles last night. I won't pry, but if you'd like to talk I'm a good listener.'

That was true all right. Rarely had Harry felt so at ease with anyone as quickly as he did with Frank.

'The trouble is, being a wildlife film-maker I was often away for long periods. In fact I used to be on location for months at a time but when I married Louise – that's my wife – I promised never to be away for longer than a month. And I kept that promise too, even on our Amazon birds programme which we'd been filming for a year, I'd fly back home every four weeks for a week or two. It added a lot to the budget of course but what could be more important than your marriage? Anyway, I thought it was all going okay, but when she picked me up from the airport after the accident a month ago something was different. She just seemed distant: I couldn't connect with her. Of course I assumed it was just the shock of it all, and her not knowing how to handle my grief. And then I started noticing a few things: like the candle wax all over the old sideboard. When I asked her about it she just said she fancied a few candles one night. But she never did that usually. Not on her own. And then after I'd been home a few days she just suddenly broke down. She told me that she couldn't stand the loneliness of me being away any longer, and had got involved with someone else. And so the wax had been from a candlelit dinner with him – in my home – while I was out in a jungle earning the money that paid the mortgage that enabled us to have the lovely cottage in the first place.' Harry paused as he felt his anger rising.

'So she'd fallen in love with someone else. It was that simple. In that last trip to Ecuador I had simply become unwanted. She only stayed a couple of days after that, and that was probably only out of pity. Then she went. To him. And I haven't seen her since. Just a message to say she would collect her things when I was feeling better. To make matters worse *he* was a friend of mine. I'd been out for a drink with him shortly before I went out to Ecuador for the last time and was telling him what a lovely wife Louise was. He obviously decided to see for himself.'

Harry suddenly ground to a halt. As on the night before, his story had just poured out and now his chest felt tight with stress and his eyes heavy with un-cried tears. He hung his head as Frank again patted his arm and offered words of sympathy as they pulled up outside Tern Cottage.

'So,' Harry sighed, 'tomorrow I think I shall go for a very long walk.'

CHAPTER FOUR

Grimes's dog was bewildered. He recognised the beach but was not sure how he got there. Grimes was nowhere in sight. Lifting his great shaggy head, the dog inhaled the cold salty air and could detect the closeness of his master. But the smell was coming from the open ocean, and Grimes never took to sea without his faithful hound by his side; protector and companion in one. The dog whimpered a little and trembled. He turned to the west and padded along the shoreline looking out to sea. Now and then he would stop and survey the horizon, sniffing the air. The scent was always there. How could the dog go anywhere else with the smell of his master, his life, still in his nostrils?

When two men came into view in the distance, the dog knew instinctively that he must not be seen. He slunk low to the ground, not easy for such a large animal, and pulled himself across the shingle towards the shrubby salt marsh plants. He hid in the undergrowth and waited as the men passed by, laughing and carrying a small wooden chest between them. When their voices had fully faded, the dog emerged from the shrubs and continued his search. He must find his master. He knew he was close.

By nightfall the dog had covered miles, backwards and forwards along the same stretch of coast. The smell he could not get away from was always out to sea. The dog headed west until his master's scent grew faint, then turned east and repeated the process. He never grew tired and he knew it was no good searching further inland. His master was out there – he just had to wait. Whenever people appeared on the beach the dog would hide, and save his whining for when the coast was clear. He craved companionship, a kind word and a warm body to curl against, but only his master would do. Loyal to the end.

Days turned into weeks. And although the smell of Grimes remained as strong in the same location, the dog gradually started to roam further afield. Finding his master, always the only thought in his head. He came inland when necessary, in order to access further stretches of beach beyond Morston and Stiffkey to the west and Cley and Salthouse to the east. Often travelling by night so as not to be seen, he would slink along the muddy coastal paths, silently padding past the upturned rowing boats and weaving in between the piles of crab pots. He was always careful not to stray too far from cover lest anyone should appear. He never slept. He no longer needed to. He would never rest again until reunited with his master.

Chapter Five

The tractor wouldn't start. Peter Wild stood back to glare at it and could feel his stress levels rising. He had enough to do without messing with engines all day. He didn't like engines. Someone had rung earlier to report a seal entangled in a fishing net – a common occurrence on the Point – and it was Peter's job to sort it out. He didn't mind that, he loved the seals, but these days he was spending too much time coaxing the temperamental tractor to life. It was time for a new one really, but of course the budget wouldn't stretch to that. A tractor was the only vehicle that could get to the Point by land – even a four-wheel drive would flounder on the shingle – and, as warden of the Nature Reserve, Peter was the only one allowed to drive there. He could go by boat of course, and had one just for this purpose, but often the tractor was of more use with the seals. Especially if he had to bring a body back.

'Dad,' came Anna's voice from the back door. 'Do you want a cuppa?'

'Please, love,' Peter replied. 'And a shotgun for this ruddy tractor – I've had enough of it.'

A few moments later Anna appeared beside her father and passed him a steaming mug. 'You know you can't shoot vehicles, Dad, don't you?' she teased.

'Well what else am I supposed to do? I need to get to the Point: there's a seal in a net. I guess I'll have to go in the boat. Tell you what, can you do me a favour and give Joe a ring and tell him the tractor won't start *again*? Tell him if he can fix it today there's a beer in it for him. I better go now or the tide will be too low to get the boat out.'

'All right Dad, will do. And you take care out there, it's getting cold now.' Anna returned to the kitchen and paused at the window of Marsh View for a moment to watch her father putting the equipment in the back of his truck to take to Morston quay: thick gloves, cutters, lifejacket, spare fuel tank and waterproofs. Although they lived in Cley, the boat was moored at Morston, just the other side of Blakeney, where the quay experienced deeper water at high tide, so allowing easier boat access to the Point.

She knew her father loved his job, but he had been increasingly stressed recently. She also knew he was supremely capable and practical, but couldn't help worrying about him all the same. It was his state of mind that concerned her. When everything had changed a year ago she had moved back home, at the age of thirty-one, to look after him. The excuse was that she would be looking after her sister Sophie, only fifteen and still at school, but it was her father who needed the most support.

Anna had been a secondary school teacher in Bristol when her mother had suffered a massive, unexpected brain haemorrhage. She didn't even get back to Norfolk in time to see her mother before she died. They had all been devastated, of course, but it was Peter who had seemed lost ever since. Only his job and love of the seals kept him going. Sophie had gone off the rails a little to start with, had started smoking for a while and bunked off school a few times, but thanks to the love of her elder sister and father she was now in better spirits, and studying hard for her exams, or so it seemed. Anna now worked part-time at the primary school in Blakeney and spent the rest of each day running the house. This often included handling phone calls from the public whenever they saw a seal in distress.

She didn't really have a plan. In the back of her mind she expected to stay at home until Sophie was old enough to leave in about three years, but she wasn't sure about abandoning her father even then, especially at about the time he should be considering retiring. Life was okay, but there were elements missing, romance for a start. For now she was just taking things a day at a time.

Anna finished her tea and went through to the front room to call mechanic Joe. The phone was near the large window that overlooked the salt marshes and she couldn't help noticing that clouds were building in the distance. Maybe her father would be back home before the rain started.

Chapter Six

Peter pulled up at Morston quay and went to check the boat before unloading his gear. It was a RIB – a Rigid Inflatable Boat – grey with a wooden floor and a thirty horsepower outboard engine. A little rainwater had collected inside since the last time he used it, but this took only a few minutes to bale out. He put on his red waterproofs, clipped on the lifejacket and turned the ignition key for the outboard. It started first time: at least some engines were reliable. He untied the bowline, pushed off, and started motoring slowly up the creek.

There were many other boats moored alongside the banks, soon to be grounded on the mud as the tide slipped away. There were only a few hours at high tide when you could get a boat of any size in and out of the quay. Peter glanced at his watch and calculated he had a couple of hours at the most – with any luck that would be just enough. Gradually the creek grew wider and soon he was steering into the natural harbour where the bigger boats were moored: several large catamarans, fishing boats, many big sailing dinghies and a disused lifeboat, now used for training. As he headed for the western end of the Point, where the seals haul out, it became choppy and the odd wave sprayed him in the face. He opened the throttle a little, although there was a speed limit of eight knots in the harbour area, and after about fifteen minutes he had reached the spot where he often landed the boat on the Point.

The bow of the RIB pushed gently up on the sand and Peter stepped out, tying the bowline to a post he had put there for this purpose. It was a good place to land, as the seals could not see him from here. He turned the engine off and took a rope, the cutters and gloves and started walking over the dunes. As it was not far off high tide the seals shouldn't be too far away, and on reaching the summit of the dune Peter spotted a number of common seals resting on the shore in their classic banana shape: head and tail pointing skywards. He lay on the dune, careful not to show his profile against the sky, and pulled a pair of binoculars from his jacket pocket. Scanning the beach, he finally saw a young grey seal, which indeed appeared to be tangled in blue netting. As so often happened, the seals would play in the water with discarded pieces of fishing net, push their heads through a hole and then be unable to wriggle out of it. If not rescued, the seals often suffered a lingering and painful death as the nylon fibres of the nets cut into their bodies and hampered their ability to swim.

Peter crawled back down the dune and then trotted along, bent low, towards where the tangled seal was lying. At the end of the dune he crept up again to look and saw that this was the nearest he could get to the seal without being seen. He slipped his gloves on, waited until the seal was looking directly away from him and then ran as fast as he could towards it. The seal heard him at the last moment and started wriggling towards the water's edge but Peter was fast. He had been too slow enough times to know that if the seal reached the sea he would have no chance of catching it. He quickly straddled the youngster and held its head pointing forwards so that it couldn't turn and bite him. The animal cried out and opened its mouth to reveal impressive teeth, but it had been weakened by its effort to get free from the net. There were only two thick strands that were gripping its body and as yet they had not cut into the flesh. Peter pulled the cutters from his pocket and carefully snipped the blue nylon. He eased the netting away from the seal's body and, when he was sure there was no serious damage, stood up and stepped back. The seal turned to look at him, showing the whites of frightened eyes, cried out again, and then made for the sea. Peter watched for few moments longer and was satisfied to see the seal swim out then turn to look at him from the safety of the water. Gathering up the netting he returned to the RIB.

An hour and a half later Peter was back at home warming his cold fingers in front of the fire Anna had lit in the front room. From outside came a metallic hammering as old Joe tinkered heavy-handedly with the tractor. Anna was busy preparing the evening meal in the kitchen, Sophie would soon be home from school and all would be well. Peter opened his logbook and entered details of the afternoon's activities. His beloved seals were safe. For the time being.

CHAPTER SEVEN

It was the sound of the gulls that woke Harry. He had been having a dream free of torment for a change, and he stretched and smiled before opening his eyes and remembering where he was. Remembering who he now was. His smile faded fast.

He swung his legs over the side of the bed and walked over to draw the curtains back. He felt heavy and stiff. The sky was blue with just a few wisps of white cloud – perfect for that good long walk he needed. After a quick shower, he filled up on a hearty cooked breakfast that Linda provided, and then packed his small rucksack: binoculars, mobile phone, bird guide book, waterproof jacket, notebook and pen – the usual kit for a naturalist.

He drove the short journey from Blakeney to Cley in his Freelander, stopping to buy a packed lunch at the delicatessen. He was surprised to find the shop full of customers, but realised why, when he saw the display of home-made pies, cakes and breads. The realisation that he could treat himself to a high-class picnic lifted his mood, and he filled his basket with a pot of queen olives stuffed with sun-dried tomato, a small loaf of lavender bread, a Gloucester Old Spot pork pie and a bottle of Norfolk apple juice. He then continued to the beach car park by the old coastguard lookout.

With the picnic added to his rucksack, he locked the car and climbed the shingle ridge to gaze at the sea awhile before turning left and heading west to the Point. He paused at a notice board showing a map of the Nature Reserve and saw how narrow the shingle spit was, before it curved round to a large sandy area at the end. This was where the seals must be. As it was still a good few hours before high tide, he could walk close to the sea's edge, where the harder, wet sand was easier going than the shingle, where every footfall sank a few inches.

He marched on with the sea to his right, the low ridge to his left. The wind was coming from the north and the sound of the waves on the pebbles was surprisingly loud. Ahead of him the beach went on as far as he could see, there was no one else in sight. He took a deep breath of fresh, salty air. It felt good to be out on a minor adventure, and to have the mission of seeing the seals.

After he had been walking for about half an hour he climbed the shingle ridge and took out his binoculars. From here he could see across the huge natural harbour to Blakeney village, and then Morston further to the right. On this side of the ridge there were many salt-hardy plants growing among the pebbles: sea-blite, prickly saltwort and sea-lavender, but nothing more than about waist-height. Harry could imagine the extreme conditions when a strong north wind picked up from the Arctic.

He returned to the sea's edge and continued. It became a monotonous trudge. Today there didn't even seem to be any seabirds to look at and, inevitably, his thoughts returned to his problems. It was as if he had run away from his previous life with no thoughts of return, and it was distressing to think that in only a few days' time he would be back in the thick of the mess. Events had all been so unexpected he didn't have a clear plan, and he wasn't used to such an unknown future. The cottage would have to be sold of course, and there would be nothing to keep him in Newmarket anymore. He'd only moved there in the first place because it was where Louise grew up and where her parents still lived, but now it held nothing but bad memories for him. It would be good to move away: somewhere completely new, start again. But where? The endless possibilities left Harry feeling lost and insecure. And what of the business? There was no way he could have finished the film for the BBC without Mike, and the project had been cancelled, leaving him in some debt. His share of the proceeds from the sale of the cottage should be enough to pay it off, but he would be left with precious little else. He wasn't even sure he had the stomach for filming any more after Mike's accident.

It was another hour's walking with little new to look at before Harry's attention was caught by a great black-backed gull standing alone at the edge of the water ahead. The aggressive-looking bird watched Harry approach, occasionally scanning around with jerks of its head as if expecting other people to appear, unsure of what to do. To Harry the bird seemed unnaturally large and he felt strangely uneasy. There was something about its solitude that made Harry feel all the lonelier too, and it suddenly occurred to him that he might be the only human being for several miles. But it was only a gull after all, and, as Harry drew too close for comfort, the bird simply opened its wings and let the wind raise it from the ground and take it effortlessly over the shingle ridge and away.

Harry took a long swig from the bottle of apple juice and then carried on. He reckoned he must have been walking nearly four miles now and his legs were starting to ache. It wasn't long after that before the ridge started flattening out and the shingle gave way to sand. Harry figured that if he kept the sea to his right he couldn't fail to reach the seals. The wind was picking up and he could see white crests of waves out to the horizon. He pulled his collar up and squinted at numerous large dark shapes on a sand bank in the distance. Surely they weren't boulders? Focussing his binoculars he could see that they were indeed seals. A rough headcount told him that there must be a couple of hundred on the bank. Harry walked as close as he could, but as the tide was not fully in, there were still a number of sand banks exposed which the seals hauled out on. At high tide the seals would have been forced on to the beach and he would have got an even closer view, but this was still a spectacle. The majority of them were common seals with their round dog-like faces, but Harry spotted the odd grey seal with its long Roman nose among them.

A few were disturbed enough by Harry's presence to slide into the water and watch him from there. Harry was aware of the strange feeling of having hundreds of eyes upon him alone. He suddenly felt the intruder that he was, and retreated from the shore to a dune area. Some of the seals were crying out; a strange high wail that cut through the sound of the surf. Harry sat down out of the wind, where the seals could barely see him, and took out his picnic. The pie was delicious and the olives were the best he'd ever tasted, but he couldn't properly relax. He knew it wasn't just his troubles, which he was utterly bored of thinking about. There was something else about this place, something eerie that he hadn't been expecting and couldn't put his finger on. The blue sky had taken on an odd yellowish tint and clouds were approaching from the north. It had been good to find the seals but Harry's solitude suddenly hit him, and he wanted to get away, quickly. He realised that, without any reason, he felt strangely … unsafe. Without the sun it was a harsh and forbidding place. He packed the rest of his food away, shouldered his rucksack and, with a last look at the seals, turned to the east and walked towards the sea's edge again: this time keeping it to his left.

It was then that he saw the blood.

CHAPTER EIGHT

At first it just looked like dark streaks on the sand, but as he came closer he could see that it was clearly fresh blood. And lots of it. He must have walked over it on the way out without noticing, which was maybe not so strange as his attention had been clearly focussed on the seals then: but it was so obvious now. The deep red had soaked into the sand and trailed several metres to the sea's edge. It must have been an injured seal that had managed to make it to the water. Or had been dragged to the water. Maybe two males had been fighting, but as Harry kicked at the sand and saw how far down the red stain had soaked, he knew this was more blood than just a few bites could release. He was sure the injured animal could not have survived this much blood-loss, but there was no sign of a body floating offshore or washed up nearby.

Harry detected an unusual smell in the air, and, standing up, was shocked to see two more trails of blood to the sea ahead of him. All three were remarkably similar. That made even less sense – if one seal had been attacked by something then surely the other two would have easily got away. Maybe it was a dog attack, and Harry's thought immediately went to fisherman Mack's dog, Prince: but it would have to have been a pack of dogs to attack three seals at once. And besides, Harry had seen no dogs on the whole of his walk. Perhaps it wasn't even seal blood at all, and for a moment Harry considered taking a sample back, but then he was overcome by an urge to get out of there. He set off, occasionally glancing back, keen to put distance between himself and the haunting cries of the seals.

As he walked, it struck him that it might simply have been birth-blood, for he knew that grey seals pupped late in the year.

But then again there was such a lot of blood, and surely it would have been unusual to have three seals all giving birth next to each other in the same twelve-hour period? The high tide would certainly clean the stained sand. He decided the reserve must have some sort of warden and resolved simply to report his findings. Then it would be problem over – for him.

The wind was strong now and Harry hunched into it as he trudged along. He had been looking forward to a bracing experience but now he just wanted it to be over. After about an hour, however, the atmosphere changed. The sky seemed to resume its previous pure blue and the wind dropped a little. The incoming tide had forced Harry to walk higher up the beach on the shingle, which made the going even harder, and he was suddenly surprised to see a house ahead of him. He must have walked right past it on the way out to the Point. True it was on the other side of the shingle ridge, nearer the harbour shore and surrounded by marsh plants and grass. But it was still odd that he hadn't seen the roof or the chimney above the ridge on his walk out. And how unusual to have just one house all on its own in such an isolated position, probably two miles to the next building.

As he drew closer, Harry could see that on the upper floor there was a single dormer window that jutted out towards the sea, and it dawned on him that this wasn't just a house but some sort of lookout post. Maybe another building used by coastguards in the past. Curious, Harry climbed over the ridge and down towards the house. It was of old red brick with a grey slated roof and a chimney in the middle. On the side facing the sea, apart from the dormer window, there were three other windows on the lower level, each covered with wire mesh. Harry peered inside but it was so dark he could make nothing out. He walked slowly round to the side of the building that faced the harbour. Here there was just one window, again meshed and dark, and a wooden door painted blue. Harry went up to the door and, although there were certainly no signs of habitation, something made him knock. No reply or sound from within. He tried turning the knob but the door was locked. About ten yards to the side of the house there was another, much smaller building, with two blue doors side by side. Someone had fixed a home-made sign between the doors which read 'Loo-with-a-view'.

A couple of old fish crates had been placed besides the door to the main building and Harry sat down on one to swig some apple juice. It felt quite different here. With the shingle ridge between the house and the sea it was far quieter, peaceful even, and the sun had swung round to warm the front of the building. The rough grass that stretched down to the marsh along the edge of the harbour was a welcome contrast to the endless shingle. How romantic it would be to live here, so close to the sea, so close to the elements. Every day, life would depend on the weather, and every tide would bring new treasures to find on the shore. What a place for birdwatching too. Harry reluctantly left the house behind and continued with his journey, but he was determined to find out more about it.

As he walked, and dreamed of living in such an amazing location, he had forgotten about the blood at the Point. The new idea lifted his spirits and before long he saw the old coastguard lookout at the beach car park in the distance. But it was still a long way and after half an hour the building barely seemed any closer. He had walked nearly eight miles by then, but his legs ached far more than they should have done. He put it down to the extra effort of walking on shingle for much of the way.

As he finally drew closer to the coastguard lookout he came across his own footprints, heading west in a patch of sand, from five or so hours earlier. He also saw some prints that looked like those of a large dog, and, in a few places, the dog-prints were actually on top of his own boot-prints. The animal must have been there after him, maybe even following him.

Chapter Nine

Harry woke from bloody dreams the next day and was shocked to find it was already nearly lunchtime. His legs were stiff from the previous day's walk as he dressed. Downstairs he found a note from Linda saying that she had gone to Norwich for the day and he was to help himself to breakfast. Harry made a bacon sandwich, feeling rather odd about doing this in someone else's house even though he had been invited to do so. It occurred to him that he was already halfway through his week's break, a depressing thought when he wasn't feeling at all relaxed or rested yet.

At the end of his walk the previous day he had taken another look at the notice board near the old coastguard lookout. At the bottom there had been the address of the warden of the reserve: Marsh View, Cley.

Breakfast finished, Harry drove to Cley, parked up, and asked at the delicatessen for directions. When he heard that Marsh View was only just the other side of the village he decided to walk the rest of the way there. It took only ten minutes before, almost opposite the road to the beach car park, he found a sign for Marsh View. He opened the gate and walked up the driveway, noticing the large front window that gave the house its name.

He knocked on the door twice but there was no response and he could hear no sounds from within. There was, however, a notice pinned to the door, which gave the warden's mobile phone number in case he was needed urgently. Not expecting this situation, Harry had left his own mobile phone in the car, but he had brought his notebook and pen and wrote the number down. Just as he turned to leave, he noticed a young woman getting off a bicycle at the bottom of the drive. She opened the gate and pushed the bike through, then stopped as she saw Harry.

'Hello, can I help you?'

'I was looking for the warden actually: do you know where I might find him?'

'Well if he's not in I expect he's gone to get some parts for the tractor: did you try knocking?'

'Yes, no answer.'

'Tell you what, if you wait a minute I'll see if he's left a note inside, he usually does.'

Harry watched the woman as she leaned her bike on the wall beyond the door and fumbled in her shoulder bag for a key. 'You obviously live here too?'

'Yes, the warden's my dad.' She opened the door and turned to face Harry. 'I'm Anna Wild.'

'Harry Lambert, pleased to meet you.' They shook hands.

'Come in a sec' while I look.' Anna led the way through a small entrance hall into a large kitchen with a solid oak table in the centre. It was covered with papers and books, and a map of the Point was laid out. Anna went to the kettle next to an old Aga range and found what she was looking for. 'Ah yes, I was right: he's gone to the garage, shouldn't be long though. Do you want to wait, or leave a message, or maybe it's something I can help with?'

'Well it's a couple of things: I walked to the end of Blakeney Point yesterday and found quite a lot of blood on the sand, I thought I'd better report it in case a seal had been injured or something. Probably several seals actually.'

'Hmm, it does happen occasionally I'm afraid, but a *lot* of blood doesn't sound good. That's a matter for my dad. You said a couple of things?'

'Yes, on the way back I came across a house, about halfway from the Point to the beach car park: I wanted to find out more about it and figured the warden would know.'

'You mean the Watch House.' Anna paused, realising what a

nice change it was to talk to a man not much older than she was. Over the last year she had seemed to spend most of her time conversing either with the children at the primary school, or harassed parents, or retired people from the village. 'Look, I need a coffee, would you like one while you wait for my dad?'

'That'd be good thanks. So do you know any more about this Watch House?'

Anna looked at Harry while filling the kettle and frowned. 'You're not a property developer or something, are you? Being on a Nature Reserve the house can't be sold or anything.'

Harry laughed. 'No, not at all, I just thought it would be an amazing place to stay.'

'That's all right then,' smiled Anna. 'I'm sure some students stayed there last year while doing a project on seabirds, so it might be possible, but you'd have to ask my dad.'

Harry watched Anna go to the fridge and take out a carton of milk. In fact he realised that it was hard not to watch her. She was dressed smartly in a maroon knee-length skirt and cardigan, her long light-brown hair tied back in a ponytail. Slim with an attractive face. A kind face. Harry also noticed her hands: long slender fingers. Hands were important to Harry. He figured she must be about ten years younger than him and wondered what she was doing still living at home in a small village like Cley. He was just about to ask when he was stopped by the sound of the front door opening.

'That'll be dad now.' Anna put a mug in front of Harry. 'Is that you Dad? There's someone here to see you.'

'Aye, it's me.'

Harry turned to see a man enter in blue, oil-smeared overalls. He was balding with greying hair round the edges, but had a strong face and a ready smile.

'Dad, this is Harry Lambert: he found something at the Point yesterday.'

The man offered his hand to Harry. 'I'm Peter Wild, warden of the reserve. So what is it you found there?'

'I found blood. Right out at the Point, opposite the sand bank where the seals had pulled out.' Harry indicated the rough position on the map on the kitchen table. 'Three patches of it actually. It just seemed unusual because there was a lot of it, soaked into the sand, but no sign of any injured animals or anything.'

'Hmm,' Peter stroked his chin. 'Yes, that does sound unusual. We do get an injured seal from time to time, but three at once sounds odd.'

Anna interrupted, 'I'm just going to get changed, I'll leave you to it.' She left the kitchen by the other door and Harry could hear her footsteps climbing the stairs.

'I wondered if it might be a dog attack, or maybe blood from pupping, but surely not that much?'

'Well I was out at the Point the day before and there was no sign of any greys pupping yet. They will be soon, mind you. And we do get the odd problem from tourists' dogs, but they rarely get a nip or two in before the seals make it to the water. They do drive me mad though – dogs – never on a bloody lead when they should be. I guess I'd better go and have a look. Too late today though, it'll be dark by the time I get there. I'll go first thing tomorrow.'

'Something else I wanted to ask you: I came across the Watch House on my walk and Anna tells me it was used by some students a year or so ago. I was wondering if it was possible for other people to stay there?'

Peter sat down at the table and indicated for Harry to do the same. 'Can I ask what your interest is first, what you do?'

'I'm a wildlife film-maker actually, but my interest in the Watch House is not really connected with that. I just thought it would be the perfect place to get away from it all and do a little birdwatching.'

'A wildlife film-maker! Really?' Peter became quite animated. 'I've often wished I'd got involved with that myself. Too old now. Anything by David Attenborough has me glued to the telly. Have you ever worked with the great man?'

'Not directly, but he has narrated a couple of our films.'

'Fantastic!'

They were interrupted by Anna's return. She had changed into a pair of jeans and a figure-hugging red pullover. Her hair now hung loose around her shoulders. Harry practically had to stop himself gawping at her.

Peter also turned to look at her. 'Hey, Anna, love. Did you know we had a wildlife film-maker in our midst?'

'Is that right?' She smiled at Harry. 'Oh, well, you've got a friend for life now. Dad loves all those programmes. Has he told you all about the Watch House?'

'I was just about to,' stepped in Peter. 'You're right, it's a great place for birds, but it's very basic you know: no electricity, phone or water. Just a fireplace, gas stove and a few camp beds.'

'I'm used to roughing it: sounds great to me.'

'Well it's managed by a committee now. I'll have to ask them, but I can do that tonight. And there'd be small rent, mind. When were you thinking of using it?'

Harry hadn't expected staying at the house to become a real possibility. But the thought of going back to Newmarket in a few days filled him with dread. 'My booking at the B&B is over in a few days, so maybe I could even move in straight after that – just for a week or something. Or would that be too short notice?'

'I can only ask. Can't see why it would be a problem. Give me call tomorrow afternoon – I should be back from the Point by then – and I'll let you know. Have you any plans for tomorrow?'

'Not yet. Birdwatching I guess. I've hardly done any since I've been here.'

'In that case why not come to the Point with me? Then you can show me exactly where you found this blood, and tell me some of the adventures you've had making films along the way. Where are you staying?'

'Tern Cottage, on the High Street in Blakeney.'

'Oh, Frank and Linda's place. I know it well. Frank's a grand guy, known him for years. Keen fisherman, often see him on the beach. I'll have to pick you up at seven sharp though, the tractor's still knackered so we'll have to go by boat from

Morston. And I can tell you what the committee said about the Watch House then.'

'Sounds great. I'll be ready at seven.'

Anna was pulling on a navy blue fleece. 'Dad, I'm just going to the deli to get some veggies for tonight. Nice to meet you, Harry.'

'I'm parked down that way, I'll come with you if you like.'

Peter took down Harry's mobile phone number in case there was a change of plan, and saw them both to the door. As Harry and Anna walked through Cley, side by side, Harry was pleased to see he was a few inches taller than Anna. And then he suddenly wondered what on earth was he doing sizing her up. Only a month ago he was longing to be in the arms of his wife, and now here he was, attracted to someone he'd only just met. He wasn't sure whether he was still in love with Louise – he certainly felt a lot of pain still – but also knew he never wanted to see her again after the way she had betrayed him.

'So, what do you do? I mean do you have a job?' Harry asked.

'I work part time as a teacher at the primary school in Blakeney. Just mornings. Still looking forward to half-term next week though. When I'm not doing that I'm looking after my dad and sister, she's just fifteen.'

Harry could sense there was a lack of a mother on the scene but didn't want to pry. Anna asked him more about his work and he explained about the film he had been making and about Mike's accident. Anna briefly touched Harry's arm when she heard about the tragedy. She was intrigued about this man who had suddenly appeared in their lives, whom her father had taken an instant liking to. She had also noticed that Harry had found it hard not to look at her in the kitchen, despite the wedding ring he wore.

'So is your wife here on holiday with you?'

'My wife?' Harry was confused for a second, then looked down at his hand and the plain gold band on his ring finger. It had never even occurred to him to take it off. He was still married after all. 'Oh, that. You know what?' He twisted the ring off, feeling his heart twist at the same time. 'That useless piece of scrap doesn't belong there any more.' He put the ring in his pocket, but had other plans for it later. 'She left me a month ago, went off with a friend of mine while I was away. Just history now. All of it is, really. I feel I'm at the start of a new phase of my life. Just need a rest and to get my bearings. That's why I'm here, I suppose.'

CHAPTER TEN

Harry left Tern Cottage at seven o'clock to find Peter waiting outside in his pick-up truck, engine running. He climbed in the passenger seat.

'Morning, Harry. Have you got any waterproofs with you as we'll get some spray this morning?'

'I've got a waterproof jacket in my bag.'

'That'll do. We need to get cracking now to catch the tide.'

On the short drive to Morston, Peter quizzed Harry some more about his life as a wildlife film-maker, then Harry raised the question of the Watch House.

'Ah, yes of course, I forgot to tell you. I spoke to the committee members last night and they're all fine with it. To be honest I think they were quite intrigued to have a film-maker staying there. I sold you well.' He chuckled. 'Maybe they're hoping you'll make a film there one day. Be good for tourism. You can move in when you've finished at Tern Cottage if you like. For up to two weeks, and they'll want a donation of a hundred pounds rent. How does that sound?'

'Sounds perfect. Do you know anything about the history of the place?'

'A little. We know it's about two hundred years old and was originally built by an organisation called the Preventative Waterguard. They had men, employed by the authorities, who patrolled the coast at night watching out for smugglers. Basically the Customs and Excise of the day. They had houses like the Watch House up and down the coast, but there's few of them left these days. They used them as a base for their patrols, and I dare say a few of them lived there too. Of course Blakeney was a busy port in those days and there was a lot of smuggling going on.'

'So why isn't it a busy port any more?'

'It just got silted up. They dredged the silt out to start with, but it was happening so fast they could barely keep up with it. And then bigger ports around the country grew faster, they stopped clearing the silt, and before too long the harbour became so shallow it was only good for smaller pleasure boats. Now, when the tide's right out, it's pretty much a dry harbour.'

'So, an anti-smuggling house?'

'Well that's the funny thing: there are stories that when the Preventative men stopped using it as a base, the smugglers then used it as a store for their contraband. Now that's what I call cheeky! Years later it was used by coastguards as a lookout post, like the one at Cley, and then in the war it was used by the army. You know, to watch for the invasion that never came. Since the Trust has owned the house it was used by the Girl Guides for summer camps for many years, and now it's rarely used. Unless people like yourself come across it and ask the right people the right questions.'

Peter pulled into the car park at Morston quay and Harry helped him carry the equipment to the boat.

'Ever driven a rigid inflatable like this before, Harry?'

'I've used smaller ones with outboards before, but not one with a central seat and wheel like this.'

'Well, slip on this life-jacket, hop aboard and I'll show you what to do.'

Harry stepped into the boat while Peter passed him the spare fuel tank, ropes and other equipment, before untying the bowline that tethered the boat to its wooden post.

'Right, you sit astride the seat here at the helm.' Peter indicated. 'And clip this red cord around your leg. See, it's attached to the control column? It's called the kill-cord and if it pulls out, the engine stops, so if you fall overboard the boat won't run off without you. Check she's in neutral. Now see the button at the end of the throttle lever? That's the trim button: controls how deep into the water the outboard is lowered. So lower it a bit until the prop's in the water. The creek's shallow in places but we can lower it fully when we're out in the deeper water of the harbour. Now turn the ignition key. Good, usually starts first time. Okay, put it in forward gear. Now push the throttle lever forward slowly and give it some revs. That's it, now just cruise gently up the creek: keep to the right.'

Harry was enjoying himself. It was good to be doing something practical for a change. And good to be out on the water. Heading away. Soon they had left the creek behind and were motoring across the open harbour. Peter pointed out some of the other boats moored here, he seemed to know who each one belonged to. A pair of cormorants passed by, flying low over the water, also heading towards the Point.

As they reached Peter's mooring post, he showed Harry how to slow the boat down and approach against the current. It was done perfectly. Peter jumped out and tied the boat up while Harry turned the outboard off, raised it out of the water with the trim switch, and then unclipped the kill-cord from his leg. The two men set off across the sand toward the dunes. The wind was increasing all the time and occasionally they had to turn away as a gust blew sand into their faces. When they reached the dune, Peter indicated for Harry to crawl to the top, as he was doing, and to keep quiet. He forgot that Harry was well used to creeping up on wildlife. Peeping over the top of the dune they saw the seals, hundreds of them. As it was high tide, Harry got a much closer view of them than when he had been there two days earlier. Again they were mainly common seals, including some youngsters from the summer's pupping season, with just a few greys dotted about. No sign of any new grey pups though.

Both Peter and Harry surveyed the colony with their binoculars, looking for any signs of trouble or any injuries, but all looked fine.

'So where was it you saw the blood?' Peter whispered.

'Further round to the right, I'll show you.'

They both crawled down from the ridge and, stooping so as not to be seen, trotted further round to the right of the dune. As they came out into a clearing by the sea's edge where Harry was sure the blood had been, they were far enough away from the seals to come out into the open.

Harry looked up and down the beach. 'Here. I'm sure it was here. Mind you, the patch of sand I was looking at might be under water now the tide's higher.'

They both walked up and down, inspecting the sand closely, kicking at it now and again. But there was no sign of any blood. Not even a faint stain. They explored the dunes further down to the right, away from the seals, but again there was nothing unusual to be seen: no prints, no blood, no bodies. For a moment Harry worried that Peter might think that he'd been wasting his time. The wind bit hard; Harry pulled his collar up and shivered.

'Well, we'd better not hang around too long now the tide's going out.' Peter looked at his watch. 'Let's head back to the RIB, but we can go back a different way – cut across the dunes here – at least then we'll be searching new ground.'

But the scream that ripped the air froze them to the spot.

Chapter Eleven

There it was again. A high-pitched scream – a chilling wail – almost human-like. The two men looked at each other. The sound was coming from an area of dunes a little further across the Point, away from the water's edge. The scream again – longer this time and more tortured – it sounded as if it were coming from something in great pain. As one, Peter and Harry started walking towards the sound, but both stopped again as they heard it once more, much louder, and this time joined by a second voice. There were two of them: whatever they were. The sound was piercing, heart-wrenching. Harry suddenly realised he was scared. He and Peter were possibly the only humans for miles around. The sounds of the waves and the wind and the screams all combined in his head and for a moment he clapped his hands over his ears. But then all he could hear was Mike screaming. He glanced at Peter, who was frowning deeply, and then followed him closer to the sound.

As they reached a ridge of the dune, the screaming had become so loud it was clear that whatever was making the sound was just the other side. Peter climbed up and looked over, tentatively at first, and then drew himself up to his full height.

'What the …'

Harry wasn't far behind him. 'Jesus Christ!'

The scene before them was a bloodbath. Three seals, all greys, lay in a depression in the dune in a pool of their own blood. A younger one lay on its side, mouth open, eyes staring, clearly dead. But the other two – full-grown adult females – twisted and screamed in agony. Both had several huge wounds along their flanks. Big chunks of flesh were missing, as if they had been bitten out. Blood flowed freely and mixed with the sand as they thrashed around in pain, making a sticky, dark-red mudbath. Whatever had happened to them must have taken place recently, and the wounds were so severe there was little chance of survival. Their muscles had been so badly damaged they could not move properly, could not get away, but merely writhed and squirmed in their own juices, their eyes bulging with terror. One of them could barely raise its head out of the bloody soup, and was snorting out lungfuls of stringy blood as it gasped for air. The close presence of the two men distressed them further and the screams grew to a horrifying, shocking intensity. The one that was drowning in blood cried out again and tensed its body against the pain. The cry was gargled and large red bubbles formed around its nostrils. It convulsed, sucked in a full lung of sandy blood, heaved once more, and was still. The other started a fresh wave of screaming.

Peter and Harry were both so shocked they had barely moved, but stood open-mouthed, stunned by the grisly scene.

'What the hell could have done this?' Peter's voice was hoarse. 'I've never seen anything like this in my life.'

As he spoke, the remaining living seal shook violently. Its body had gone into spasm and drops and strings of blood flew in all directions as it convulsed and shuddered. Then, it too, suddenly tensed and fell still, its body sliding back to rest alongside the others in the bath of death. Harry felt sick and for a moment turned away, afraid he was going to vomit.

As the initial wave of shock passed, Peter stepped down into the depression and Harry watched as he examined the bodies, crouching for a closer look, his hand over his mouth as the smell of fresh blood enveloped him.

Eventually he stood. 'I think we've been here long enough.' He sounded shaky. 'Let's get back to the mainland. I'll come out here later in the tractor and collect the bodies. That's assuming Joe's got it running.'

The two of them walked back towards the RIB, both glancing back just once.

Harry was confused. 'What do you think? Any idea what did

that? Do you think they were bites?'

'Oh they were bites all right. I could see teeth marks. But I can't think for the life of me what did the biting. Too vicious for another seal, besides that's usually male-on-male anyway. Only animal I can think of that bites out great chunks of flesh like that is a killer whale. But of course they only attack in the water, and with wounds like that the seals could never have crawled that far inland. Killer whales haven't been seen in these waters for years anyway. It must have been a land animal, but what?'

'How about a dog?'

'Did you see the size of the bites? What sort of dog could take out chunks like that? And I noticed that the flesh removed wasn't there any more. Whatever it was has eaten it. Eaten them alive.' He paused. 'When I get the bodies back I'll take them to the vet; see if he can shed any light on it.'

Harry could tell Peter was distressed. His jaw muscles flexed as he internalised his pain. His protection of the seals had failed somehow. Harry again thought of Mack's dog, Prince, though he knew from the size of the bites that whatever had done the damage had to be considerably larger than an Alsatian. And what dog was? He then remembered Frank's story of the spectral hound.

'Frank was telling me of a huge ghost dog that's seen around here: Black Shuck?'

Peter turned on him angrily. 'We'll have no talk of that now.' His eyes blazed for a moment then he carried on striding with an urgent pace. Harry was surprised and confused. He thought they were in this together, and had been enjoying the companionship, but Peter had suddenly put up an impenetrable barrier. During the boat ride back to Morston, and the drive back to Blakeney, Peter barely spoke. He wouldn't look Harry in the eye and just grunted replies when Harry said anything. The last part of the journey was made in an uncomfortable silence.

The men parted with minds rattled by visions of torn and bloody carcasses. But what they hadn't seen, just a stone's throw from the slaughtered seals, were the other bodies. The partly clothed, lifeless bodies. Half hidden under a large shrub and still clinging on to each other, chunks of flesh ripped from their legs and bellies. Shattered bones spiking upwards, still wet with blood, through blue jeans.

CHAPTER TWELVE

There had never been a more devoted cur. For well over four hundred years Thomas Grimes's dog had patrolled the coastal paths and beaches of North Norfolk searching for his master. The scent ever in his nostrils. So faithful was he that he couldn't pass to the other side until he had found him. It was just a question of time before the two spirits could leave this realm where they no longer belonged. Together. But after such a long time the hound was feeling a stronger pull.

Initially, after his death, Grimes's dog was careful not to reveal himself to any living being, mainly conducting his searches by night. But then one evening, as he was hiding in a thicket of young willows, he saw a coachman approach along the narrow muddy track. There was something different about this man. The dog knew instinctively that the death of a loved one was imminent: that the man's wife had only hours to live. He stepped out from the thicket, and stood in the path.

The man was tired after a long journey driving the coach and horses to Norwich and back. He was looking forward to sitting in front of the fire in his small cottage; his wife would be expecting him and would have a stew of sorts, bubbling in a pot. There'd be trouble if she hadn't. But there rarely was trouble. After nineteen years together and eleven children she was still a good wife, knew what her old man needed after a hard drive. They were honest folk with simple needs and pleasures. The cottage was in sight in the distance – he could almost smell that stew.

But suddenly, before him, blocking his path, was the mighty hound. There were plenty of dogs in the village but never in his life had he seen one so huge. And those eyes – red and glowing – that just wasn't natural. The coachman stopped in his tracks. He had no weapon on him should the dog choose to attack, yet he didn't dare look away from those blazing eyes to search for a suitable piece of timber or a branch to beat it off if need be. Smaller mutts could just be kicked out of the way if they were troublesome but there was something deeply sinister about this beast. Its size alone led the coachman to fear for his life. But after a few moments the dog merely turned and disappeared into the bushes.

Without realising it, the coachman had been holding his breath, and now let out a heavy sigh. Just to his right a broken oar lay on the ground – he picked it up and held it like a club as he gave the bushes a wide berth. But there was no sign of the dog. No flash of black shaggy fur through the branches. The dog just seemed to have melted away. Reaching home without further incident, the coachman had a new story to tell his wide-eyed children as they all sat around the hearth, eating steaming bowls of pottage.

That night there was a heavy frost. The next morning the wife left the cottage early to fetch water, but never returned. When the coachman went to search for her he found a couple of neighbours wailing at the side of the well. His wife had slipped on the ice while heaving up the heavy bucket and had fallen in after it – head first. She lay at the bottom, floating in the freezing water, neck snapped, stone dead.

The story quickly spread through the village but no link was made between the appearance of the hound and the death of the coachman's wife. No one knew whom the hound belonged to. Someone said it sounded like the cur of an old sea-trader named Grimes, but both had died at sea some time ago so that couldn't be the case.

It was only after two more deaths in the village were preceded by appearances of the massive black dog that people started to make a connection. And so it continued and the legend grew. As time went on, the spectral hound was given a number of names but it was *Black Shuck* that stuck, from the local word *shucky* which meant shaggy or hairy.

Encounters with Black Shuck became favourite tales at the inns of the region. Stories were embellished and exaggerated: some said that the hellhound was dragging chains or disappeared into thin air, gave chase or let out blood-curdling howls. But the basic theme – that the phantom was a portent of death – continued. Another popular version was that sight of Shuck foretold your own death within twelve months. Fear of the spectral hound was passed from generation to generation and, as he continued to appear, the legend remained strong. It spread to other villages, and indeed Shuck did wander further afield in his search for Grimes. Occasionally the story became confused when people ran into large living black hounds – some of which actually attacked. But none were the size nor had the glowing red eyes of the real Black Shuck.

However, as centuries ticked by, Shuck became weaker and felt the dark calling. Something had to change.

Chapter Thirteen

It was Harry's last full day at Tern Cottage and he decided he would spend it birdwatching. He needed time to think. The seal carnage at Blakeney Point had left him shocked, but Peter's reaction when Harry had mentioned the ghost dog had left him baffled. Surely no one believed in ghosts these days anyway? He had meant to ask Frank about it the night before, but Frank had gone to bed early, not feeling well. He seemed bright enough in the morning, though, and showed Harry a few recommended spots for birdwatching on the map.

The visit to the delicatessen at Cley to collect a superior picnic was now almost routine, and certainly something to look forward to. Queen olives had become a necessity, but this time Harry supplemented them with a slice of feta and spinach pie, a bottle of Norfolk-brewed beer and a piece of baklava, laden with almonds and dripping with honey.

Harry soon found the small car park that Frank had recommended, less than a mile east of Cley. He swung his rucksack on his back and walked along the bank that stretched from the coast road towards the shingle ridge that hid the sea from view. On his left lay an expanse of marsh, thick with reeds. He paused to look at a pair of large brown birds circling above the area. From their behaviour he could tell immediately they were birds of prey, and examining them through his binoculars – followed by a quick flick through his guide book – confirmed them as marsh harriers. The breeze from the north was enough to support them without any need for wing-flaps as they performed slow aerobatics above the reeds.

To his right was an extensive meadow with a herd of large black cattle grazing peacefully, including a single bull with its massive thick neck. Among them a number of greylag geese, with their large orange bills, sat by a small creek that ran through the meadow, and a few pairs of Egyptian geese wandered about, pecking at the grass. Further along the bank, on the right, there was a lagoon of salt-water known as Arnold's Marsh, which Frank had indicated was a perfect site for watching waders and seabirds. Harry climbed down the bank a little, spread his jacket on the ground and settled down.

In front of him a few black-headed gulls drifted about on the water. In winter plumage their black heads had become white with a smudge of grey, but the red bills gave them away. Behind them a large group of waders probed the mud beneath the shallow water. At first they all looked similar, but after studying them for a while, and frequently referring to his book, Harry identified redshank, black-tailed godwits, curlews and a few exquisite avocets with their long bills curving upwards and black and white tunics. Further in the distance, on a sandy bank, he could see a group of cormorants, several of them extending their wings to dry in the breeze. And, to their right, a large group of widgeon, shelduck and teal. Harry could understand why birdwatchers came here from all over the world.

Tucking into his picnic, Harry mused over the last few days. Tomorrow he had to leave Tern Cottage, and although the plan was to go straight to the Watch House, he had made no definite arrangements with Peter, whose help he would need. There was certainly no way he felt like going back to Newmarket yet. Maybe he should phone Peter from the cottage that night: find out what had upset him, make some plans.

Having popped the last piece of baklava into his mouth, Harry wiped his honey-sticky fingers on the grass and took a swig of beer. Norfolk was growing on him in ways he hadn't foreseen. Not only was he falling under the spell the landscape – wild and bleak yet fascinating – but also his unexpected interactions with some of the local people had made him feel involved. He wasn't the unidentified loner he had expected to be on this get-away of recovery. Despite Peter's coldness at the end of their trip to the

Point, Harry felt more at home in Norfolk now than in Newmarket: the town of pain. And to a small degree the holiday was working; this new involvement and the strange events were helping to put some distance between Harry and his tragic past.

Loading up his rucksack he walked further along the bank to where it met the shingle ridge. Climbing up, slipping back one step on the loose pebbles for every two he climbed up, he finally saw the sea. It was an overcast day and the water looked grey and unwelcoming. He settled on the top of the ridge and scanned out to sea with his binoculars. The wind from the north was good for birdwatchers as it often blew seabirds closer to the shore. In the distance a number of gannets with yellowish heads were diving for fish as the odd greater black-backed gull flew past. A few dark patches floating on the surface proved to be rafts of razorbills and guillemots.

Eventually the wind became too chilling and Harry retraced his steps to the car. As he journeyed back towards Cley he drove past Marsh View and considered dropping in, but thought his original decision to phone was wiser, and continued back to Blakeney. He would change, pack his belongings, ring Peter, and then go to the King's Arms for supper.

As it happened, when he opened the door to Tern Cottage, Linda had just returned from shopping and was carrying several bags of groceries through to the kitchen.

'Here, let me help you.' Harry reached for one of the bags.

'Oh, hello Harry,' Linda turned and smiled. 'I'm glad I've caught you. We're having the Wilds over for dinner tonight and hoped you could join us as it's your last night. Be a bit of a party! We're sorry to see you go, to be honest, but the person coming after you has confirmed their booking and the other room's still not ready. I wish Frank would finish painting it but he's been a bit tired recently. Always got the energy for fishing, mind you.'

Harry hesitated. Maybe the Wilds had been invited before he and Peter had gone to the Point. But then Peter hadn't mentioned it. Hopefully this meant that whatever had upset Peter wasn't serious – and the meal might be the perfect way to regain a good footing in their relations. 'Thanks, I'd love to.'

'Good. Frank will be pleased; he's taken a shine to you. We've known Peter and the girls for years. Have them round every few weeks or so for a meal. Of course it used to be Mary too, God rest her soul.'

Harry was just about to ask what had happened to Peter's wife – presumably the Mary whom Linda had just referred to – when the front door opened and Frank came in with a box of mackerel.

'I couldn't stop them biting today, look at this lot!

After admiring Frank's catch, Harry went upstairs and changed into a clean pair of jeans and had a good wash in the bathroom. It was dark now and from his bedroom window he could see the lights along the side of the quay: to stop people wandering off the edge at night, into the black water. He could make out a small group of people walking in the street below, and sure enough there was soon a loud knock at the front door followed by Linda's calls of welcome. Harry felt a twinge of apprehension: would Peter still be cold towards him, would Anna still be friendly? He took a deep breath and went down the stairs to the kitchen where everyone had gathered.

He was surprised that the first person he saw was a girl he didn't recognise, but remembered Anna had a sister. Everyone turned to look at him and to his relief they were all smiling.

It was Linda who spoke first. 'Ah, here's our guest of honour. Harry you've met the Wilds already, haven't you?'

'Well, most of them.'

'Harry, this is Sophie,' Anna helped out. 'My little sis'.'

Sophie glared at Anna and then turned to Harry, beaming. 'Hello.'

At fifteen years of age she was nearly as tall as her sister, but had blonder hair, tied back in a long ponytail. She, too, was going to be a beauty. Anna was looking stunning in black jeans and a red cardigan under a long black coat, her hair loose and freshly brushed.

'Right, who's for a drink?' asked Frank. The kitchen was

suddenly full of activity as coats were taken off, drinks were organised, and Linda bustled around with the cooking.

Anna touched Harry's arm and, with a serious expression, whispered, 'Harry, can I have a quick word?' She nodded towards the front room, which led off the hallway by the bottom of the stairs.

'Sure,' replied Harry, leading the way and flicking the light switch in the room. He turned to face her.

'It's about my Dad,' she spoke quietly. 'He feels badly about the other day but I'm not sure he's up to apologising himself. He told me what happened – I mean about storming off after you mentioned…' Anna paused and looked to the floor. '…Black Shuck.' She spat the words out as if with great hatred. 'He knows you meant no harm: that you were only trying to help. It's just that … he's got so much hurt inside.'

'I don't understand.'

'Well, it's only a year ago that my mum died. It was really sudden and unexpected: a brain haemorrhage. The thing is, a couple of days before she collapsed, my Dad saw a big black dog on the beach near the car park. Do you know about the legend?'

'You mean that if you see Black Shuck you or someone in your family will die soon afterwards? Yes, Frank told me.'

'Yes, well, of course my dad, being my dad, never believed in nonsense such as that. He only remembered the dog because it was so large and shaggy and seemed to have no owner nearby. He tried to follow it in case it strayed too close to the seal colony, but it vanished in the shrubs. Then when my mum died, he remembered the dog and thought about the legend. It was weeks before he could even bring himself to tell me about it. Ever since then if anyone mentions Black Shuck it just brings it all up again for him.'

'I'm so sorry, I must apologise to him.'

'No need, you didn't mean to upset him. Best let things lie now.'

'If you're sure?' Harry touched Anna's arm gently. 'And I'm sorry for you, too: for your loss.'

'Thanks.' Anna held Harry's gaze for a moment. Her eyes were sad but the corner of her mouth turned up in a half smile. 'We'd better join the others – before they get suspicious!'

Back in the kitchen, Linda was emptying pots of steaming vegetables into large serving-dishes and Frank was pouring wine.

Sophie sidled up to her sister. 'And what were you two up to?'

Anna merely gave her a withering look.

As wine glasses were handed round and several conversations started up, Peter came over to Harry. 'Listen, about the other day, I know you meant nothing, I'm sorry for my reaction. Let's just put it behind us, eh?'

'No problem. I'm sorry too.' Harry raised his glass and clinked Peter's. 'Cheers.'

Feeling much relieved, Harry sat at the large kitchen table, now laden with a feast. Frank carved two roast pheasants while bowls of roast potatoes and parsnips were passed round, followed by cabbage and carrots and jugs of gravy. Wine seemed in endless supply and the atmosphere lightened by the minute as the lively conversation veered from teasing Frank about his fishing obsession to laughing at Peter's mischievous tractor.

It was a long time since Harry had felt so involved with a group of people he genuinely liked very much. He felt sad to be leaving Tern Cottage so soon; he would gladly have remained longer if it had been possible, and he was determined to stay again another time. But he was also excited at the prospect of staying at the Watch House with just a few passing seabirds for company. Excited but at the same time a little apprehensive.

All too soon the meal was over and, after coffee and a few whiskies, the Wilds prepared to go home.

'I think I'll be driving tonight,' Anna said, patting her bleary-eyed father on the arm.

'I think you will,' Peter chuckled then turned to Harry. 'I'll meet you at Morston quay at about eleven tomorrow and take you out to the Watch House in the RIB, okay? Don't forget to have all your supplies ready, food, bottled water and so on.'

'Thanks, look forward to it.'

As Anna passed Harry to leave, she smiled at him. 'See you.'
'Hope so,' he replied.
For Harry, the bloodbath at Blakeney was becoming a distant memory. But memories have a habit of resurfacing.

Chapter Fourteen

Linda was up early the next morning as she had much to do. First there was the weekly visit to her elderly aunt, then stocking up on groceries for the week ahead, and she wasn't forgetting having to prepare Harry's room for the next guest. There was a two-hour window between Harry leaving and the expected arrival of the new lodger. Still, it was a well-worn routine, and that was ample time to spruce up the room, strip and remake the bed, and clean the bathroom.

She left Frank snoring gently beneath the duvet. Since retiring from crab fishing by boat, he seemed to have aged rapidly. Despite being only in his early sixties he needed more sleep these days, and had less energy for tasks around the house – such as decorating the other guest room. They could do with the extra income. Perhaps she would give him a gentle nag later. Just a reminder; she was not the nagging sort and he didn't deserve anything more stern. He had been a good husband for thirty years and was a kind soul, the sort people would describe as not having a bad bone in his body: happy to help anyone. For some reason she briefly reflected on their sadness at being unable to have children, something she hadn't thought about for some time: he would have made a lovely father.

She stepped quietly down the stairs, not wanting to wake Harry either. She would miss him and was glad he was staying in the area a little longer, but nevertheless hoped he would vacate his room by ten, so that she could tackle the cleaning.

Leaving Tern Cottage, she walked down the street to the quay. Turning left and walking along the edge, she shivered and pulled her collar up. Autumn was really setting in and there was a low mist on the surface of the water. It was early enough for the quay to be deserted. There was no rain, but the air felt heavy with moisture. Perhaps this was the last time she would walk to her aunt's via the marsh path: soon that would become muddy and slippery. For the rest of autumn and winter she'd take the longer route along the side of the coast road – but with no pavement that had its own dangers.

At the end of the quay she turned right and walked carefully along the dilapidated wooden boardwalk before stepping down on to the path. Now, on the edge of the marsh, the mist was unusually thick and low, lying over the sea lavender like a dense blanket. Her feet made swirls in this covering; she could almost feel the weight of it, as if she had to drag her legs through treacle. A distant lone curlew called out, eerily the only sound across the marsh.

Not that she resented her weekly visits: it felt good to be useful and Eileen, her aunt, was truly grateful. It was her regular carer's day off, and, despite her frailty, Eileen still liked to get up early, though she could no longer do so without assistance. At the age of eighty-one she had a collection of health problems, the majority brought on by a life of being overweight. She was now diabetic and had a weak heart, not to mention her arthritis and regular bouts of gout. Linda was now her only remaining family and Eileen looked forward to her brief visits.

Arriving at the back door of the small bungalow, and glad to have the marsh behind her, Linda let herself in with her own key.

'Eileen, hello, it's just me: Linda,' she called as usual.

After a pause came a small croaky reply. 'Oh, hello dear. I was having a little dream.'

Linda went through to her aunt's bedroom. Eileen lay under a thick duvet in a pale floral cover, propped up on a large number of pillows. She seemed barely able to turn her head towards Linda, but looked at her out of the corner of her eyes. Her face looked more gaunt than usual, her thin papery skin stretched tight.

'Morning, love,' Linda leaned over and kissed her on the

forehead. 'How are you feeling today?'

'Oh not so bad you know.' Eileen coughed and winced with the pain it caused. 'Just a bit more tired than usual. Not sure I feel like getting up today.'

'Why don't you have a day in bed for a change? I could make you some sandwiches for lunch and leave them ready for you.'

'Yes, all right dear.' Eileen looked distractedly towards the window.

'Okay, you just rest. I'll bring in your Weetabix.' Linda sounded bright but was concerned. This was not like Eileen at all, who was usually keen to get up and dressed and sit by the large window in her front room where she could spy on people walking along the marsh path.

Back in the kitchen she put Eileen's regular single Weetabix in a bowl with lots of milk. She carried this into the bedroom on a tray and helped Eileen to sit up higher in the bed. She sat on the edge of the bed and chatted about the mundane comings and goings of life that Eileen loved to hear about, but couldn't help becoming misty-eyed as she saw how Eileen was struggling. Just raising the spoon of cereal seemed an effort and Eileen's hands shook more than usual. After just a few spoonfuls she lay her head back and closed her eyes.

'I think I've had enough thanks, dear,' she said in a slow, slightly slurred voice.

Linda took the tray away and busied herself in the kitchen, washing up a few items from the day before and making a couple of Marmite sandwiches, crusts cut off, for Eileen's lunch. She left these with a banana and a glass of sugar-free orange squash on the bedside table and helped Eileen into the bathroom for a wash and to use the toilet. Back in bed, Eileen seemed a little brighter and talked about how she was looking forward to the summer. Next summer: that was such a long way off Linda couldn't help but fear Eileen might never see it. She had never seen her as weak and lethargic as this. After chatting a little longer, Linda made sure Eileen had everything she needed and that the telephone was close to the bed.

'Now just remember to phone me if you feel poorly or if you need anything. Call me any time, day or night.' She worried for a moment that she might have sounded too concerned, but Eileen's eyes were already closed again as she fell into a doze. Linda decided she would telephone Eileen that afternoon to check she was all right; maybe call the doctor out if she didn't sound too good.

Leaving the bungalow, Linda was surprised to find the mist over the marsh was just as thick as when she had arrived. The sky above was clear: surely the sun would burn it off soon? As she walked along she felt a great sadness about Eileen's deterioration. Normally she was such a jolly soul, despite having lived on her own for thirty-odd years after her husband had left her for a younger woman. She had been in Blakeney nearly all her life, and, until she had grown too frail, filled her loneliness by becoming involved in village community activities. Although it was just a weekly visit, her death, when it came, would leave a hole in Linda's life.

Ahead of her, for a moment, Linda thought she could see two red lights, shining weakly from a shrubby area to the right of the marsh. Bicycle lights maybe? But a strange place for them to be. She carried on but slowed slightly when she thought she saw a dark shape moving in the shrub. Then a brief flash of red lights again. She stopped. Maybe she should go back to the bungalow and walk home along the road instead. But that was silly. It was probably only a couple of children on their bikes. Maybe meeting for an illicit cigarette on their paper-rounds. Besides, this was a safe place, just a holiday village, sleepy now the summer was over.

She started walking forwards but after a few steps saw the black shape again. It almost looked as if it were an animal turning around under the shrub. Again the two red lights, close together, always the same distance apart, and this time they flashed twice. It was almost as if they were eyes blinking at her. Linda felt a coldness flood through her body, and was suddenly aware of the stillness all around, and of her isolation.

'Hello,' she called out, instantly regretting the quaver in her voice. How daft to be afraid of a couple of paper-boys. But when the red lights blinked at her again she knew she really was afraid: deeply afraid in a way she hadn't experienced before. She wanted to turn away, to go back to the bungalow, to *run* back. But she couldn't move. She tried to call out again but no sound would come. Her eyes were locked to those red lights that seemed to be boring into her.

And then it revealed itself.

From under the shrub a large black animal moved on to the path in full view, its feet hidden in the same thick mist that seemed to be anchoring Linda to the ground. It looked like a huge hound with a thick shaggy coat. Like a wolfhound but even larger, stockier. It slowly turned its massive head towards Linda and again those big red shining eyes penetrated her body and blinked twice. Linda wanted to run, to scream, but could do nothing. Another icy wave passed through her body. For what seemed like many minutes the beast stood its ground and stared deep into her. Then, just as Linda thought she was going to pass out with terror, it turned slowly and seemed to fade away into the mist. And it was then that Linda suddenly realised what this demon was. What it was telling her.

CHAPTER FIFTEEN

The alarm, set on Harry's mobile phone, woke him with a start. He had been in a deep sleep and now found his head muggy from the wine and whisky of the night before. Sitting up, he could tell from the illumination of the curtains that it was a bright day, and as he gradually remembered that today was the day his adventure at Watch House was to start, he became invigorated. Adventures, however small, were what Harry lived for.

Tern Cottage seemed strangely quiet as Harry breakfasted. He didn't want to leave without saying goodbye to Linda and Frank, so he decided to shop for his provisions next and then return to the cottage for the farewells.

Leaving his small rucksack, he took his packed holdall and coat and locked them in the back of the Freelander on the way to the village stores. He knew the Watch House had a cylinder gas stove, luxury compared to some of the conditions in which he had had to cook for himself, and he was used to stocking up on supplies for an expedition. He chose a selection of tinned goods and other foods, then a few essentials including candles, matches and bottles of water. If he was feeling energetic later in the week he could always walk from the Watch House to the delicatessen at Cley and stock up on some classier fare. His groceries were packed into a cardboard box, which he took straight to his car before returning to Tern Cottage.

Opening the front door, he was surprised to hear the sound of crying coming from the kitchen. He could also hear Frank's voice mumbling soothing words. Not wanting to pry, Harry went straight upstairs to his room. He checked the bathroom and packed a few remaining small items into his rucksack. After a final check in the drawers of the chest in his room he carried his rucksack downstairs. He knocked gently on the kitchen door.

Frank opened it. 'Harry, you know there's no need to knock. Are you ready for the off then?'

'Yes, all packed.' Harry could see Linda beside the stove, wiping her eyes with a pale pink hanky. 'Is everything all right?'

'Linda's just a little upset about her aunt,' replied Frank.

'Don't mind me, love,' sniffled Linda. 'I've just had a bit of a shock that's all. My poor old auntie's on her last legs, I'm afraid. I don't think she'll be with us much longer, and I'm not very brave when it comes to losing loved ones.'

'Sorry to hear that.' Harry felt awkward. 'I'm all ready to go so I should leave you to it. I just wanted to say thanks for looking after me: for the meals and treating me like family.'

Linda came over and surprised Harry by giving him a hug. 'It's been lovely having you, Harry. You will drop by and say cheerio properly before you leave Norfolk won't you?'

'Of course I will.'

Frank grasped Harry by the hand and shook it warmly. 'You take good care in the Watch House, Harry. I'll keep an eye out for you when I'm fishing at Cley. I should be there tomorrow as a matter of fact. But today I've promised the old dragon I'd do some more to the other guest room.' He glanced at Linda, making sure that his teasing would not upset her further, and put his arm round her shoulders.

'Old dragon, indeed!' Linda chuckled, but Harry could see the sorrow in her eyes. And something else: something more disconcerting than sadness that he couldn't put his finger on.

CHAPTER SIXTEEN

Harry walked to the Freelander, threw his rucksack on to the passenger's seat, and set off towards Morston. The week at Tern Cottage had flown by, and had been filled with many unexpected occurrences, which had certainly helped take his mind off troubles at home. Even thinking of Newmarket as 'home' seemed ridiculous now, and he determined to move from the area as soon as possible.

As he pulled into the rough car park at the far end of Morston quay he could see Peter, leaning against his truck. He pulled up alongside.

'Morning, Harry,' Peter smiled. 'Have you got everything you need before I maroon you?'

'I think so,' laughed Harry. 'Enough for a few days anyway. It's not as if I'll be hundreds of miles from civilisation.'

'The RIB's all ready, so let's get your stuff loaded and we'll set off,' Peter glanced up at the sky. 'It's going to be a fine day.'

True enough, the sun was shining brightly now and all traces of early mist had been burned off. Peter helped Harry carry his holdall, rucksack and supplies to the RIB where they were stowed in the bow area. He then showed Harry where he could park his Freelander while he was away – further back from the quay car park which was occasionally flooded by an unusually high tide. Back at the RIB they donned life jackets and cast off. Harry was happy to take the role of passenger this time as Peter took the helm. The engine started, and Peter steered the boat down the creek.

'Did you manage to collect those seal bodies from the Point the other day?' Harry asked cautiously.

'I did. Joe managed to get the tractor working – for a little longer anyway. So I picked the bodies up and took them to the vet's. As it happens he rang this morning before I left the house.'

'Did he have any ideas?'

Peter stroked his chin. 'Nothing unexpected. He confirmed that the seals all died of blood-loss from their wounds, and that the wounds were caused by something biting chunks out of them. He found plenty of tooth marks all over the bodies, some caused by other seals, but the majority of marks around the wounds were from long canines that were closer together than those in seals. More like you'd find in a dog, but he agreed it would have to have been a very large dog. There's also the matter that all three seals must have been attacked at the same time, so it must have been either a pack of dogs or … or a dog that could move like lightning. Bite like lightning.'

'Christ! And has anything happened since?'

'No, been as quiet as usual. And what's more I haven't seen any dogs around the reserve and there have been no reports of strays: packs or otherwise. It's a bit of a mystery for now. But my shotgun's all ready at home should anybody see a rogue hound. I'll do my damnedest to make sure something like that doesn't happen again.'

Out on the open water of the harbour, Peter steered the RIB in between the last few moored boats that had not been taken away for a winter of dry storage. The Watch House came into view – a small square shape, dark against the horizon. As they drew closer the water became shallower, and Peter had to slow down and raise the outboard slightly as it occasionally bumped along the muddy bottom. There was a mooring post ahead on the edge of a reedy area: the closest they could get the boat to the house. As they drew near, Harry leaned over the bow and secured the boat with the line before stepping out.

The two men walked towards the house, Harry carrying his rucksack and holdall, Peter carrying the box of provisions. They put these down outside the door as Peter fished in his pocket and produced a large key. He unlocked the door and gave the key to Harry.

'I've just got a couple of things to show you, Harry, then I'll leave you to settle in.' He handed over another smaller key. 'While you're staying here you can take off all the wire mesh covers on the windows – this key fits the padlock for each one – they're to stop people breaking in while the house is empty.'

Peter opened the door, lifted the box of supplies, and carried it into the house. The entrance led straight into the main room, which had only a large oak table and two chairs for furniture. Peter slid the box on to the table, which was under the window overlooking the marsh and harbour towards Blakeney. Opposite the window was a small fireplace in the centre of the building.

'Feel free to use the fireplace; you'll find plenty of wood washed up on the beach: old fishing crates and the like. Now, down here is the stove.' Peter led the way down a narrow corridor that led from one of the four internal doors of the main room. At the end was a small cooker above a large orange gas cylinder. He lifted the cylinder to gauge its weight. 'There'll be plenty enough gas there for your stay. Just turn the valve here to let the gas through, then shut it off when you're done. There's a small cupboard here with cooking pots and plates and so forth. The only other thing I've got to show you is outside.'

Harry followed Peter outside and around to the side of the house where there was a large circular water tank. Peter lifted the lid of the tank and peered in.

'This tank's full of rainwater fed from the roof. You can use it for washing yourself and washing dishes, but not for drinking.' He nodded towards the small brick building a few yards away: the loo-with-a-view. 'And in the toilet you'll find a bucket you can fill from this tank to flush.'

Harry smiled. 'Everything seems to have been thought of.'

'Well, it's basic, but you're a survivor. Now I best be going while there's enough water to get the boat off. You know where we are if you have any problems; I assume you've got your mobile phone with you?'

'Fully charged.'

'Good.' Peter turned and started walking back to the RIB.

'Thanks for dropping me off.'

Peter stopped and turned to face Harry. 'You know, you might be a useful lookout. It goes without saying that if you do see anything unusual – like a dog or pack of dogs – you will let me know.'

'Straight away.'

Peter waved and carried on to the boat. Harry watched as he climbed in, untied the mooring line and motored off without a backward glance.

Harry turned to face his new home. He was alone at last, the sky was clear blue, the smell of the sea was in the air, and he was master of the beach. First he would explore his new domain properly. He took his rucksack and holdall inside the house and dumped them in the main room. The first internal door led to a small bedroom with one camp bed, the other two rooms were slightly larger with two camp beds in each. There was no other furniture in the house; the walls were bare with peeling paint, the floors were of ancient boards. It was basic indeed, but Harry had roughed it far worse in the past.

One of the bedrooms had an old iron ladder that led up to the lookout room. Harry climbed up to investigate. The room was surprisingly small – bare and empty with wood-panelled walls stained a dark brown. It had just the one window: looking north out to sea. The glass was so filthy it was hard to see much, and there was no way of opening it. Harry could just imagine the Preventative men of centuries ago, taking turns to sit up here and watch for smugglers trying to sneak their boats into port.

Back on the ground floor, Harry chose the smallest bedroom and unpacked a few of his belongings. He then carried the box of provisions through and left it on the floor next to the stove. There was no sign of any mice or rats; he supposed there was so rarely any food here that they would have nothing to live on. He picked up an old metal kettle, rinsed it out, and filled it with water from one of his bottles. Turning the gas valve on, he successfully lit the stove, and left the kettle to boil while going outside to take off the metal window-guards. Once he had done this he leaned the large sheets of mesh against a wall in the main room.

Having made a mug of tea, he carried it out and sat on a fishing crate that had been placed by the front door. He could see Blakeney village in the distance, but it was too far away to make out the movement of any people. The only sounds were the wash of waves on the shingle beach from the other side of the house, and the occasional call of a gull. He stretched his legs out and could start to feel the release of tension. His troubles felt far away. Old troubles.

But hundreds of miles to the north of where Harry sat, an area of low depression was brewing trouble of a very different kind.

Chapter Seventeen

It was a strange rattling noise that woke Harry the next morning. He lifted his head and winced at the pain in his neck – the lack of pillows had forced him to sleep on his rolled-up fleece. He purposely hadn't set his alarm and was shocked when his watch told him it was already past ten o'clock. After a sausage-supper in front of a small crackling fire the night before, he had felt unusually tired and had gone to bed early. He must have fallen asleep instantly and slept for more than twelve hours. Not like him. Maybe it was the sea air.

He rubbed his neck, pulled on his jeans and padded over to the front door; the rattling seemed to be coming from outside. It was an irregular twanging metallic sound. Opening the door he was momentarily blinded by the sunlight; it was another bright autumn day. The sound was coming from just around the left corner of the house. The air was still, so it couldn't be anything vibrating in the wind. Still bare-footed, he stepped cautiously forward to peer around the corner. There, he was surprised to see an Egyptian goose flapping awkwardly on the ground, its leg caught in a piece of wire that was rattling against the wall of the house where it was attached. When the goose saw Harry it started making a high-pitched call: 'Hur, hur, hur,' and flapped its wings all the more. At this rate it was going to do some serious damage to its leg.

Harry darted back in the house and grabbed his towel from the bedroom. He approached the goose quickly and covered its body with the towel so that he could hold its wings closed and stop it struggling. The bird immediately calmed down and fell quiet.

Harry spoke to it gently and soothingly. 'All right, all right, let's get you untangled then. How on earth did you get in this mess, eh?'

He sat on the ground with the bird in his lap and investigated the long pink leg. With his free hand he gently loosened the wire, which had formed a noose, pulled tight above the webbed foot like a snare. But it wasn't a snare surely – here on a nature reserve?

With the wire removed he inspected the leg carefully, but despite the wire having cut through the skin there was no sign of bone-breakage or permanent damage. Setting the goose down on the ground he slowly removed the towel. The bird limped a few paces away and then turned to look at Harry. It shook its wings out and hobbled a little further away as Harry stood up and started coiling the kinked and rusty wire. He pulled the coil as hard as he could to try and detach it from the wall, but it wouldn't come free. So instead he wound it into a tight ball and buried it by the side of the wall, with a few large stones on top for good measure. Perhaps he would borrow some wire-cutters from Peter in a few days and remove the hazard completely. The goose was watching him warily all the while. It seemed reluctant to move off. Maybe it just needed a little time to recover.

Harry went back in the house, dressed properly and put the kettle on. He made a couple of honey sandwiches for his breakfast and took them outside with his mug of tea to eat in the sunshine. The goose was still there. Harry sat on the crate and took a large mouthful of sandwich. Now that he had time to look at the bird properly he could see what a beautiful animal it was. The body was largely buff-coloured but it had reddish-brown wings with a white flash. There was also a distinctive dark patch around the eye and a narrow neck-band. He was used to seeing Egyptian geese in pairs – maybe this one had lost its mate.

He tore off a small piece of bread and threw it in front of the bird. It hesitated then stretched its neck out cautiously, watching Harry all the time, before gobbling the morsel down.

'Are you a hungry fellow then? Would you like some more?' A second piece went the same way, so Harry fetched a whole slice from the house, broke it into pieces, and fed them to the bird.

When finished, it sat gingerly down on the ground, just a few yards from where Harry was sitting. He expected the damaged leg was hurting the bird, but it should heal in time. After a rest it would probably be on its way.

Having finished his breakfast, Harry wandered over the shingle ridge and down to the edge of the sea. The tide was starting to recede and had left a fresh collection of stranded items on the beach: driftwood, plastic bottles, a light bulb, clumps of seaweed, a starfish. The wood would be useful for a fire later and Harry determined to set a daily ritual of collecting driftwood and laying it out to dry in the sun. He picked up the starfish – pink and rough to the touch – a common starfish with five thick arms. It was still moist and probably still alive, but would soon dry out in the sun despite the chill in the air, so Harry took it to the water's edge and threw it gently in.

Sitting on the pebbles and squinting out to the bright horizon, Harry's thoughts wandered to the difficult tasks ahead once he returned to Newmarket. He needed a plan. Just needed to be organised about it all. He would put the house on the market as soon as possible, divide up the possessions, find somewhere cheap to rent. His share of the house sale should settle his debts, and he always had his cameras to sell if need be.

He kicked out at the pebbles, suddenly angry that it had come to this. Angry with Mike for dying and leaving him, angry with Louise for wanting someone else and leaving him, angry with being abandoned by his most important people. He'd thought they'd had a pact. Louise knew full well he was going to have to work overseas, and he had made a huge effort to make sure it wasn't for too long at a time. All those occasions he had left Mike in the field to fly home and be with Louise for a week or two had been a waste. Everything had been a waste. All the effort – both in work and love – had been made and it was time to reap the rewards, but now he was worse off than ever.

He glanced down at his sun-bronzed hands, a pale band where his wedding ring had been until that brief walk with Anna a few days earlier. He reached in his jeans' pocket; the ring was still there. Pulling it out he turned it over in his hand, remembering the pledges made as it was put on his finger.

Suddenly he was on his feet and hurled the ring as far as he could into the sea, yelling: 'Good riddance – bitch!'

His chest was heaving with the effort and the stress. The realisation of what he had done, what it meant, sent waves of heat through his body. He felt his face flush. He could smell his own sweat – different from the normal perspiration of exercise but the more pungent sweat of stress. He slipped his shoes off, rolled up his jeans and stepped into the water. It was cooling, soothing. Looking up and down the beach there was no one in sight, so he stripped off all his clothes, throwing them behind him on to the shingle, and waded into the water.

A wave reached his waist. 'Jesus!' It wasn't soothing any more, it was freezing. Now his hot body was fully in the water he gasped for breath. Plunging headlong he swam a fast font-crawl, parallel to the shore, turned and swam back again. He did it again and again until he was exhausted, spent.

Enough. Time to get out. But as he turned to the shore he was surprised to see someone on the beach: a woman in a red dress. She wasn't close enough to see any detail and was walking away from Harry – back towards Cley – but he couldn't figure out how he hadn't seen her before when he had scanned the beach before stripping off. She must have been the other side of the shingle ridge behind some shrubs. An odd place to be.

Up to his neck in water, he shuddered with the cold and swam back and forth at speed a couple more times to warm up and let the woman get further away before he exposed himself. But when he looked again there was no sign of her at all. There was no way she could have walked fast enough to be out of sight, so must have gone the other side of the ridge again. At least he could get out now that she was gone.

He crawled towards his discarded clothes and sat on the shore, panting, holding his side where a stitch nagged at him. After the pain had subsided and his breathing became more regular he stood, to find his legs wobbly from the exertion. He gathered his clothes, and, shivering, jogged back to the house. He barely registered the goose, still sitting in the same position. Inside he quickly towelled himself dry, dressed, lay on his bed and was rapidly overcome by sleep.

Two hours later he awoke with an urgent need to relieve himself. Walking to the loo-with-a-view, he felt lighter, clearer-headed. Maybe the manic swim had done him some good: exorcised some anger. He wasn't the sort to see a counsellor; he preferred the punch-bag approach.

It was on his way back that he noticed the goose. It watched him nervously, but made no attempt to stand. Harry found a bowl in the kitchen, filled it with water from the rain-tank, and placed it slowly in front of the bird. After he had backed away it dipped its beak in the water and lifted its head to let the liquid slide down its throat. Harry fetched some more bread and his guidebook. Sitting close to the bird, he read the page on Egyptian geese. He discovered that though the different sexes had the same plumage, it was only the female who made a high-pitched call such as the one he had heard earlier, the male's being a husky wheeze.

'So, you're a girl are you? What shall we call you?' Initially Harry struggled to think of any Egyptian name, then it hit him. 'Cleopatra. How's that? Maybe Cleo for short. Cleo? That suits you just fine.'

Cleo gobbled the bread down and took another long drink. Harry stayed sitting next to his new friend awhile and surveyed the scene. Out in the harbour he could just make out a man climbing from a small dinghy on to a large catamaran. Possibly preparing it for winter storage, or taking it on a voyage into the unknown, or stealing it! On the mooring post by the reeds a greater black-backed gull stood motionless. After a while, a few lights came on in the windows of the hotel on the quay front. There would not be much daylight left, which reminded Harry of the need to collect firewood.

Back over the shingle ridge, on the tide line, he picked up an armful of bits and pieces of driftwood, and nearer the house found a smashed wooden fish-crate, which was dry and would get the blaze going quickly. He carried them into the house and laid them next to the fireplace. It had only been a day and the isolation wasn't bothering him at all. In fact when he did see a group of walkers through his bedroom window his instinct was to remain hidden. He shinned up the ladder to the lookout and spied on them through the grimy window.

There were four in the group: two in bright red jackets and two in blue. They all wore sturdy hiking boots and carried small rucksacks. Professional ramblers. They were walking towards Cley, away from the Point, so they must have passed the Watch House in the other direction while Harry had been sleeping. Although some distance away, they stopped and looked at the house. They were clearly talking about it; one of them was pointing but there was no way they could have seen Harry through the dirty glass in the dark room. For a moment he thought they were going to come to the house and the thought of making small-talk to strangers filled him with horror. He wanted to be alone. This was his domain. He also feared they might frighten Cleo away if they came closer. But after a while they simply moved off, back towards the car park at Cley beach.

As the sun set, the temperature on this clear day dropped quickly. Harry ripped a couple of pages out of his notebook and crumpled them up in the fireplace. On top he placed some strips of cardboard, torn from the box his groceries had come in, and then some slivers of wood from the smashed crate. Lighting the paper soon produced the desired result and he sat cross-legged in front of the flames, feeding them with larger pieces of fish-crate and then lumps of driftwood until the heat forced him further back.

In the kitchen he concocted a stew by mixing cans of chopped tomatoes, sweetcorn and tuna and heating them in a pan. Sitting at the oak table, eating by candlelight, he imagined himself there centuries ago. Fuelling up before a night-time patrol of the beach. Perhaps he would catch some smugglers tonight. Maybe he would be carrying a sword to protect himself.

Harry stared into the flames a long while, feeding the fire with driftwood until it had all gone. His thoughts drifted from history to the present and back again. One minute he was wishing he lived in the past, when everything had been simpler, the next he was lamenting the present and plotting a better future. He thought of Anna too, and of how easily she had lifted his spirits. He could see her long hair in the flames, her beautiful face. The more he stared, the more he became one with the fire, and the more the external world ceased to exist. The universe became just him and the fire and nothing else. Two life forces locked together.

As the embers gradually faded and the room cooled, he walked the few paces to his bedroom and lay down – hoping sleep would again come quickly.

But it didn't.

At first it was a busy head that kept him awake, and then, as the heat from the fire dissipated, it was the cold. He heaped all his clothes on top of the rough blankets that had been provided on the camp bed but still felt the chill. And then, just as he was starting to slip away, the noises started.

CHAPTER EIGHTEEN

First was the rustling. Slight at first. So slight that he had to strain to hear it, holding his breath. Then it grew a little louder, a little more frantic. It seemed to be coming from inside the house. Maybe a mouse had found its way in, after all. Slowly and quietly, Harry swung his feet over the side of the camp bed and stood up. He reached in his rucksack, pulled out his small Maglite and twisted the head to switch it on. Stepping into the main room he played the slender bright beam around the floor, in the corners. Nothing unusual to be seen, and the noise had stopped. He twisted the torch off and stood still for a moment. It started again. This time he was sure it was coming from the corridor that led to the stove. Must be a mouse in his box of food.

Harry tiptoed toward the corridor in the dark, feeling his way with his hands. He touched along the fireplace's mantelpiece, past the two doorways that led to the other bedrooms, and down the rough brick of the corridor. When he had turned the corner to face the stove, and the rustling was continuing right in front of him, he twisted the torch on. The grocery box was illuminated and the noise stopped instantly. But there was no movement: no tiny brown body darting for cover. Harry shone the torch all around the floor, in the cupboard, even in the stove itself, but there was nothing to be found. He sorted through the box's contents but nearly all the goods were tinned. In fact there wasn't really anything that could make a rustling sound – the loaf of sliced bread, in its plastic wrapper, had been left on the oak table in the main room after he had last fed Cleo, and the noise definitely wasn't coming from there. All was now silent. Harry shivered and went back to bed.

At first he lay, acutely aware of the silence, almost willing the sound to start again. But then gradually his body relaxed as his concentration waned. He was just about to drift off again when he heard a twang, which jerked him alert. An isolated old house in the middle of a nature reserve was bound to have strange noises all around it – he just needed to switch off, he told himself. Another twang. From outside surely? And then a continuous twanging rattle. He realised it was exactly the same sound the wire had made when Cleo was tangled in it. Maybe she was caught up again, or something else was. But what could have dug up the buried coil and unwound it?

Harry stood up, pulled on his jeans, grabbed the torch and switched it on. He stepped quickly to the front door, opened it, and directed the beam to the spot where Cleo had been lying when darkness had fallen. Sure enough she was no longer there, and the rattling sound became more desperate. He ran the few steps forward to peer round the corner of the house just in time to see the wire whip back towards the wall, as if someone – something – had stretched it out and let go. But shining his torch all around illuminated no goose, no creature, no person. He inspected the wire, to find it was still attached to the wall and did indeed appear to have been dug out of the ground – there were scraping marks where it had been buried and the stones had been shifted some distance. No way a goose could do that. Why would it, anyway? Harry felt a chill ripple through his body: partly the cold and partly being spooked by the unknown. Something was out there.

He stood perfectly still and played his torch over the marsh plants that surrounded the house. No movement. No sound. Satisfied that whatever it was had gone, he held the torch in his teeth and coiled up the wire again, shoving it in the hole and covering it once more with the stones. This time he placed the old fish crate on top as well.

There was still no sign of Cleo. She must have recovered and flown off to find others of her kind. Maybe even her mate. It was best for her.

Harry went back in the house and closed the door. He listened for a while but there were no further sounds. Still feeling unsettled, he found the large key and turned it in the keyhole to lock himself him. Or rather, to lock out whatever was out there.

This time the silence lasted long enough for him to fall into a doze, so when a new noise started he didn't respond immediately. It was loud enough to disturb his sleep though, and in a half-awake state he thought the noise was part of his dream. But there was something wrong. Despite his not being fully alert there was something about the sound that told his brain to be afraid. Afraid in real life, not in a dream. His consciousness slewed into wakefulness. There it was again. A long, slow scraping noise. It sounded as if someone was dragging a sharp instrument down a piece of wood. It paused for a few seconds then started again. The front door: it was coming from the front door. Harry, fully awake, heart now pounding, stood and lunged for his Maglite, twisting it on with trembling hands. At first he wasn't sure if the sound was coming from the inside or the outside of the door, and for a terrible moment he considered that maybe while he had been outside coiling up the wire, whatever it was that had dug it up had slipped into the house – was locked in the house with him!

But stepping forward and shining the beam on the door he saw there was nothing there. The noise continued: a slow, regular scratch. That was not a noise an animal would make, surely? It wasn't a scrabbling double-pawed scratch like a dog would make if trying to get in or out of a door. Too slow, too regular.

Harry switched the torch off and stepped up to the window above the table, stretching to try and see the outside of the door, but he couldn't make anything out. It was too dark and the angle was not right. The scratch again: firm and loud. Whatever was making the sound was strong – was pushing hard with whatever was scraping the door. Somehow Harry couldn't bring himself to fling the door open. Thank God it was locked. He considered dashing up to the lookout room, but what good would that be? It overlooked the other side of the house, not the doorway.

The scratching stopped. Harry froze, straining to listen for any sound: footsteps on the pebbles, heavy breathing, anything. But there was complete silence. A trickle of sweat ran down his forehead despite the cold. He reached up to wipe it out of his eye, and was disappointed with the extent his hand was shaking. He'd confidently slept in many a noisy jungle before now – but something about this was different. He was a prisoner and something was trying to get to him.

The silence continued. Harry decided he was being pathetic – he simply had to open the door and see what was there, shoo it away. He switched the torch back on, stepped towards the door and put his hand on the key. Still no sound from outside. He turned it slowly until it clicked unlocked. Hand now on the door handle he paused, heart hammering. Then at speed he twisted the handle, flung the door open and shone his torch around the area in front of it. Nothing there. He leaned forward and peeped to the left and right, sweeping the beam back and forth. But there was nothing. He shone the torch at the outside of the door, expecting to see great gouges down the wood, but again nothing. That wasn't possible.

He stepped out, this time shutting the door behind him, and cautiously walked forwards until he could see where the wire was buried. It still was – the fish crate still on top of the stones. He returned to the house and made a final sweep of the marsh. All was normal. Frowning and still shaky he locked himself indoors. Had he been imagining it all? No way. He wasn't going crazy.

Harry lit two candles and placed them on the oak table. He sat for a while, wishing he'd collected more wood to light another fire, his breath coming out in clouds in the candlelight. It was too cold to sit for long, so after a few minutes he went back to bed and snuggled beneath the pile of clothes and blankets. He was too alert to sleep, and lay for a long time, just listening. It must have been hours but no further sound came.

As the sun rose, and daylight brought a feeling of safety, he finally fell into a fitful sleep. But after just a few hours, a distant cry snapped him awake.

Chapter Nineteen

Harry felt groggy and confused. He remembered the night before but now wasn't sure how much of it had been real and how much his imagination. Everything felt different with the darkness gone.

Then he heard it again. A faint cry – a human cry – maybe a child or someone shouting. He stood up, rather shakily, and pulled his jeans on. On unlocking and opening the front door the first thing he saw was Cleo, sitting in exactly the same spot she had been the day before.

'Hello, Cleo. So you've come back have you? Where were you last night then?' The goose eyed him warily but made no effort to move away. 'Would you like some more bread and water?'

Just as Harry was about to turn back to the house he heard the cry again. But this time it was louder, closer and he could make out the words.

'Helloooo!' It was a woman's voice. 'Harry.' It was Anna's voice!

Harry walked a few paces towards the beach as Anna's head appeared over the shingle ridge. She waved as she saw him and held up a bag she was carrying. Harry was suddenly aware of how rough he must look: bare-chested, hair-tousled, obviously just out of bed. He had no idea what the time was.

'I bring supplies, and company if you'd like some.' Anna surreptitiously admired Harry's physique as she approached.

'Oh, great – yes, fantastic.' Harry thought for a moment of leaning forwards to kiss her on the cheek but felt that was too forward, especially in his state of undress. 'Look, I'm afraid I've only just woken up. Had a bit of a bad night. Come in while I sort myself out.'

Anna noticed the goose sitting a little way behind Harry and nodded towards it. 'I see you've got some company already.'

'Ah, yes, this is Cleo. Cleo, meet Anna.'

'Pleased to meet you, Cleo.' Anna turned to Harry. 'There I was worrying about you all alone and you've already sorted out a female friend.'

'Well she found me really. I'll tell you all about it – just need to get a top on – it's a bit nippy. Come on in the house.'

Anna followed Harry inside and sat at the oak table while Harry went into his bedroom and pulled a t-shirt and a fleece on. Anna had decided the day before that she would pay Harry a visit. There was something about this newcomer; she felt a desire to find out more about him. She could also feel his sadness, but was wary of crowding him. Maybe he needed to be alone and she was disturbing him. She was suddenly filled with doubts about whether it had been a good idea surprising him with a visit.

Harry appeared from the bedroom, fastening his watch around his wrist. 'God, it's gone twelve. I just need a quick wash to wake me up properly – back in a tick.' He walked around the side of the house to the water tank, filled a bowlful, and splashed handfuls of the stimulating liquid into his face.

Anna stood up from the table, wondering if she should actually just leave the supplies and go.

Harry returned, rubbing his face with a towel. 'I'm glad you've come. I know I've only been here two days, and I've been to a lot more remote places than this, but – there's something about the place. Good of you to walk all this way.'

An awkward pause followed, Harry struggling to find the right words for what he wanted to say.

Anna could feel the tension but also relaxed in the knowledge that she was welcome after all. 'So, tell me about your bad night.'

Harry hesitated. To say he had been scared of strange noises seemed pathetic. To say he had thought that something was trying to break in to get him sounded distinctly paranoid. 'Just a noisy night really. So I didn't sleep well. I guess I haven't got used to the sounds of the house yet. Maybe I've got a house mouse.'

'You're bound to hear unusual noises in a place as exposed as this. You know you can always phone if you're worried.'

'I'm sure it's nothing to worry about. But thanks.' Harry suddenly remembered Cleo. 'How about a cup of tea? I was just going to feed the goose – my goose.'

'Well, I don't know if you're ready for lunch yet but I have an alternative to tea if you fancy it.' Anna pulled a bottle of white wine from her bag.

'Hey, now you're talking. Shall we take a picnic and sit on the shingle where we can watch the waves?'

'Good idea – and I've got a picnic here all ready.'

'Great, okay, I'll get some glasses for the wine.' Harry had a quick look in the cupboard but there were no glasses at all, so he chose the two cleanest-looking mugs. Taking a couple of slices of bread from the packet that was still on the oak table he carried them out to Cleo. He broke the bread into small pieces and held them out on his palm. Cleo hesitated a moment and then eagerly wolfed them down.

Anna was watching from the doorway. 'My, you're on friendly terms already.'

'She does seem unusually tame. Or maybe just starving hungry. I found her tangled in a wire just by the side of the house yesterday.'

'That's why she lets you get close then – you're her hero – she trusts you.'

'Actually it sort of looked like a snare that she was caught in – attached to the house. I don't suppose any of that happens legitimately around here?'

'No, not on the reserve. I'd better tell my dad about that. Where is it now?'

'I buried it – just under that crate.' Harry neglected to say that he had had to bury it a second time the night before. 'It's tough wire though. Perhaps your dad could bring some wire-cutters next time he's passing, get rid of it for good.'

Harry refilled Cleo's water bowl and left it in front of her. 'Shall we go then?'

'Ready when you are.' Anna fetched her bag from the table.

Harry shut the door, locked it, and put the key in his pocket. He led the way over the ridge towards the sea and they found a spot where the stones looked dry. Sitting down, Anna passed the bottle of wine to Harry.

'Oh – bottle opener.' But as he said it, Anna pulled a corkscrew out of her bag and waggled it at him.

'I wasn't sure if there was one in the Watch House, so thought it better to be safe.'

'I can see you'd be perfect to take on an expedition.' Harry uncorked the wine and filled the mugs.

Anna pulled out a paper bag containing two pasties and passed one to Harry. 'From the deli. And there's apples and chocolate brownies too.'

The couple munched and chatted and relaxed in each other's company. It was another fine day and the sea looked bluer than Harry had seen it before. Anna told Harry about her father's continuing battle with the tractor, which seemed to be serviceable only every other day. Then she explained a little more about her past, about how the death of her mother had completely changed her life. It hadn't been an easy decision to leave her teaching job in Bristol, but it had coincided with the end of the academic year and the school hadn't put up too many barriers. She didn't know if she wanted to go back to teaching full-time now. She quite enjoyed it but it had never felt like her life's calling. Norfolk wasn't a bad place to be – it was home – but there was also a part of her that felt slightly claustrophobic from having moved back. A part that needed more adventures.

Before she knew it she was talking more about herself than she had done for a very long time. Harry was a good listener and there was something about him that made Anna want to bare her soul. He understood. Maybe only someone else who had suffered loss and hard times could understand.

Harry broke into her thoughts. 'So, did you have a bloke in Bristol?' And it was only when he said this that he realised that she might still have someone in Bristol: someone she saw every now and again. He didn't mean it to sound like a leading question but it had just blurted out.

'Well there was a guy I was seeing. We even talked of getting engaged. This is about eighteen months ago now. But I was never a hundred percent convinced about him and one day he suddenly dumped me. I never really found out why, but apparently the bastard had another girlfriend very soon after, so you never know. That wasn't the reason I left Bristol of course, but sometimes it's good to leave bad memories behind.'

Harry told Anna about his plan to sell up in Newmarket and start again somewhere else. Time flew. Wine flowed. Before they knew it they had finished the whole bottle between them. A slight breeze blew in from the north and Anna shivered. Harry wanted to put his arms around her, to warm her, but he just couldn't.

'Are you cold? We could go inside if you like – have a hot drink?'

Anna looked at her watch. 'Actually, I hate to say it, but I'd better be heading back or it'll be dark before I get home.'

Harry stood up, swaying slightly from the effects of the wine. Anna offered him her hands and he pulled her up. She, too, staggered slightly and they both giggled.

'At least let me walk you back; I need the exercise.'

'No, really – it's miles there and back – there's no need.' Anna protested.

'I've been cooped up here and I've got a torch; I don't mind coming back in the dark.'

Anna hesitated. 'All right – you can help me not to fall over!'

They returned to the Watch House where Harry packed his coat and torch into his small rucksack.

As they set off on the two-mile journey back to Cley they both felt connected to each other's thoughts. They walked close together and, thanks to the wine and the sliding shingle, occasionally bumped lightly into each other, which caused more giggling. Their hands occasionally touched as they walked and, the more it happened, the more Harry wanted to hold her hand. It was such a simple thing to do but it felt so difficult. So loaded.

After a mile or so, the old coastguard lookout at the car park in Cley came into view. Their hands touched again and this time, unable to put it off any longer, Harry hooked a finger into Anna's palm. She held it, and after a few paces adjusted it to a proper handhold. Neither spoke for a while.

The journey certainly felt a lot shorter and quicker than when Harry had walked it by himself. At the car park they turned right, up the path towards Marsh View. Daylight was starting to fade. Harry reflected on what an unexpectedly lovely day it had been: banishing the ghosts of the night before. But the loveliness had to end. The news that waited for them at Marsh View was the last thing either of them expected.

CHAPTER TWENTY

Anna knew there was something wrong the minute she opened the door. She was expecting the house to be empty – Sophie was having a sleepover at a friend's and her dad was supposed to be fishing with Frank. Instead he was standing in the doorway to the front room, staring towards the window; he didn't even turn towards Anna and Harry as they entered the house.

'Dad?'

'Mmm?' Peter sounded distant. Anna could see in the dimming light that his face was grey and drawn.

'Dad, what's wrong? Why haven't you put a light on?' She reached up and flicked the hall light-switch.

Peter slowly turned to face them and spoke in a monotone. 'It's Frank.'

'Frank? What about Frank?'

'He's – he's dead.'

'Dead!' Anna almost shouted the word in her surprise. 'Oh my God! How? When? No – wait – Dad, come and sit down in the kitchen and I'll make some coffee, then you can tell us about it properly. Harry was just going to have a drink before going back to the Watch House.'

Anna took her father by the arm, led him into the kitchen and settled him on a chair. Harry followed, switching the light on, and sat next to Peter, who continued to stare into space.

Harry felt awkward, not knowing what to say. He put his hand gently on Peter's arm. 'Peter, are you all right? You look awful.'

'Still in shock, I guess.' Peter rubbed his hand over his face.

'Poor Dad.' Anna bent and kissed her father on his forehead. 'And Linda – oh God, poor Linda. What the hell happened?'

'It was Mack who found him. He called an ambulance and then called me. It can't have been long after you left for the Watch House. I was there in minutes but Frank was already dead. Mack was beside himself: he'd been on his way to Frank's when he saw this pair of legs sticking out from under an upturned boat by the side of the marsh path. He went over for a closer look and it was Frank: in a pool of blood.'

'Oh my God!' Anna pushed mugs of coffee across the table towards Peter and Harry. 'Did he fall? Could the ambulance men say how he died?'

'As it happened Doc Kelly turned up before the ambulance. He said Frank was too far gone to try and resuscitate. Just said it looked like death from blood-loss.'

'How come Frank was under a boat?' Harry asked.

'Only partly under. His hands were still gripping the sides of the boat – as if he'd dragged himself under, trying to get away from someone, or something.'

'Where did the blood come from?'

'From his legs.'

'His legs! Jesus! Had someone attacked him?'

'I don't think it was someone, Harry.' Peter, for the first time, looked Harry straight in the eye. 'From what I saw of his legs the wounds looked exactly the same as the ones we saw on those seals the other day.'

Harry felt a chill ripple through his body. 'Oh my God! So you think it might have been an animal? A dog?'

'Can't say. Police have been there all day, taking photos, and statements.'

'And what about Linda? Did the police go and tell her?' Anna asked, her voice catching.

'No, I did. I thought it would be better from a friend. But she went hysterical before I could even finish telling her. Almost as if she was expecting something to happen. And then she ran all the way to the marsh path and fell on his body, weeping and wailing. I couldn't stop her. The police had to pull her off. Screaming she was. Never seen anything like it.'

'Where is she now?'

'She's at home. Friends are there with her.'

Anna glanced at Harry. 'We should go and see her.'

'I'd leave it a bit.' Peter said wearily. 'Maybe tomorrow.' He looked into his coffee and shook his head slowly.

Anna put her arm round her father's shoulders. 'Dad, you look exhausted, why don't you go to bed? I'll bring you up some supper.'

'I think I'll have to. I'm done for today.'

Anna took her father by the arm and led him towards the stairs and up to his bedroom. Harry busied himself washing up the mugs – unsure of what to do. It was fully dark now and he didn't feel like the long walk back to the Watch House after such shocking news.

Anna came back down the stairs, into the kitchen, and surprised Harry by walking straight up to him and putting her arms around his waist as he turned to face her. She buried her face in his shoulder. Harry folded his arms around her and held her close; he could feel her body trembling.

Eventually Anna lifted her head and looked at Harry, tears on her cheeks. 'God, I'm glad you're here, Harry.' She pulled a tissue from her jeans pocket and wiped her eyes. 'You wouldn't help me make some soup would you? I don't feel like cooking anything major.'

'Course I will.'

'And will you come with me to see Linda in the morning? I'm not sure I could face that alone.'

'Sure. Just tell me what time to come back and I'll be ready.'

'Come back?' Anna had forgotten that Harry had planned to return to the Watch House. 'Oh no, stay – please stay.' She looked into Harry's eyes. 'Sophie's away so you can sleep in her room tonight. Please stay.'

Harry stroked her hair. 'I didn't fancy walking back anyway now.'

Anna reached up and kissed him briefly on the lips, then gave him another squeeze before letting go to fetch soup ingredients from the cupboard.

Harry chopped vegetables, glad to have something practical to do, while Anna stirred a large pot on the stove. They didn't talk much, lost in their own thoughts. Between them they produced a hearty broth: comforting nourishment for shocked bodies and minds. Anna took a bowl up to her father and then returned to sit opposite Harry at the kitchen table.

Harry blew on a spoonful of steaming soup. 'Sounds like Linda took it really badly. As you would. But really hysterically, from what your dad was saying, which somehow feels unexpected from Linda, she seemed so … in control.'

'I know. It's not going to be easy tomorrow. Knowing what to say, I mean. I'm glad you'll be there with me.' Anna reached out her hand to touch Harry's fingertips across the table.

After supper, Anna phoned Sophie at her friend's to check she was all right, but decided against telling her about Frank until she was home the next day. Going up to retrieve her father's soup bowl, she found him fast asleep, spoon still in his hand. She pulled the duvet up under his chin and noticed how old he looked. He seemed to have aged ten years in a day. The sudden thought of one day being parentless brought tears to her eyes again. Back downstairs she poured large brandies for Harry and herself and they sat on the sofa together. After a while Anna closed her eyes and rested her head on Harry's shoulder.

A couple of hours later, Anna came to from a shallow sleep to find herself enveloped in Harry's arms. 'We'd better get to bed.' She murmured sleepily, rubbing her eyes.

She took Harry by the hand and led him upstairs, showed him where Sophie's bedroom and the bathroom were and found him a new toothbrush. While he cleaned his teeth, she changed into her nightdress in her bedroom.

Harry finished his teeth, washed his face, and went into Sophie's room. It didn't feel quite right sleeping in a teenage girl's bedroom, but he was grateful for a warm bed for the night. The room was a mixture of little girl and adolescent: posters on the wall alternating between semi-clad pop stars and fluffy kittens. The dressing table was overloaded with make-up equipment yet the bed was covered with teddies and cuddly animals. Harry stripped down to his t-shirt and pants, switched off the light and climbed into bed.

A few minutes later the door opened quietly and Anna appeared. She knelt by the side of the bed. 'I just came to say goodnight. And thank you.'

Chapter Twenty-One

'Hey, sleepy-head. Time to wake up.'

Harry opened his eyes. He had slept deeply and had been dreaming of Louise when the voice woke him. It felt as if he had been asleep for only minutes but it had actually been nine uninterrupted hours. In a strange bed and looking into Anna's eyes, he was momentarily confused. Then a warmth flooded through his body as he remembered the new closeness they had found. For a moment he had forgotten the tragedy of the day before and their difficult task ahead. He smiled and stretched.

Anna was already dressed. 'I'll get some toast on while you return to the land of the living. See you downstairs.' She ruffled his hair before walking to the door.

After dressing and washing, Harry joined Anna in the kitchen. Peter was already out and Sophie was still at her friend's.

Anna passed him a plate with two thick slices of toast on. 'I thought we could pick up some flowers on the way to Linda's.'

'Mmm – good idea. How was your dad this morning?'

'Better than last night but still looking – sort of – haunted. Frank was a close friend. It'll take him some time to get over it – it took him a long time to get over losing Mum.'

'How shall we get to Linda's? My car's still at Morston.'

'We can go in Dad's truck, he's gone out to the Point on the tractor, to check on the seals.'

Breakfast finished, Harry and Anna set off, picking up a large bunch of mixed flowers *en route*. They parked on High Street in Blakeney and walked to Linda's cottage. Just as Anna was about to knock the door opened and a large woman, whom Anna recognised as one of Linda's neighbours, came out.

'Hello,' the woman said. 'You're the warden's daughter aren't you – Annie, isn't it?'

'Anna – yes, we've just come to see how Linda is doing.'

'She's not good I'm afraid. I've been with her all night and she's hardly slept. Nor have I for that matter. I was just going home to get some shut-eye. She's got the doctor coming over later, and another friend, but I'm sure she'll be glad to see you. She's in the kitchen at the moment. She won't eat but I've just made her a drink.'

The woman turned and wearily shuffled off towards her house. Anna and Harry went in the open front door and through to the kitchen.

Linda was sitting at the table with her back to the door. Anna spoke gently. 'Hello, Linda. How are you doing?'

She turned towards them. Both Anna and Harry had to control themselves not to look taken aback at the sight of the changed woman before them. Linda's face was puffy and swollen, her eyes red and sore. Her hair was all over the place, and she clutched a damp tissue in a shaky hand.

Anna walked up and put her arms around her. 'We're so sorry to hear about Frank. What a shock.' Linda let out a sob and held the tissue to her eyes.

Harry sat opposite and took Linda's other hand in his. 'Yes, so sorry Linda, is there anything we can do?'

'What can anyone do? It's too late now isn't it?' Linda's voice was quiet, strained and hoarse: barely recognisable.

'Linda, love.' Anna stroked her hair. For a few moments no one knew what to say.

Then, in a tiny voice, Linda spoke. 'I just didn't think it would be him.'

Harry and Anna glanced at each other with puzzled expressions.

'I'm not sure what you mean, Linda.' Anna said.

'I thought it would be Eileen.'

'What did you think would be Eileen?'

'Eileen, who was going to die.'

'But what made you think anyone was going to die?' Harry asked, still confused.

'Because I saw HIM,' Linda almost shouted in her agitation.

'Oh God,' sighed Anna as the penny dropped.

Harry was not there yet. 'I don't understand – saw who?'

'Him – Black Shuck!' Linda held the tissue quickly to her mouth as if she had surprised herself by saying the dreaded name.

'Black Shuck?' Harry repeated. 'The ghost dog? When? Where?'

'A few days ago. On the marsh path. Near where they found – found Frank.' She let out another sob. 'I'd just visited Eileen – you remember, Harry, I told you. She looked so poorly, so frail, I was afraid she was at death's door. So when I saw *him* on the way home of course I assumed poor old Eileen was about to leave us.'

'So, that's why you were so upset on the day I left,' Harry understood now. 'Because you'd just seen Shuck.'

Linda nodded. 'I didn't even tell Frank. I didn't want to upset him.'

'And what did you see exactly? What did Shuck look like?'

'Just a big black dog. In the mist. Huge red eyes he had – just stared at me, then disappeared. I was terrified. Never seen anything like it before in my life.'

Anna hadn't spoken for a while and was now standing at the window, staring out, her arms folded. It was only then that Harry remembered that Peter had seen Black Shuck shortly before his wife – Anna's mum – had died.

He stood and put an arm around her shoulders. There were tears on her cheeks. 'Are you all right?'

She wasn't, but she had to be strong for Linda's sake. She nodded but seemed unable to speak. She didn't want Linda to see that she was crying too.

Harry turned back to Linda. 'Does Peter know – that you saw a big dog I mean?'

'Yes, I was cursing Black Shuck when I saw Frank on the

marsh. Cursing and cursing. Oh, Frank.' She dissolved in a fresh wave of sobs.

Just at that moment there was a knock on the front door. Harry went through to answer it. A young man, tall and thin with spectacles, introduced himself as the doctor and followed Harry back into the kitchen.

Anna was giving Linda another hug. She looked up, recognising the doctor. 'We'd better leave you to it, Linda. But call us if you need anything won't you? Or if you want to come and stay at Marsh View?'

Back in the truck Harry looked across at Anna's tear-stained face. He reached over and stroked her cheek. 'How are you doing?'

'That was really hard.' She sniffed. 'And it also explains why Dad was looking so grim last night. It's not the first time Shuck has raised his head since a year ago.'

'No?'

'No. A woman who works at the stores in the village saw him a little while back. Lost her husband the same day.'

'Oh, yes, Frank told me about that.' Harry thought for a while 'But I'm still confused, as far as I understand it Black Shuck appears to warn someone of the death of a loved one.' Anna nodded. Harry continued. 'But Shuck is a ghost dog, right? I mean, what's the connection between that and the fact that Frank, and the seals for that matter, were actually attacked by something?'

'I don't know,' said Anna. She put the truck into gear and pulled out on to the road back to Cley.

'So it might just be a coincidence, that there might be a big dog or some other animal – a real one I mean – that's attacking people and seals at the moment, nothing to do with the Shuck legend.'

'Funny coincidence,' said Anna miserably.

Back at Marsh View they found Peter, stern-faced, cleaning his shotgun with an oily rag. Cartridges were laid out on the table in front of him. He looked up as Anna and Harry entered the kitchen but said nothing.

'Dad.' Anna leaned towards her father and kissed him on the cheek. 'What are you up to with that?'

'Going hunting,' he answered gruffly. 'Hunting dog.'

'What do you mean? Where?'

'I've just got back from the Point and I found more bloodstains on the beach.' He glanced up at Harry. 'Looked like the ones you described to me last week, Harry. Fresh too – fresh this morning I'm sure. No bodies. I reckon whatever attacked Frank is still out there – feasting on my animals.'

'What are you planning to do?' Anna frowned at her father.

'Mack and I and some of the other fishermen are going to do a sweep of the Point. I didn't see anything from the tractor but there's so many places something could hide. With enough of us we might be able to flush it out though – if it's still there, that is.'

'You think after attacking Frank yesterday it headed out to the Point?' Harry asked.

'Looks like it. Maybe that's where it spends the night; perhaps it's got a lair somewhere out there.'

'Dad, you will be careful, won't you?' Anna was looking worried.

'Don't you fret, love. We've a few guns between us. Not that the police know what we're planning. Best they don't. But the sooner we get this beast the better. And the sooner we get going the better too: we need to trap it on the Point before it strays away again.'

'I'm coming too,' said Harry. It was a simple statement, not open for debate.

Peter looked up at him for a moment. 'The more eyes we have the better.'

'Harry!' Anna protested.

'It's all right, I want to help.' Harry placed a hand on her shoulder.

It was only at that moment that Peter understood there was a deeper connection between Harry and his daughter than he had realised. He often worried about his daughter's quality of life:

being stuck in a tourist village looking after her old man. He felt guilty and several times had tried to persuade her that he was fine and that she could go back to teaching full time – move out. Maybe even back to Bristol. But on the other hand he knew he would struggle to bring up Sophie on his own. He didn't really want Anna to go away at all.

She broke into his thoughts. 'Then I'm coming too.'

'No, love, no. You stay here. Sophie will be back any minute. I need you to stay here and look after her.'

Anna folded her arms crossly. She knew she had no choice.

Peter stood up from the table and pocketed the cartridges. 'Right, Harry, we'd better go. I don't have a spare gun for you I'm afraid, but there are some staffs in the shed we'll take – for beating the shrubs as we go: flush anything out.' He neglected to say that the staffs might also be needed for self-defence.

Harry followed Peter towards the door but Anna caught his hand and pulled him back. She turned his face so that he looked her in the eye. 'Promise me you'll take care – of yourself as well as Dad.'

'I promise. Don't worry.' Harry leant forwards and kissed her, then turned and joined Peter who now had an armful of staffs as well as his shotgun. He passed a couple of the staffs to Harry and the two of them set off towards the track that led to the beach car park.

Anna watched the men march off with their weapons. It was as if they were going to war.

Chapter Twenty-Two

Following Peter down the track, Harry could see a small group of men waiting by the old coastguard lookout. As they got closer he recognised Mack, but the other four faces were new to him. Rugged, weather-beaten faces with grim expressions. Harry considered how he wouldn't like to run into this lot on a dark marsh path. But he also knew that they were probably all salts-of-the-earth – like Frank had been. These were Frank's friends, and although they were out to rid the area of a dangerous animal, they were also out for revenge.

They wore dark clothing, collars turned up; two were in camouflage jackets. One was carrying a stout walking stick, two had shotguns hanging over their arms, the others kept their hands in their pockets. The day had become overcast and cold, and a wind was picking up.

Peter stopped in front of the group and appraised the men. He nodded slightly in approval. The men stood in a semi-circle, watching Peter as if expecting orders. It was clear that Peter was to be the leader of the operation, and he knew it.

'Right, boys.' Peter sounded grave but confident. 'Thanks for turning out. This is Harry who's also going to join us – he's staying at the Watch House.' Several of the men raised their eyebrows at this. Harry nodded a greeting to the group. 'Harry, this is Mack, Joe, Joe's son Wayne, Roddy and Steve.'

They were mostly of a similar age to Peter – late fifties/early sixties Harry reckoned – except Wayne, who looked to be in his late twenties. Peter passed staffs to Joe and Roddy, and Harry passed his spare one to Wayne, who took it with no acknowledgement. Mack and Steve were the two carrying guns in addition to Peter.

'Right, here's the plan.' It was as if this were a regular task for

Peter. 'We'll form a line across the spit, from the harbour on our left to the sea on our right. We walk forwards together and keep the line straight. I'll go in the middle, with Mack on the far left and Steve on the far right: to spread the guns out. Keep an eye out for walkers. If you do see any, ask them if they have seen any dogs, and report to me. If you see a dog then shout out – and if there are no walkers about we shoot. Remember, and this most important, we only shoot forwards: away from the line. No accidents – understood?' The men nodded. 'Right, let's go.'

There were few other people about. A small number of birdwatchers stood on the shingle ridge, their scopes trained out to sea. They looked on with curiosity as Peter's men spread out across the shingle, formed a line, and started walking to the west. Harry was near the centre with Peter on his left and Wayne on his right.

Wayne seemed to be enjoying himself: beating his staff on his hand as if about to tackle an opposing gang. He looked at Harry. 'All right Harry? Ready for a Shuck-hunt?'

Peter immediately stopped and turned toward Wayne, fuming. 'This is no Shuck-hunt! We're not looking for a non-existent ghost, we're looking for a real dog – a killer. Is that understood?'

Wayne blushed and looked towards the ground.

The group straightened their line then continued the march forward. At first the shingle spit was narrow so the seven of them were only a few yards apart. As it grew wider they naturally increased the spacing between each other. The pace was quite fast to start with and hard going on the sliding shingle. At this stage there were few shrubs anything could hide in, so the men scanned far in front of them as they marched. There were no other people in sight; it might be that the Point was deserted today. Peter hoped it was; he didn't want to frighten any tourists or have his armed hunt reported to the police.

After a while the area to the left of the ridge became covered in low-growing salt marsh plants. The men on that side poked the small shrubs with their staffs as they walked but it was clear there was nothing substantial enough to hide a large dog.

Before long the Watch House came into view. Harry wondered if Cleo were still there – missing her feed. As they drew level with the house, Peter raised a hand for the men to stop. He searched around the outside of the house, checking any possible hiding places: behind the water tank, even under the old fish crate.

Harry remembered the wire that had caught Cleo and walked over to Peter. 'I forgot to tell you, Peter. I found some wire attached to the house, it had a goose caught up in it the second day I was here. I meant to ask you to bring some wire-cutters. I can't work out what it's for.' Harry took Peter to the edge of the wall where the coil of wire was still buried and dug it up.

Peter tugged at it. 'Hmm, that's well attached isn't it?'

'Yeah, I couldn't break it off. Do you know what it is?'

'No idea – never seen it before – but it's obviously been there a while from the look of the corrosion. I'll bring cutters next time I'm passing.'

Harry looked around but was sad to see there was no sign of Cleo. He walked back to his place in the line and they started moving forward again. Harry thought about whether he should tell Peter about the noises he had heard at the Watch House at night – the scratching at the door – but decided against it. Now he wasn't convinced about any of it, and there were no marks, no proof of anything.

The marsh plants grew more thickly now, which slowed their advance as they strode over the shrubs, beating them with staffs. But nothing was flushed out. Harry was hungry and thirsty; it was past lunchtime now and none of them had brought any sustenance.

As they came within a half mile or so from the end of the Point it widened dramatically. They had to spread out further until there was quite a distance between each man. As the area was more overgrown here it meant that there were shrubs that remained unbeaten between the men. Peter became increasingly anxious that their quarry could slip through the net by lying low and getting lucky.

Suddenly, in a thicket of shrubs ahead of him, Harry thought he could see something moving. Something black. Despite the staff he was carrying and the company of men with guns, he felt strangely unprotected now the group was so spread out. He glanced over towards Peter, but when he looked back the black shape had gone. Had he imagined it? Had it been a shadow? He didn't want to draw everyone's attention to nothing. Wayne, to his right, was whacking at a small shrub in front of him and clearly hadn't seen the same thing. They moved further forward. The thicket was directly in front of Harry but still thirty or so yards away.

There it was again. Definitely something black moving. Harry stopped dead. Despite the exertion of the walk he felt a chill spreading through his body. He looked over to Peter who had seen him stop and had come to halt also.

'Anything?' Peter shouted.

'In the bushes ahead – something black – something moving.'

CHAPTER TWENTY-THREE

Peter signalled that he was going to converge on the thicket, holding his gun now with two hands, at the ready. Wayne also heard and understood – the other men were too far away. The three of them closed in on the thicket. Harry, adrenaline flowing, could still see glimpses of black, but as they got nearer it took on an unnatural quality. It was as if it were trembling – shaking. No, it was almost as if it was fluttering. And it became shiny.

Peter got to the thicket first and had obviously seen what it was, as he strode forward, gun now back over his arm, and reached down. He pulled out a large piece of black plastic: an old bin-liner that had blown into the thicket and become snagged on the branches. He held it aloft for the others to see then screwed it up and put it in his jacket pocket.

'Sorry,' Harry said, feeling rather sheepish.

'Don't be sorry, Harry. I'm glad you've got your eyes open. Let's keep going.'

They formed their well-spaced line once more and continued the sweep. Soon the shrubs gave way to dunes as they neared the end of the Point, ahead of them, the large, flat expanse of sand and the many dark shapes of hauled-out seals. The tide was out so the seals had moved away to sandbanks off the Point, where they could rest with no danger of being bothered by walkers – or dogs. It seemed the hunt had been fruitless. Harry felt a pang of disappointment and knew that Peter must be feeling it far worse. Now all he could think about was his hunger and the long walk back.

But his feeling of deflation was interrupted by a shout from the right. Looking over, Harry and the rest of them could see Steve, standing on the edge of a depression in the dunes, waving an arm above his head and pointing to something below. The men all started moving towards him – Wayne, keen for action, broke into a run. Harry was the second to arrive, closely followed by Peter. As they reached the edge they looked down to see what Steve and Wayne were staring at.

In the depression – lying in a pool of blood – the carcass of a large seal. The same wounds that Harry and Peter had seen before, large chunks of flesh missing from its flanks, bitten out.

'Fuck's sake, what's done that?' Wayne gawped at the spectacle.

'That's what we're trying to find out,' replied Peter. 'That's why we're here.'

By now, all seven men were standing around the edge of the depression. Harry realised it wasn't very far from the scene of the bloodbath he and Peter had discovered the week before.

'Is this where you saw the bloodstains this morning?' Harry asked.

Peter shook his head. 'No, that was nearer the shore – not in the dunes. This is new: recent.'

Wayne stepped down and jabbed his staff at the seal's body. The instant the wooden pole made contact, the seal reared up, screaming hideously, splashing blood around the clearing.

'Shit!' shouted the shocked Wayne, scrambling backwards up the sandy slope. All the men had jumped back in surprise. Wayne dropped his staff and clamped his hands over his ears as the ear-splitting screams continued. Most of the other men were frozen in horror, but Peter stepped forward and levelled his shotgun.

'Stand back!' he shouted.

The explosion from his gun as he let loose hundreds of pellets into the seal's skull was deafening at such close range. Blood spurted up as the body crashed down into the pool below. Wayne, being the nearest, was sprayed with red droplets. He turned his face to one side but was too late.

'Shit!' Wayne said again, wiping blood from his eyes with his sleeve. 'I thought it was dead! I thought it was fucking dead!'

The words sounded muffled and distant to Harry as his ears were ringing from the gunshot. Peter looked up and scanned the horizon all around, but there was nothing unusual to be seen.

'Damn!' Peter flipped the safety catch back on his gun. 'Damn! Whatever it is that's done this … it's given us the slip.'

CHAPTER TWENTY-FOUR

The trudge back from the Point seemed longer than ever. The men still took up their sweeping line but it was a heads-down, half-hearted affair. Wayne, in particular, seemed sulky and lagged behind, occasionally wiping at his blood-smeared face.

Peter called out encouragement now and again but Harry suspected that they were all just looking forward to getting home. It would be dark in an hour or two and he, for one, was famished.

As the Watch House came into view, Peter turned to Harry. 'Well, Harry, you may as well stop off here. I doubt we'll see anything today now, and the spit's narrower from here on anyway.'

Harry hadn't been sure whether Peter was expecting him to go all the way back to Cley or not and was privately relieved that his part in the hunt was over. 'Okay, Peter. I'll keep a look out for anything unusual.'

'Yes – do that – and if you see anything resembling a large dog for Christ's sake don't approach it – ring me straight away.'

'Will do.' Harry waved to the rest of the men and watched for a while as they trooped off towards Cley.

He unlocked the door and stepped in to find a stale, musty smell – unusual as the house had only been shut up for a day. He checked all the rooms, even the unused bedrooms, but nothing seemed out of place. No one – or nothing – had been in since Harry locked up the day before. The day before? So much had happened in between, it already felt like several days since Harry had been here last.

He filled the kettle from a bottle of water and lit the gas ring beneath it. A hot drink was needed urgently. While it was boiling he checked his mobile phone but there were no messages. He switched it off again, wary of running the battery low as there was no way of recharging it here.

Sitting at the oak table in the main room, gazing out of the window over the harbour towards Blakeney where a few lights were beginning to come on in houses and the hotel, Harry reflected on the past twenty-four hours. The new-found closeness with Anna, learning of Frank's death, visiting devastated Linda, and then the long haul to the Point searching for … who knows what? After all that activity the Watch House now felt quiet, isolated and, Harry hated to admit, rather creepy.

Tea finished, Harry left the house and walked towards the sea in search of firewood before it grew too dark. He was lucky to find what looked like half an old chest of drawers that had been washed up on the previous tide. The wood was dark brown and varnished, so had not soaked up too much water to make it unusable in a fire. He dragged it to the house where he leaned it against the brick wall and kicked at it to break it up. The wood panels were thin and splintered easily; some of the smaller pieces would make perfect kindling. There wasn't much for that night but Harry was tired anyway and looking forward to his bed. Tomorrow he would go on a longer search for firewood. He carried the pieces in and stacked them by the side of the fire.

Before shutting and locking the door, Harry looked into the sky. No sign of Cleo – she must have found some friends. Harry didn't expect to see her again now.

Rummaging through his box of supplies revealed little choice for supper. He should have picked up some more provisions while he was in Cley. He emptied a tin of mushroom soup into a pan and set it on the hob to warm up while he built the fire. Harry crumpled paper and some more cardboard from the grocery box to start the fire off. He lit the paper with a match and quickly added some of the slivers of wood from the old chest. They caught light easily so he pushed the larger pieces on top. As the flames licked over the varnished surfaces, the wood crackled and spat.

Harry fetched his soup and sat cross-legged in front of the fire. As the flames warmed up his exterior, the soup heated him from the inside. His mind couldn't help but wander to Anna. What would she be doing now? Preparing supper for Peter and Sophie? Would she be thinking of him in the same way? He decided to ring her the next day to see if she'd like to get together again – for a walk or a meal maybe. For the moment he needed to snap out of this dreaming, or he might build himself up for a fall.

He stood, to carry his soup bowl outside to wash, but something made him look into his bedroom first. And what he was to see from his bedroom window was curious indeed.

CHAPTER TWENTY-FIVE

Anna stood in the kitchen of Marsh View washing up the dinner plates. The mood in the house was dark. Sophie had returned in the afternoon as planned and Anna had broken the news of Frank's death to her then. She had barely reacted but was quieter than usual over the evening meal and had now gone to bed early. This was the first death of a close acquaintance since their mother had died and Anna knew this would bring back difficult memories for Sophie – as it did for her.

Peter had returned from the hunt, exhausted and despondent. He had told Anna that it had been fruitless but little else. When Anna asked about Harry, Peter just offhandedly said that he seemed fine and had stayed at the Watch House. Anna couldn't help but feel disappointed. Although nothing had been arranged she had hoped that Harry would return with her father, maybe even stay another night at Marsh View.

She didn't like the idea of his staying alone at the Watch House. She knew he was a survivor at heart – but recent events had unsettled everyone. She knew there was something dangerous out there – something that prowled the Point killing seals, and maybe the same something that had killed Frank. And Harry's hideaway couldn't be more central to this sinister activity.

Having finished the washing up, she poured a small whisky for her father and took it through to the lounge, only to find him asleep in his armchair. She sat on the sofa and watched him for while, sipping the drink herself. He was still looking older than his years; she feared that if this business with the seals being killed wasn't resolved soon it might have serious effects on his health. The seals meant a great deal to him, and to have lost one of his best friends, possibly to the same killer, had hit him hard.

Her thoughts strayed back to Harry. She knew he had a mobile phone so could ring if he was in any difficulty, but there had been no calls or messages left. She resolved that if she had not heard from him by tomorrow afternoon she would give him a call.

Chapter Twenty-Six

Harry stood at his bedroom window in the Watch House looking at the figure walking along the beach at the edge of the sea. He could tell that the distant figure was a young woman, from the long hair, the shape of the body and the clothes. And that was the odd thing, the thing that made him stare and wonder who she was: the clothes. Whereas all other hikers out here at this time of the year would be wearing thick, often brightly-coloured jackets, usually with trousers and walking boots and a rucksack on their backs, this woman was simply wearing a thin red dress. Harry could tell it was thin by the way the fabric was fluttering in the breeze. She must be freezing. It also struck Harry how similar she appeared to the woman he had seen on the beach a couple of days earlier when he had been swimming in the sea.

He lost sight of her as she passed behind a few shrubs that grew not far from the Watch House. Without realising what he was doing, he nipped into the second bedroom and shinned up the iron ladder to look through the lookout window. Here he had a better view, as he could see over the tops of the shrubs and she had moved a little nearer to the house. It was hard to see much detail as the light was fading into early evening. But he was pretty sure that she was barefoot and wasn't carrying anything. Barefoot! That was even more curious. Walking on shingle with no shoes or boots on was a painful occupation at the best of times. Those who tried it would often look as if were walking on hot coals, wincing and muttering oaths as they wobbled along. It was usually reserved for the summer, and then just the short trip from the laid-out-towel to the sea for a swim. Yet this girl seemed to be strolling along with ease, as if on soft grass.

Perhaps she was part of a larger group and was lagging behind. But why would they be out walking at this time of day? It would be pitch black within an hour.

Harry needed a closer look. He climbed down the ladder, went out of the front door and walked around the side of the house towards the sea. The woman came into view again but by now was walking away from Harry. She was indeed barefoot, yet stepping smoothly and casually. Her long, wavy black hair reached halfway down her back. Her dress looked somehow dated, reaching down to her knees, but tight around her tummy and with short sleeves. It was more like a summer dress, however, and even Harry was shivering in his fleece. Why wasn't she cold? Her gait was as carefree as if it were a summer's day.

Harry trotted forward but lost sight of her as he rounded a clump of shrubs. As he came back out into the open he couldn't see her as he expected. There must be a dip in the shingle – it was hard to see over the ridge. He ran to the top of the ridge from where he would be able to see her wherever she was – especially in that red dress which stood out even in the rapidly dimming light: but there was no sign. Puzzled, Harry ran a little further forward, there were a few smaller shrubs along the shingle spit but certainly nothing large enough to hide a person.

He cupped his hands to his mouth and shouted. 'Hello! Helloooo!'

CHAPTER TWENTY-SEVEN

When Peter had left the other men at the old coastguard lookout in Cley, he had assumed they were all going home. Back to warm houses and welcoming wives. In fact not even Joe knew that his son had been hatching a new plan on his way back from the Point. Wayne had been about to set off to stay with some mates in Norwich for a few days when his father had co-opted him to help sweep the Point, and so had taken his own car, an old but souped-up Golf GTI, to the car park at Cley, so that he could go straight to town from there. But now he had other ideas.

He didn't want anyone else to know what he was up to, so pretended to be shaking stones out of his walking boots while the others said their brief farewells and drove away. He told his dad he'd see him in a few days and waved him off before opening the back of his GTI and withdrawing the weapon wrapped in an oily cloth.

Wayne had felt humiliated when Peter had shouted at him for calling their search a 'Shuck-hunt', and then again when he had shown his fear when the bloody seal had reared up and screamed at him. He was angry. Angry with Peter for not letting him get further out of the way before he had blown the seal to hell. He was sure Peter had done it deliberately to teach him a lesson. And now he was covered in splashes of seal blood and wasn't ready to leave the matter there. He was going to catch the killer-dog on his own. That'd show them all. He'd be a local hero.

Satisfied that no one was watching, he also took the large torch he kept in the car and set off back towards the Point. It would be dark soon but he'd stay out all night if needs be. He figured that as they hadn't found the dog on the Point that it would probably head out there during the night. For another seal-feast. Only this time Wayne would be waiting. Waiting with the large hunting knife he carried in its wrapping. A bit of poaching now and again was one of Wayne's little hobbies, and that knife had been used to kill and skin many an animal – some legally, some not. He was a strong lad and knew how to use a knife to kill. A dog would be no problem.

After about a mile from the old coastguard lookout, he found a small depression in the shingle surrounded by shrubby sea-blite: a perfect hiding spot. The spit was still narrow enough here for him to easily spot any creature trying to slink past. He settled down, pulled his collar up and started his vigil, torch in one hand, knife in the other.

By the time a couple of hours had passed he was enveloped in darkness and the cold was eating away at him. The longer he stayed, the more he wondered what the hell he was doing when he could be sitting in a lively pub in Norwich with his friends. What if the dog never turned up? What if it did but ran off before he could slit its throat? He determined to give it another hour before heading off.

He laid the torch and knife down, his fingers numb from the cold, and pulled the sleeves of his jacket over his hands to warm them up. And then, despite the sound of the waves breaking on the pebbly shore just a stone's throw away, he was convinced he could hear something panting.

Chapter Twenty-Eight

Having given up his search for the woman in the red dress, Harry had returned to the Watch House and re-warmed himself in front of the fire before retiring to his bed.

It was only as he lay there in the dark that he started thinking about huge black dogs. Straining to hear any sounds, he couldn't help but imagine a beast out there: prowling around. Maybe the seals would be attacked again that night; maybe he would even hear their screams from here despite its being a couple of miles to the end of the Point.

Harry had never seen a ghost in his life. In fact he had never really thought a great deal about whether he believed in them or not. He was naturally open-minded, but also practical and straightforward. He had never before had a reason to explore the possible reality of ghosts in any depth. He couldn't even remember talking to anyone who had thought they had seen one. Until meeting the people of North Norfolk.

He turned on his side and remembered his plan to ring Anna the next day.

It was then he heard the first footfall.

It was the unmistakable sound that shingle makes as you walk on it – except just the one step. It seemed to have come from fairly close to the house – maybe just a few yards from his bedroom window – between the house and the sea. He didn't move a muscle but tuned his ears in, ready to analyse the next sound. For a while there was nothing, but Harry could think of few explanations for a one-off footstep in shingle. He had heard nothing approaching. Maybe something had blown over and landed just beside the house – like a piece of wood – but the wind was light tonight, too light for that. Maybe a bird had landed on the shingle, it would have to have been a heavy bird like a goose – it could have been Cleo. But there had been no sound of wing flaps before the crunch.

There it was again: same place, same sound. Harry raised his head slightly to hear better. Two more crunches, then another. There was something out there in the night. Outside his bedroom window. But was it human or animal? Perhaps it was looking in through his window right now. Harry tilted his head back slowly to look at the window, but could see no face peering in. Not from that angle anyway, besides it was so dark it would have been hard to see anything in the house through a window and there was no sign of a torch or any other light outside. What was it doing out there? Maybe it was the woman in the red dress, but surely she would have made it back to Cley by now?

Harry slowly pushed the blankets off his body and swung his legs silently over the edge of the bed, all the time looking towards the window in case he could make anything out. Bit by bit he lifted his weight from the bed and stood until he could look properly through the window. But the glass was so grimy and the night so dark that he couldn't see a thing. It occurred to him that he might get a better view from the lookout room: from there he could scan down over a larger area and might be able to make out some movement.

He stepped slowly and carefully towards the door to the main room, desperate not to make any noise. Feeling his way, he moved along the mantelpiece but stopped as he heard more crunching shingle from outside. Maybe whatever it was had seen him leave the bedroom. Maybe it had excellent night-vision.

Moving into the room beneath the lookout, Harry felt along the wall until he touched the iron ladder. Holding the sides of the ladder he stepped up, wincing as it made a knocking sound against the wall. He climbed up and into the lookout, crawling to the window on all fours. The window here was filthy too, but the clouds hiding the moon seemed to have thinned a little now and he could just about make out the dark outlines of the shrubs around the house. Ahead, the sea looked pitch black, with just a couple of tiny lights on the horizon where container ships made their way across the North Sea.

Again the crunching: sounding quieter now as Harry was further away. He looked down towards the source of the sound – the *apparent* source – but could see nothing. In his desire to make no noise himself, Harry had left his torch in the bedroom and now chastised himself for having nothing to shine downwards. More footfalls in the shingle, this time seemingly heading along the side of the house towards the right. Harry shivered, his mouth dry. He remembered his promise to Peter to look out for anything unusual and now here he was hiding in pathetic fear. He had just decided to go back down, fetch the torch, pull his jeans on and go out to see what was there, when he heard whatever it was heading off, now at a run. The shingle crunches came close together and grew quickly fainter as their maker sped off in the direction of Cley.

The curious thing was the odd rhythm of the sounds. Harry couldn't tell whether they were made by a two-legged or a four-legged creature: man or beast. It was a running-sound, that was for sure, but strange – unnatural. Maybe it was something, or someone, injured – limping – but clearly capable of speed nevertheless.

Harry climbed back down the ladder and felt his way to his bedroom. He turned his Maglite on for the momentary relief of being able to see properly. He was disappointed with himself that something had been out there and he hadn't identified it – had nothing to report to Peter. It could have been so many things: a dog, some other animal, a burglar, a bored teenager, a lost walker, a woman in a red dress – all seemed improbable now.

CHAPTER TWENTY-NINE

Wayne, still in the depression in the shingle, very slowly pushed his hands out of the ends of his sleeves and reached for the torch and knife. The panting was not only clearly audible now but very close. Yet he was sure he had heard nothing approach.

His right hand closed firmly around the handle of the knife but his left failed to find the torch in the blackness. He silently patted the area where he was sure he'd left it; he didn't want to look for the animal until he could illuminate it. Maybe shining the light in its eyes would dazzle it enough for him to get close for a throat-slash.

The torch continued to elude him and the panting was now so near that the dog, if that's what it was, must be almost upon him. He turned his head slowly towards the sound, not wanting to scare the animal away with a sudden movement. But the two large red shining eyes that stared back at him instantly turned the tables when it came to being scared. Not only was the animal fully aware of the young man's presence but was within striking distance. From Wayne's prone position the owner of those burning eyes towered over him.

'Holy fuck!' Wayne held his knife out towards the hound while his other hand frantically scrabbled behind him for the torch. He made a slashing movement with the knife but made no contact. It must be just out of reach. Finding the torch at last, he pointed it at the red eyes and switched it on with trembling fingers.

The shaking beam made little difference: the eyes were too bright and the thick shaggy fur of the animal so black – so deeply black – it seemed to absorb all light. But he could now see the jaws. This was no ordinary dog: twice the size of a wolfhound with a massively wide mouth. And the teeth: canines as long as his knife-blade, dripping with saliva.

'Jesus Christ!' Wayne's bladder gave way, but he didn't even notice the hot liquid spreading around his groin. He slashed again with the knife and this time the dog rushed forward, seizing the arm holding the knife just below the elbow and, with one flick of its mighty head, ripping it clean off. Wayne let out a high-pitched scream, staring at the torn tendons and vessels emerging from the stumped elbow. Blood spurted out in rapid pumps as his heart raced, but there was no pain. No pain, oddly, until the dog moved to his legs. It bit deeply into Wayne's left thigh and came away with a mouthful of camouflage trousers, skin and the entire muscle of the upper leg. And this time it felt to Wayne like a leg *had* been ripped away: the pain was so intense, so unbearable, so *hot*.

Wayne screamed further, his bowels now erupting. He tried to beat the animal's head with the torch but it slipped from his bloody fingers. And just as the dog moved to his other leg, poised for a second bite of thigh, Wayne's vision started to dim. He groaned and fell back on the shingle into a cocktail of his own juices. He could feel the lower half of his body being pulled from side to side. Being dismantled.

CHAPTER THIRTY

Harry sat bolt upright, streaming with sweat. Sunlight beamed through the dirty bedroom window. The few hours of sleep he had managed had been ravaged by his friend Mike's screams and massive hounds hunting him down. Jesus, when would these nightmares end?

It took a few moments for the transition from dream-world to real-world to complete. Waking mid-dream always leaves the strongest memories and Harry felt the pain of losing Mike all over again. The guilt was refreshed too. He knew he could have saved Mike – if only he hadn't hesitated to save that damned camera. Effectively he was Mike's killer. And now he was dreaming of killer dogs too. Perhaps he did need therapy after all.

Harry wiped the sweat from his eyes and stood up, a little shakily. Peering through the window he could see it was a bright day, the sun twinkling on the crests of small waves out to sea. He pulled on his clothes and walked through to the main room. There was that strange musty smell again so he unlocked the front door and pulled it wide to let fresh air in.

He was immediately met with a nasal, 'Hur, hur, hur.' Cleo was back, sitting in her usual spot just a few yards in front of the house.

'Hello, Cleo.' He took a few steps towards her. 'It's good to see you again. Would you like some more bread then?' The bird swayed its head a little, eyeing Harry but making no effort to move away.

Harry went back indoors to find only two slices of bread left in the packet, and they were pretty stale by now. He took them outside and refilled the water bowl.

'Here you go, Cleo. Look, I'll break the bread up in the water and make it softer for you.' He placed the bowl where Cleo could reach it without moving and stood a few paces back. The bird stretched her long neck forward and took a piece of bread, mashing it rapidly in her beak before swallowing. Harry sat on the sand and watched her finish it all, then take long sips of water before shaking her feathers out and settling down to preen.

'I wasn't sure I was going to see you again, you know. But I'm glad you're back.'

Harry then remembered the noises from the night before. Maybe it had been Cleo arriving after all, but surely the sound of running footsteps couldn't have been made by a goose. No, it had to have been something larger. Harry walked all around the outside of the house, studying the ground for signs. He was used to tracking animals in the bush while film-making, but shingle was a difficult surface to read. It was covered with many natural indentations and Harry could see no pattern that might suggest footprints or something running away.

Back in the house he saw how low his provisions were. He didn't feel like walking to Cley and back today, but it would be a good excuse to ring Anna – to tell her he was coming to Cley – and that in turn would provide an excuse for them to see each other, maybe the next day. Why he needed excuses he wasn't sure.

First job of the day though was to collect more wood for the fire, and a decent amount this time to keep him going. He set off on his mission, initially heading west towards the Point. The receding high tide had left the usual mixture of flotsam and jetsam: pieces of blue netting, plastic bottles, an empty chemical drum that might make a useful seat. There were plenty of natural items along the strandline too: a mermaid's purse, a cuttlefish bone, strikingly white against the dark pebbles, hundreds of broken razor shells, piles of almost-black seaweed, a few dead starfish and the wing of a long-dead gull. A little further along he found half a smashed wooden palette that would provide some excellent firewood, so he dragged this back to the house.

Returning to the high tide mark, Harry now walked to the east, shells crackling beneath his feet. He found several small pieces of driftwood: this time tree branches that were worn smooth and curvy from months at sea, maybe years. He placed them in a pile until he had enough for an armful to carry back. Further along there was another curling branch, this time sticking out from the shingle as if an entire tree might be growing beneath. Harry grasped the end and pulled. There was just enough give to tell him that it would pull free but would require some effort. He placed his feet either side of the branch and straightened his back, using his leg muscles to draw the branch slowly from its stony grave. The last part came away suddenly, causing Harry to stagger a few steps back to steady himself. The end of the branch was hooked and as it dragged across a pile of seaweed it became entangled. Harry twisted the branch to free it and the action uncovered what at first seemed to be a white stone. Nothing unusual in that, but something made him take a second look.

The partly-covered stone had a deep hole on one side and a row of small white shapes along the other. Could those be teeth? Harry lowered the branch to the ground and went down on his knees for a closer inspection. This was no stone, this was a skull – but from what? He cleared the seaweed from around it and could then see how elongated the skull was, with large canines. Must be a seal's skull. Common around here, surely? He picked it up with both hands but then automatically dropped it immediately as his fingers pushed into squishy meat hanging on to the underside of the upper jaw. He rolled the skull over. Sure enough there was still flesh attached to the bone, and it looked fresh too. But then why was the rest of it so clean if it had died recently? Or been killed.

Harry could see a number of grooves on the top of the skull – possibly caused by large teeth scraping meat from the surface. Certainly another seal would not have done this, it had to be a dog. *The* dog. The lower jaw was missing altogether so Harry started poking around in the seaweed to find it. More cuttlefish bones and dead crabs but no seal teeth. Just as he was about to give up, he spied what looked like a small broken branch, but unusually pale, sticking upwards. Pulling it out of the shingle he saw it was part of a bone, with one rounded end where it used to fit into a joint socket. Possibly from a seal's front flipper; Harry was no expert at seal skeletons. But again he could see the same grooves near where the bone was broken. It was the same colour as the skull too and probably came from the same animal. What was for certain was that if an animal had crushed that bone to break it, it must have had incredibly powerful jaws. The only creature Harry knew that could bite through a bone like that was a hyena: the strongest mouth in Africa.

He explored the area for some time, pulling the seaweed aside and digging in the shingle with a piece of driftwood, but no further evidence came to light. Eventually he gave up and carried the skull and bone back to the house, then made two return journeys to carry armloads of wood.

He also fetched the empty drum he had found earlier and set this up outside the house, placing the skull on top. But as he broke up the wood for the fire he couldn't help but feel the skull was looking at him. The gruesome empty sockets seemed to follow his every movement. He turned his back on the skull but it felt as if there were someone standing right behind him, a real presence that made him spin round again to face this new demon. The skull still stared. There was no way he could carry on with his task under this devilish scrutiny. He realised it would be stupid to leave the bones outside anyway: they might attract unwanted visitors, maybe even the perpetrator of the crime. Besides he needed to keep them safe to show Peter. He carried them into the third bedroom, placed them on the floor in the corner, and firmly closed the door.

Cleo watched calmly as Harry broke up the rest of the wood and carried it into the house to pile beside the fireplace. There should be plenty for a couple of days now. After swigging some water, he fetched his mobile phone from the bedroom, switched it on, and went outside to sit on the drum while making his call. Waiting for the phone to ready itself he suddenly felt apprehensive. What would he say? What if Anna wasn't there?

The phone picked up a strong signal and Harry left it long enough to see if there were any messages or texts for him. Nothing. He was also concerned to see that the battery was half used-up already. That was strange: he had barely used it since it had been fully charged. Still, there should be plenty of juice for two or three more days, and he was due to stay at the house only a few more anyway. He just had to be careful not to let it run too low, so that it was always there for emergencies.

He had previously entered Anna's number into the phone's memory. As it rang he looked at Cleo, her head now under her wing as she rested. He was glad she felt relaxed enough to sleep in his presence, but worried for her should there be any further unwelcome visitors at night. Maybe she would fly off to roost anyway.

It had now rung six times and Harry was just expecting the answering service to kick in when there was a click followed by Anna's breathless voice. 'Hello.'

'Hi, Anna, it's Harry.'

'Harry! I've been worried about you. I was going to give you a call soon in fact. How are you?'

'Fine, fine, no need to worry.' As he said these words he realised this wasn't the time to mention the skull and bones, nor the noises at night. 'How are things at your end? How's Peter?'

'He's not great. Keeping busy but hardly talking about anything. Sophie's grumpy too. It's not a lot of fun here right now.' She sounded pretty low.

'I'm sure it's not. Look, I'm running out of supplies here, so I need to take a trip to Cley tomorrow – perhaps we could meet up?'

'As it happens I was planning to pay you a visit tomorrow – if you wanted one that is. I can come in the RIB, so why don't I bring supplies with me, save you carrying them all that way?'

'That'd be great.'

'I could do with a breather from this place, all a bit gloomy here. So what sort of things do you need?'

'A pack of bottled water, large loaf of bread, then I guess just a few tins of easy things like beans. Oh, and maybe a pack of sausages. And some biscuits.'

'That sounds like meagre rations to me – I bet I can do better than that. Leave it to me.'

'What sort of time shall I expect you?'

'With the tide it's going to be about mid-morning.'

'Okay, great.' There was a pause. The phone call so far was more like an order to the local grocery store rather an intimate conversation. Suddenly he couldn't think of a thing to say.

Anna broke the silence. 'Well, I guess I'll see you tomorrow then.'

'Yes. Take care in the meantime.'

Harry pressed the red button to end the call and again to close the phone down. He slapped his forehead and shook the tension out of his body. The conversation had felt stilted and awkward, and there was so much he had wanted to say and hadn't been able to. But at least they had spoken and would be together the next day.

He jumped to his feet startling Cleo from her sleep. Harry blew her a kiss before taking the phone back into the house. But just as his hand reached out for the door handle he saw a flash of red out of the corner of his eye.

CHAPTER THIRTY-ONE

Anna was stirring a pan of curry on the stove when Peter came in and looked over her shoulder.

'I'm glad you're back, Dad. This'll be ready in about fifteen minutes. I just need to put the rice on.'

'Good. Well done, love, smells delicious.' He put a hand on her shoulder and kissed the side of her head.

Anna stopped stirring and looked at him quizzically. It was the first time he'd kissed her since – she didn't know when. 'So how are you feeling today?'

'Oh, a little brighter. Been busy on the tractor with Joe and it seems to be running fine now. Good to be doing something practical – you know. Where's Sophie?'

'She's upstairs. Been playing music all day and doing something on her computer. I expect she's missing her schoolmates. If you're going up can you give her a fifteen-minute warning for food?'

'Will do.'

'Oh, and Dad, I've just been speaking to Harry on the phone and he's running out of supplies. So I said I'd take him some over in the RIB on the morning tide if it's still okay for me to use it.'

Peter ran his finger down the tide-table pinned on the kitchen wall. 'High at ten-thirty tomorrow, yes that's fine. Mind you, I don't want you walking back on your own – not with recent goings-on. Tell you what, why don't you leave the RIB with Harry? He can run you back to Morston in it then go back to the Watch House on his own. He's a capable chap – I've seen him helm the RIB and he's fine. Just make sure there's plenty of fuel, fill the spare tank right up on your way.'

Anna frowned. That would give her only a couple of hours with Harry before the tide would be too low for him to get to Morston and back in the boat. She was hoping to spend longer with him. 'But what if you need the RIB in a hurry?'

'Well it's only for a few days and the tractor seems more reliable now, so I should think we'll be okay.'

'Hmm, all right then.' Anna didn't sound pleased. But then maybe Harry wouldn't want a long visit anyway; maybe it would be interrupting his rest.

Peter went off upstairs to change for dinner while Anna resumed the stirring of her curry. She wanted to spend more time with Harry before his holiday was over, before he headed back to Newmarket, but obviously tomorrow wasn't going to offer that opportunity. Never mind, at least they'd get some time together and she would enjoy choosing him some fancy supplies – something a bit better than baked beans.

Chapter Thirty-Two

Slipping the phone in his pocket, Harry looked over to the left and, sure enough, there was a figure in red walking behind a clump of shrubby sea-blite. It was her again: the woman in the red dress, he was sure of it. Only this time she was heading in the opposite direction, towards the Point. He was determined to catch up with her this time, but to get closer had to run round the other side of the house and up over the ridge. When he reached there he couldn't see her in the direction she had been heading.

He turned and looked back to the east towards Cley – maybe she had somehow doubled-back while he had been racing round the house – but there was no sign of her in that direction either. He scanned all around, but there was nothing to see. It was impossible. How could she just vanish into thin air? There were certainly no other walkers around either, she was alone. And why the red dress? Always the same red dress.

He stood for a few minutes longer, looking back and forth, but it was fruitless. It was when he started heading back to the Watch House that it occurred to him that the only remaining possibility was that she had gone into the house herself. He couldn't imagine how she could have sneaked past him so swiftly, but surely that was the only explanation now? Maybe, somehow, she hadn't seen him, and – lost and cold – had taken refuge inside.

He quickened his pace, feeling oddly unnerved that a stranger was in his house right now – going through his belongings even. As he walked round the side of the building he noticed that Cleo had gone. Funny, he hadn't seen or heard her fly off. The woman must have scared her as she approached the house.

He called again so as to warn the woman of his arrival. 'Hello!'

The door to the house was shut. He could have sworn he had left it open. For a moment he feared she might have locked herself in – locked him out. As he had left the key on the inside of the lock it would have been easy to do, but when he turned the handle the door opened.

'Hello?' It was more of a question from Harry this time. Was anyone in?

No reply. Everything looked untouched. Harry looked in his bedroom, almost expecting the red beauty to be curled up on his bed, Goldilocks-style, but of course it was empty. He looked in the second bedroom and up into the lookout room, he even turned down the corridor where the stove was. Nothing. That just left the third bedroom. Why had he left that until last? She had to be in there. He turned the handle and pushed the door fully open.

The face that stared at him caused him to step back with a sharp intake of breath. But it wasn't the face of a young woman with long black hair. It was the face of a dead seal: the skull with its dark hollow eye-sockets and grinning teeth. He had forgotten it was in there. Harry shut the door firmly. He wasn't too happy about having that gruesome object in the house.

So she wasn't there after all. Again he left the house, walked to the top of the shingle ridge and looked all around. It was nearly dark now and there was nothing to be seen but the grey shapes of shrubs, buffeted slightly by the growing wind, and the distant black waves rolling in from the North Sea. Somehow she must have got past him and returned to Cley – but how she did that without being seen was a mystery. Harry pulled his collar up and turned back towards the Watch House.

CHAPTER THIRTY-THREE

Sophie lay on her bed listening to music, probably a little louder than her father would like, but he hadn't complained yet. She had just spent twenty minutes pushing one of her sister's vile curries around her plate before leaving the table and walking off without saying anything. She hadn't even asked if there was a dessert. It was some time since she had felt like eating much anyway.

She hated the half-term break. Not because there was no school – she hated that too – but just because of the boredom, the feeling of being trapped, not seeing her friends. Living near the sea was okay in the summer but now it was colder there was just nothing to do. Why couldn't her family live somewhere exciting like a city? Not that it was much of a family now; her dad had been distant and subdued ever since her mother died a year ago. She was glad to have her sister around, but they never really connected. Anna had been working in Bristol for too much of Sophie's childhood for them to have developed a strong bond. At least now Anna was here she could do the chores around the house and talk to Dad. If it had been just Sophie and Dad at home it would have been even more miserable, and Sophie would have felt extra guilt from not feeling able to support her grieving father. She was grieving too – could nobody see that?

Sophie had always wanted to ask her mother why there was such an age-gap between her and her sister. But now she couldn't. Could it be that Sophie had been a mistake – unwanted – simply the product of a failed contraceptive? She didn't feel she could ask her father. Who cared anyway, she was here now.

There was a knock on the bedroom door, just loud enough to be heard above the music. She didn't respond.

The door opened, it was Anna holding a bowl. 'Apple crumble – do you want any?'

'Nope,' Sophie monotoned.

'Are you sure – you hardly ate any of the curry?'

'Sure.' Sophie stared at the ceiling, not wanting to make eye contact with her sister.

'Everything okay?'

'Yip.'

'I know you're bored. Is there anything else wrong?'

'Nope.'

'You don't want to talk about anything?'

'Nope.'

'You know, it wouldn't hurt to socialise with your family a bit more now and again – we do care about you.'

'You know, it wouldn't hurt to leave me alone.' It almost sounded like a shout, above the music.

Anna looked at her sister for a few moments, fumbling various replies in her mind, then left, closing the door. She'd been through this too many times to think she could win. She could remember feeling grumpy and uncommunicative herself when she had been a teenager, but hadn't had the added complication of dealing with the loss of a parent. She knew she could never be a replacement mother for Sophie, yet she did want to help somehow, just didn't know how. She just found it impossible to communicate properly with her. Maybe it would come with time now that they were living in the same house.

Sophie exhaled noisily with frustration. God, she needed a cigarette. She had started smoking when she was just fourteen, after her mum died, but had led her dad and sister to believe she had given up, just to stop their nagging. So now it was a sneaky puff now and again, hanging out of the bedroom window or when she was away from the house, followed by handfuls of mints to get rid of the smell on her breath. She had even taken to washing her own clothes often, to remove the smokiness.

What was wrong with it anyway, all her friends smoked? Well, lots of them, and her dad had said he had smoked when he was younger. She'd stop before it made her ill.

Besides, that wasn't the half of it. Her family certainly didn't know she'd been smoking cannabis as well – *blow* as she and her friends called it. This had begun only a few months ago when she and a couple of her girlfriends from school started hanging out with a bunch of older local boys. Her best friend, Lara Diggory, had a nineteen year-old brother named Ewan who was the main culprit. Not that anyone knew him as Ewan – even his sister called him Digger. He and his mates, Alex and Tom, worked together in a boatyard a few miles away and were enjoying the company of some younger girls on the occasional evening or at weekends. Digger was into blow and seemed to come across a steady supply. He and Lara lived with their parents in Salthouse – the next village on from Cley and within easy walking distance. Especially when you were bored out of your mind and dying for a smoke.

Truth be told, Sophie had quite a soft spot for Digger. His friends were boring, dead-end, but there was a rebel in Digger that made Sophie buzz inside, though she tried not to let that show. The boatyard was just temporary for him, to earn a bit of cash before he started his big adventures. The only reason she had started smoking blow in the first place was to impress Digger – or rather not to let him think she was a pathetic child – but she had actually grown to like it: to want more.

Sophie had spent much of the day lying on her bed, texting Lara on her mobile phone. The trouble was that she couldn't tell Lara how much she liked Digger in case she told him. Which she would, of course. But Lara was her best friend and she really needed to talk about it with someone. Lara went on and on about how much she fancied Digger's mate, Alex. It wasn't fair.

Sophie had been hoping to persuade them to get together as a group tomorrow to share a smoke, but Digger and the others were working and Lara was going shopping with her mum. The day after was sounding more promising, though, as it was Digger and Alex's day off. They could all meet at their usual secret place. At least Sophie had something to look forward to now.

CHAPTER THIRTY-FOUR

The fire in the main room of the Watch House blazed and crackled as Harry pushed another piece of driftwood into the flames. It was the biggest fire he had created since taking up residence and he let the heat soak into his body. He brought a blanket through and spread it on the floor so that he could lie close to the inferno in relative comfort.

He had eaten his last tin of soup and last bar of chocolate, but was still hungry. Fetching a jar of honey he had bought from the stores in Blakeney he dipped his finger in, licking off the sticky goodness, which helped calm his pangs for a while. If only he had brought a case of beer too, or a bottle of whisky. It hadn't even occurred to him to suggest to Anna that she should bring some alcohol the next day. He was used to spending long periods without booze – it was often hard to come by in the jungle – but he really felt like a good drink right now. He had such a head full of all the bizarre recent events that he could do with something to blur things a little, help him relax.

His thoughts went back to the girl in the red dress. There had been something unsettling about her, something almost surreal. He had seen walkers pass the house before and barely given them a second glance, so why was he so curious about her? Was it just that she was barefoot, or inappropriately dressed, or that it was always the same red dress? Or was it that it was an unusual time for anyone to be walking towards the Point? Or more basic than that: simply that she had looked gorgeous – even from behind?

He took another fingerful of honey and stuck it in his mouth. Of course he'd probably never know now. The young woman would be back at her hotel, or B&B, or home with her family, and he would never see her again. Besides it was Anna he wanted to be thinking about now. Not a faceless stranger who was already in the past.

He pushed another piece of wood on the fire and lay back on the floor. He liked this basic living. Building a fire took a little time but he would rather that than flick a switch for soul-less central heating any day.

He yawned. It was a long time since he had had a really good night's sleep. Recently they were either interrupted by strange noises or troubled by nightmares. Tonight was going to be different, he was determined. He would go to bed in a few minutes, think about Anna for a while, and then fall into a long peaceful sleep until morning. And then Anna would arrive.

And it was precisely at that moment that the knock instantly extinguished his smile and sent a shiver through his body. A single knocking sound – but not from the door.

'Oh, for God's sake, what now?' he said aloud.

The sound seemed to have come from the other side of the house, possibly from the second or third bedroom. But he couldn't tell whether it had come from inside the rooms or outside the house. It hadn't sounded like someone knocking on the window though – it was more like a knock on wood.

He quietly stood up from the floor and fetched the Maglite from his bedroom. The flames from the fireplace were bathing the main room in a flickering orange glow, which until that point had been comforting and cosy, but now were spooky. He stepped slowly and quietly until he was standing outside the two adjacent doors that opened on to the other bedrooms, and cocked his head to one side to listen intently. The fire hissed and occasionally made small spitting noises, but otherwise all was silent. The wind had dropped so there were no sounds from outside the house. He stayed like a statue for some minutes.

Just as he was about to sit back down in front of the fire, a second knock sounded so close that he stepped back in alarm. It was coming from the third bedroom – definitely. But there was nothing in that room, except an empty bed and the dead seal's skull and bone in the corner. It had sounded like someone knocking on wood again, but not on the door – on the wooden floor. Or maybe something falling to the floor. But there was nothing in there to fall, the skull and bone were on the floor already.

For a moment he wondered if he had properly looked under the bed when he had checked the room before. Perhaps he had been not been thorough enough in his search. Could it be that the girl in the red dress had been hiding under the bed all along and had just decided to make her presence felt? Perhaps she didn't speak English and was afraid. Perhaps she was a runaway – an illegal immigrant on the run, even.

And then Harry became cross. Angry with this damned house and its noises, angry with himself for his constant analysis rather than action. He seized the door handle, twisted it, and kicked the door open. He was keyed up by now, fist clenched in case self-defence was required.

'What the hell do you want?' he shouted. But there was no one there.

The room was indeed empty apart from the bed and the skull. Just the skull? Yes, it was true, the bone was missing. Harry had placed it next to the skull earlier, but it was no longer there. He shone the torch under the bed and in all the corners of the room but there was no sign of it. He even lifted the skull, which felt strangely heavier than before, but the bone was not underneath. Where on earth could it have gone? Could something have come in and taken it? An animal? But he hadn't left the door open – that just wasn't possible. He would search the house and surroundings properly in the morning.

He sat down in front of the fire and pulled his knees up towards him. Perhaps the night was not going to be as uneventful as he had hoped.

CHAPTER THIRTY-FIVE

Anna woke early, excited. She had a mission: not only to re-supply Harry but also to negotiate the journey to the Watch House on her own. Not that she wasn't used to helming the RIB, she had done that several times before, but usually with someone else to help, and in calm weather. Today the wind was up a little so it would be choppy, even in the natural harbour.

Just as she was finishing a quick breakfast, Peter came into the kitchen.

'Morning, Dad. I'll be leaving soon: have you got the truck keys?'

Peter fished in his pocket and handed a bunch over. 'Now you will be careful out there won't you?'

'Yes, Dad.' She indulged him with a warm smile.

'And don't forget to leave within two hours of high tide or you'll never get back.'

'I know.'

'And take plenty of fuel, more than you think you'll need.'

'Yes, Dad.'

'And wear the waterproofs, you'll get spray today. And take your mobile phone.'

'Stop it, Dad!' They both laughed as Anna slipped out of the door.

Her first port of call was the delicatessen in Cley. In the bustling shop she filled polystyrene pots with olives and houmous, chose some pizza breads and a couple of bottles of apple juice before queuing at the pie counter.

On her way past Blakeney she stopped at the village store to pick up more mundane items: bottled water, bin liners, tins of soup, milk, bread, biscuits, and a bottle of whisky in case he needed a warming shot in the evenings.

The petrol station was just past Blakeney on the coast road to Morston. In the back of the truck were two plastic fuel tanks, one of which was the spare to take on board the RIB. She filled both to the top with unleaded. Then on to Morston quay where she parked near where the RIB was tethered. Anna tore a black bin liner off the roll and put all the provisions inside to keep them dry on the journey. She stored this and the spare fuel tank in the stern of the boat and then filled the outboard tank to the brim from the second plastic can. As she put on her waterproof jacket she watched a small queue of anorak-clad tourists board one of the seal boats. The skipper, in his bright orange top, checked tickets as people tentatively manoeuvred along the wooden walkway towards the vessel. Numbers were down now that the summer was over, but they still ran trips nearly every day, even throughout the winter.

Anna locked the truck, zipped the keys and her mobile into her jacket pocket and approached the RIB. A gull had momentarily perched on the outboard housing and flew off lazily as she came near. A breeze blew her hair in front of her face so she pushed it inside the back of the jacket. Fuel-tap open – turn ignition key – outboard kicks into life. She untied the bowline from the wooden post, sat astride the central seat and clipped the kill-cord around her leg before easing the RIB into the main channel leading out to the harbour. As she passed the large blue-and-white seal boat, the punters were still taking their seats and listening to the skipper's briefing.

The channel widened and as the RIB entered the harbour area Anna opened up the throttle. The water was a little rough and she felt the first taste of salt as a fine spray hit her face. To her left, in the distance, where the edge of the harbour gave way to reed beds, she could see a large raft of black and white birds, but they were too far away for her to identify with naked eyes. A lone gull passed overhead, calling as it flew out to sea.

Anna had been so busy with her preparations she had barely stopped to think about how the liaison with Harry might go. It was now two days since they had been together – the last time she had seen him he had been setting off on the dog-hunt with Peter – and in that time they had had just one stilted phone conversation. She hoped he didn't think her posh supplies were too fussy, too mothering. She bit her lip as she steered the RIB between moored boats bobbing in the waves. It was only then that she realised that she hadn't checked her mobile that morning. What if there were a message from him saying that he had already walked to Cley for supplies and didn't need anything after all?

With one hand she unzipped her pocket, withdrew the phone and switched it on. She put it back in the pocket to keep it dry while it fired up and checked for messages and texts. She had to be careful here: there were numerous unused mooring buoys and underwater ropes in this part of the harbour and it would be easy to foul the propeller if she didn't concentrate. The choppy water made it difficult to see dangers beneath the surface.

After a couple of minutes she pulled the phone out again. No signal. That was odd – there was always a good signal here, it was so flat there was nothing to block it. She stared at it for a while, expecting the signal bars to leap suddenly into life, but nothing. The phone was zipped back into its temporary home. She would just have to head to the Watch House and hope for the best.

But what would the best be for damaged people? Harry was damaged for sure, she knew that, and recently too, but her own experiences of love had not left her unmarked either. She had had a series of relationships in her late teens and twenties that had fizzled out, but it was Simon who had really destroyed her innocent notion of love.

She had been in her late twenties, teaching in Bristol, when she had met him. He was the instructor at a badminton evening class she had joined. Good-looking, fit and energetic, as Simon was, it was not surprising all the girls fell for him. And despite her gut instinct, Anna had fallen too. It hadn't taken Simon long to take notice of the slim-legged, beautiful Anna either, and after just a couple of sessions he asked her out for a post-badminton drink. It all sounded textbook stuff now: a meal out together another day, a walk in the countryside another, then supper at his flat followed by the big seduction. It had all seemed too easy somehow, too practised.

In fact it was so smooth that at the time she kidded herself that it was simply meant to be. They never actually lived together but would stay round at each other's often, and even got to the point of talking about getting engaged. Of course now, in retrospect, she could see that the danger signs had been there. Simon never introduced her to his family, and always seemed to be too busy to come to Norfolk for a weekend to meet hers. He was shy of showing affection in public – especially at the badminton class where he treated her the same as everyone else. At the time Anna had just put this down to professionalism. Then there was the way he would turn his phone off whenever they saw each other, he said it was just so that they could have uninterrupted quality time together. But it was the talk of engagement that signalled trouble. In an ideal world there wouldn't even have been any talk about it – he would just have proposed one day – and it was she who always seemed to be raising the subject. At first he sounded keen, but she could now see that once he had time to think about it the end became inevitable. He seemed to get busier, they saw each other less, and when they were together he was more distant. They never had a row but one day, when she confronted him with the fact that – considering they had been discussing engagement – it was odd that he had less and less time for her, he snapped. He told her that he had decided that marriage wasn't his thing and he needed to cool things off a bit. The next day he sent her a text saying that he had thought it over and decided that their relationship had come to 'a natural end'. *Natural* indeed!

Within a week he was seen by a friend of Anna's in a restaurant with another girl, barely out of her teens. They had left hand in hand.

Anna had been hurt and confused and had gone into

emotional hiding for while. Then, not long after that, her mother's death turned her life upside down. In the months that followed she had no time to think of romance.

Chapter Thirty-Six

As it turned out, Harry had an unexpectedly good night. Despite the bizarreness of the mystery girl-in-red and the missing seal bone, he had fallen quickly into a deep sleep that had lasted until dawn. If there had been further strange noises in the night they hadn't woken him. He rose feeling rested and bright, and was pleased to see Cleo was back. A very brief dip in the cold sea cleansed his body and woke every cell that might have still been sluggish. He even ran up and down the beach a little, to warm up and get the blood flowing.

After this he carried out an inspection of the property, studying the ground around the house for tracks or anything unusual. A thorough search inside the building did not unearth the errant bone. Something or someone must have come in and taken it, surely it was the only explanation, but who? And why? The skull still sat in the corner of the third bedroom, staring hauntingly forwards.

Harry checked his mobile phone in case Anna had sent a message and was surprised at the lack of signal. Odd, when there had been such a strong one the day before. He glanced at his watch – shouldn't be long before Anna arrived. There was no mirror in the house but his hair was short enough to look good even when unbrushed: the tousled look.

He was looking forward to Anna's arrival and the prospect of spending some time alone with her, but realised that he wasn't sure how long she was staying. If she were returning in the boat on the same tide it wouldn't be for long at all: maybe just a few hours at most. Hopefully she would be able to leave the boat at the house and he could walk her back to Cley in the evening like he had done a few days ago. Maybe she was even expecting to stay the night at the Watch House with him. He quickly tidied up the house, putting the bedroom in order, washing the used mugs and bowl from the night before and clearing out the fireplace.

When everything was as ready as it need be, he went outside to see if there were any signs of the RIB. Cleo looked up at him expectantly.

'I'm sorry, Cleo old girl, I've got nothing left for you. But Anna should be here soon and with any luck there'll be lots of bread that you can share with me.'

Looking down towards the harbour he could see a small boat approaching the mooring post at the edge of the marsh. The figure that expertly steered the boat to the perfect position and moved forward to tie up the bow was wearing a large red waterproof jacket, but he could tell that it was Anna.

As Harry looked on, the figure hauled a black plastic bag out of the boat and started walking towards him. The bag flapped in the wind; the figure stopped to readjust her hold. Harry realised he was just standing and staring when he could be helping.

He waved and set off to meet her. A little closer and he could see that she was grinning. When he was within a few yards of her she put the bag down. Harry walked straight up and put his arms around her. They squeezed hard for a few moments, both laughing.

'Hello, you,' Anna said.

Harry looked down at the bin liner. 'I see you've brought me some rubbish then.'

'Oh, it's not for you, it's all for Cleo.' Anna had already noticed the goose next to the Watch House in the distance.

Harry laughed, picked up the bag, and the pair walked towards the house.

'So, how have you been coping with isolation?' Anna asked.

'Not too bad actually, I even had a good night's sleep last night. Cleo's kept me company now and again.'

'Been up to anything interesting?'

'Beachcombing, collecting firewood, swimming in the sea.'

'Gosh, you're brave.' She leaned over and kissed his cheek as they walked. 'I thought I could taste salt on you.'

As they approached the house, Anna stopped to greet Cleo. As she did so, Harry thought about the innocent description of his time here. He didn't want to go on about bad dreams and noises at night – he wasn't one of life's whiners. He had also decided not to mention the missing bone or the girl-in-red. Apart from not wanting to worry Anna, he also felt that the mention of the young woman might make her jealous. Why a stranger walking past the house might make Anna jealous, someone whom Harry had neither spoken to nor even seen properly, was curious. He realised that actually it wasn't her potential jealousy, but it was his own guilt for being intrigued and strangely attracted to the girl.

'Let's get this stuff in the house.' Harry took Anna's hand with his free one. 'How long can you stay?'

'Well, do you want the good news or the bad news?'

Bad news? Harry hadn't been expecting any bad news. 'Good then bad.'

'The good news is that I can leave the RIB with you. Dad doesn't mind for a day or two as the tractor's working okay now. Might be useful in an emergency, plus you can putter around the harbour if you get bored – you just need to keep an eye on the fuel.'

'And the bad?'

'The bad news is that you'll need to take me back to Morston in it while the tide's still high enough.'

'Oh, right, how long does that give us?'

'Better say two hours to be on the safe side.'

Harry was disappointed. 'Couldn't I walk you back to Cley later on today or something?'

'I'm afraid I need to get the truck back to Dad, and it's parked at Morston quay.' She ruffled Harry's hair. 'Maybe we can plan something nice for before you go home.'

Home. Harry knew she meant Newmarket but that certainly didn't feel like home any more. And it didn't feel like somewhere he wanted to be heading to in a few days' time. 'Did you have anything in mind?'

'I've got a lot on tomorrow, but the day after is free. If you bring the RIB back to Morston I could meet you there in the morning, then we could spend the day together and go for a meal or something in the evening. You could stay the night at Marsh View again if you like, if you don't mind kipping on the sofa.' The idea had come tumbling out and Anna suddenly wondered if it all sounded too pushy. 'Just a suggestion,' she added.

'Sounds great to me.' Harry brightened.

'Good. I suppose the day after that you'll be heading back to Newmarket anyway.'

'I guess. Though it's the last thing I feel like doing at the moment.' Harry lifted the bag of supplies on to the oak table in the main room of the house, suddenly keen to change the subject. 'So, let's see what goodies you've brought me.'

Anna pulled out the contents one by one, describing them and enjoying Harry's reaction and happy surprise.

'Wow, what feasts shall be had!' he said at last. 'Now let's get that starving goose fed.'

He took a couple of slices of bread from the wholemeal loaf Anna had brought and they went together to crumble them up into Cleo's water bowl. The goose gobbled eagerly, even taking a couple of pieces from Anna's hand.

'You're honoured,' said Harry. 'She must like you.'

Anna laughed, but shivered as a gust of wind blew over the shingle ridge.

'You're cold. Let's go inside.' Harry suggested. 'And I'm hungry. I was going to suggest another picnic on the beach but I think it's too nippy for that. Why don't I build a fire and we can sit in the house in front of that?'

'Okay, that sounds much more cosy.'

Back indoors, Anna set out feta and spinach tart on plates and opened the pots of houmous and olives while Harry laid a fire. Before long they were munching through their feast and drinking apple juice in front of a small blaze.

'So what's the news from Marsh View?' Harry asked.

'Not much really. Sophie's spending most of her half-term break in her bedroom listening to music. Dad seems brighter though. I guess it's good that he's had the tractor to meddle with to take his mind off other things.'

'Any more dog incidences?'

No, nothing. Maybe that's the last we'll hear of it. And no further news on Frank either – not that *I've* heard anyway – you know, on what exactly killed him.'

'And Linda – how's she?'

'I've not seen her but Dad has talked to her on the phone. She's still pretty shocked, on tranquilisers from the doctor now. It'll take some time I guess. I must go and see her soon, maybe I'll fit it in tomorrow.'

'Hmm. I should see her again before I go.'

Anna pulled a sad face at this. 'I don't like the sound of that. You going I mean.'

Harry pulled her towards him and folded his arms around her. 'I don't like it either.' She turned her face and kissed him full on the mouth.

When they finally pulled apart, Harry saw there was a tear on Anna's cheek. He reached forward and brushed it away with his hand. 'What is it?'

'Oh, you know.' Anna sniffed. 'Just snatched moments. Don't want to go.' They kissed again.

Eventually Anna had to stop and look at her watch. 'Oh God, I'm sorry but we've really got to go. If the water gets too low before you get the boat back you'll be in all sorts of trouble.'

The couple stood and packed away the rest of the food in silence. After locking the house and saying goodbye to Cleo, they walked to the RIB. Harry took the helm, so that he could be sure he remembered how to operate it; Anna untied the bowline from the post and stood next to Harry in the boat. As he motored slowly away from the reeds into the harbour, gradually lowering the engine with the trim switch as he did so, Anna put her arms around him and held tight. They said nothing for the whole journey.

The channel leading to Morston quay was shallower now and Harry knew he had to turn the boat round quickly to get out again. Safely moored, they went to Peter's truck where Anna gave him the other petrol can, which was still half full.

'Just fill the outboard tank up again with this then you'll have plenty to see you through a couple of days. No long voyages though.'

Harry filled the tank to the top and returned the empty can to the truck. Anna had taken her red jacket off now and was standing by the open driver's door. After a last hug, she climbed into the driver's seat and pulled away.

Harry knew he had to get back to the Watch House as soon as possible. He fired up the outboard and took the RIB along the channel – scraping the muddy bottom as he approached the deeper harbour.

Chapter Thirty-Seven

As the Watch House came into view it looked cold and uninviting. Heading away from Anna made Harry feel dismally lonely. He reflected on how his birdwatching trip to Norfolk had turned out so differently from what he had been expecting.

After tying the RIB securely to the mooring post, he walked towards the house. Cleo was still there and waggled her tail as Harry passed her, almost like a dog pleased to see its master. Inside, Harry felt a need to check every room, despite having locked up before returning Anna to Morston. What was he expecting? All the rooms looked as normal, but the third bedroom still made him hesitate, and then shudder slightly at the sight of the skull gazing back at him blankly. The bone was still missing. He had actually planned to show the skull to Anna, maybe even ask her to take it back to Peter, but with the short time they had together he had forgotten all about it. It didn't feel good having the skull inside the house. It wasn't just bone and enamel with shreds of withering flesh; it had an unnerving presence.

Harry thought of himself as being spiritual rather than religious, but had no clear ideas about the spirit world – or even if it truly existed. He just couldn't stand the thought that once you die that's it: nothingness, blackness, forever. So he did believe that there was a soul that continued after death, and therefore must pass into other states, possibly before being reincarnated. But he had never seen a ghost or spirit, as far as he knew. Yet he had felt things he couldn't explain, and right now he felt that this skull was more than just a dead object. Perhaps the nature of the death had meant that the seal's spirit was not ready to move on and was somehow hanging around the skull. But waiting for what? The thought that the third bedroom of the Watch House was haunted by a seal's spirit was not a welcome one.

Harry liked seals though, so even if the strange presence was caused by a seal's spirit, that didn't explain why it made him feel so uneasy. The presence felt malevolent in some way: dark and restless. The more he thought about it the more he wished he had given the skull to Anna to take away. What else could he do with it now? He thought about burying it in the shingle outside the house where he could dig it up later to give to Peter, or he could leave it in the RIB. But neither would be safe. Whatever had taken the bone could easily take the skull too if it wasn't locked up in the house. He would just have to live with it for now.

For a while he sat at the oak table in the main room looking out of the window. Cleo was sleeping with her head under her wing, feathers occasionally ruffled in the wind. Marsh plants were buffeted slightly, low clouds rolling past at some speed. Perhaps a storm was brewing. He thought about Anna and how brief the visit had been. Now she was gone, it felt as if they had seen each other for only a few minutes. He was glad to be seeing her again in two days' time but right now that felt like an age away. His stay in the Watch House, instead of being a peaceful rest in an isolated rugged location, had become peppered with strange occurrences; now it just seemed like a waiting room until he could see Anna again. He must snap out of this. Must enjoy his last few days here, maybe do some more birdwatching, relax. Perhaps tomorrow he would take the RIB for a spin round the harbour. At least he would eat well tonight with the fresh supplies. Maybe have a glass of whisky too.

But even while he had all these thoughts he had an overwhelming feeling that there was someone in the third bedroom, that he wasn't alone in the house. He even looked in the room again, only minutes after he had previously done so, but as before there were just the hollow eye sockets staring back from the corner.

He sat back down at the table and this time saw through the window that Cleo had woken and was on her feet, looking around expectantly. Perhaps she was still hungry. Harry took another slice of bread from the packet and went outside.

But as he approached Cleo, she surprised him by suddenly launching into the air, calling loudly as if alarmed. 'Hur, hur, hur.'

She flew low, heading south towards Blakeney, her strong wings and the breeze taking her swiftly away from him. She had never behaved like that before. Harry felt stupidly upset at this desertion. But why had she taken flight? Surely *he* hadn't startled her? She was used to him by now.

As the goose disappeared into the distance, Harry turned back towards the Watch House. But as he did so he glimpsed what seemed to be someone's head just disappearing beyond the shingle ridge. Maybe that would explain Cleo's rapid departure, she had seen someone walking behind him and it had spooked her. Still odd though: Anna hadn't scared her at all.

He left the bread in Cleo's bowl in case she came back, and walked up to the ridge to see if he could see who was there. At first there was no sign of anybody, and he even wondered if he had imagined seeing a head, but then he heard a scrunch of shingle from beyond a clump of shrubs to his left. Turning, he was dumbfounded as the young woman in the red dress appeared yet again, walking away from him towards the Point exactly as she had done the day before.

He quickly trotted up the ridge; he was not going to let her out of his sight this time. As she came into full view, some thirty yards in front of him, he was staggered by the feeling of *déjà vu*. It was the same red dress, despite the chilly wind, and again she was barefoot, yet strolling smoothly on the shingle as if it were a soft carpet. Harry followed at a fast pace in order to catch up.

She turned to the right and walked to the edge of the sea where she stopped, looking out at the waves, the red material of her dress flapping and her long black hair blowing in the wind. Harry was not far from her now. His footfalls were loud on the pebbles, despite the sound of the waves, yet she didn't turn towards him. She must know he was there: must have heard him or sensed him, but she had never once looked in his direction. He stopped. He suddenly felt like a pursuer, he was harassing her for God's sake – the poor girl might be terrified of him, all alone on a deserted beach with a madman giving chase.

He wanted to give her a gentle warning of his presence. He called softly, 'Hello.'

There was no reaction. 'Hello.' A little louder this time. Still nothing. It occurred to Harry that maybe she was deaf. That would explain why she hadn't reacted to his footsteps. He walked down to the sea's edge, slowly this time, keeping a distance from her so as not to shock her when she realised she was not alone.

Drawing level with her, he could see the side of her face for the first time. It was a striking face: surprisingly bony with a strong jaw-line. She continued to look out to sea.

Harry took a couple of steps forward and called again. 'Hello.' This time he waved as well, hoping she would notice this movement from the corner of her eye, even if she couldn't hear him.

And then she turned her head, very slowly, to face him.

'Hello,' she said, her expression not changing at all. At least that's what Harry thought she said, but it was spoken very quietly, and against the background noise of the ocean it was hard to make out.

He stood transfixed. For a moment he could not respond nor react, so taken aback was he by her strange form. Her face was somehow disturbing: deep brown eyes, cherry-red lips curled in a half-smile. Harry could not help but notice her long figure, the thin material of the dress skin-tight as the wind blew it against her body.

Harry practically had to shake himself physically out of his trance. 'Hello,' he said again, moving closer. 'Can you hear me?'

'Of course I can hear you.' Her voice was soft and calm with a rich Norfolk accent.

'Oh, good. I just thought … I just wanted to check that you were okay: not lost or anything.'

'I'm not lost.'

'Good, good.' Harry felt like a nervous schoolboy, unsure of what to say. 'So, are you just out walking? Are you local?'

'Yes, I'm walking and yes, I'm local.' Still that half-smile, as if she were mocking him; perfectly self-assured and at ease, and still talking at a slow, measured pace. She was clearly not the slightest bit afraid at being confronted by a stranger on a deserted, windswept beach.

'Right ... I'm Harry, by the way: I'm staying at the Watch House.' He gestured back towards the house, but she didn't turn to look.

'Yes, I know who you are.'

'You know?' Harry wasn't expecting this at all.

'Oh, yes.' Her voice was remarkably deep and husky for a young woman.

'How? Do you know Peter?'

'Peter?'

'Yes – Peter Wild – the warden.'

'Oh, Peter. Yes I know Peter.'

'Right, I see. So, do you live in Blakeney?'

'Thereabouts.'

It wasn't exactly easy, getting information out of this woman. But then again she didn't know Harry from Adam – apart from seemingly having heard about him from Peter. A gust blew her hair across her face. She slowly raised her left hand and pulled it back, turning her body fully towards Harry now and smiling just very slightly more. There was something unnervingly magnetic yet dangerous about her whole being. Harry found it hard to take his eyes from her, hard to drag himself away. She appeared perfectly relaxed in his company yet seemed to have no desire to ask him anything.

Harry shivered as the wind cut through his fleece. 'Aren't you cold?'

'I never get cold.'

'Oh, right. Are you on your own then? I mean, did you walk up from Cley – it's quite a long way.'

'I like walking. I walk a lot.'

'Yes, I think I saw you here yesterday, didn't I, and a few days ago?'

'I often walk along here.'

'Right, I suppose that's why you know Peter then?'

'Yes.' Still the smile. And still she didn't take her eyes from his.

'You didn't tell me your name.' Harry stated.

'No.' For a moment Harry thought she was going to leave it tantalisingly at that. She seemed to be in thought. Then she added, 'Trash'.

'Trash!' Harry almost laughed. 'That must be a nickname or something.'

But she just continued to smile at him, eyes twinkling. Harry felt supremely self-conscious, awkward – incredibly drawn to her and yet desperately wanting to get away at the same time. It was as if there was a mighty electric charge between them that he could barely endure any longer.

'Well as long as you're all right then,' he said. 'I'll leave you to it.'

He hesitated a moment longer as she nodded slowly at him, then turned and walked in the direction of the Watch House. As he walked he could feel the electric charge reduce gradually. He realised he had been more tense than he could ever remember being, had been barely breathing throughout the encounter, so tight was his chest. It reminded him of an occasion a few years previously when he had been filming woolly monkeys in the Amazon and, deep in the jungle, had come face to face with a jaguar. For a full minute he and the huge cat just stared at each other, only yards apart, neither sure what to do. He had felt that same static tension then. On that occasion, just when his lungs were screaming for breath, the jaguar slowly turned and silently disappeared into the undergrowth.

Halfway up the shingle ridge, Harry turned to look back towards the girl. She was still standing in the same spot and still staring at him, one hand holding the hair away from her face. Harry gave her a small wave that she didn't respond to. He carried on walking. The whole encounter had been so bizarre, so curious, so unexpected, that he almost felt in shock. His mind was spinning. Not with the basic facts – there was nothing particularly odd about a local walker who had heard from Peter that Harry was staying temporarily in the Watch House – but it was the way she had made him feel that threw him.

As he walked round the side of the Watch House he noticed that Cleo was still missing: she probably wouldn't return until tomorrow now. He also found he had left the front door wide open – of course he had only been going to feed Cleo in the first place. He felt a compulsive need to check all the rooms yet again. All seemed normal as he climbed into the lookout room from the second bedroom. Looking through the window towards the sea there was no sign of the girl now. Again he had left the third bedroom until last, but there was only the skull within, as before. Except – or was it his imagination – had it moved slightly? The angle at which it was looking just seemed slightly changed from before. As if someone had picked it up and put it down in a minutely-altered position. Or maybe it was just the different direction of the late afternoon light that was fooling him now. He closed the bedroom door.

But the vision of the girl-in-red, of *Trash*, would not leave him. He could still feel that she was out there, that he was no longer alone on this stretch of the shingle spit. He just had to go out and check again, see which way she had gone. If he bumped into her he could always ask if she wanted a drink or something, not wanting her to think he was following her.

This time he was careful to lock the front door as he left. But as he reached the top of the shingle ridge, from where he had a good view in all directions, he could not see her to the left or the right. Surely that bright red dress would have stood out a mile? Wherever she had gone she must have gone at great speed.

Chapter Thirty-Eight

On her way home, Anna made a snap decision to drop in and see how Linda was getting on. She parked the truck on the high street in Blakeney and walked to Tern Cottage only to find the front door was already open. Doc Kelly was standing in the doorway with his back to Anna, talking to someone within the cottage; he appeared to be on his way out.

'Hello,' Anna said.

'Oh, hello again.' He turned to face her.

'I've just come to see Linda, how's she doing?'

The doctor stepped outside and pulled the door to, so he couldn't be overheard. 'Not too good I'm afraid. The shock has rather unhinged her and at the moment we're not too sure of the way forward. She's on tranquilisers but that's just a temporary solution.'

'Is there anything I can do?'

'Well, her neighbour's with her at the moment and happy to be so in the short term. But Linda really shouldn't be left alone, so if there's no improvement in a day or two we need to think of something else.'

'Like what?'

'Like a spell in hospital, so she can be monitored more closely. A mental health hospital where specialists will know better how to treat her.'

'Oh no, poor Linda.'

'Look, I must be getting on, but do go in and see her, I'm sure it would help.' Doc Kelly turned and walked off, black bag in hand.

Anna pushed open the door and walked in. 'Hello, it's just Anna.'

'Through here.' It was the voice of the neighbour, coming from the kitchen.

Anna went through. Linda was sitting at the kitchen table, in exactly the same position she had been when Harry and Anna had visited her two days previously. The neighbour was standing with her hand on Linda's shoulder and looked up at Anna with great concern on her face. Linda was rocking back and forwards very slightly, clutching a tissue to her mouth, staring ahead.

The neighbour spoke loudly and clearly, as if to a small child. 'Linda, Linda, Anna's come to see you – that's nice isn't it?' Linda didn't respond at all.

Anna sat opposite her and took her hand. 'Hello Linda, how are you feeling now?'

Linda continued to stare at the teapot on the table. Her face was still red and puffy and she looked a good deal older than the last time Anna had seen her. She was muttering constantly under her breath. Anna could not make out what she was saying but certainly heard the word 'Shuck' repeated over and over.

Anna stayed for a little while longer, talking about Harry and the Watch House, Peter and the tractor, despite her own shock at seeing Linda in such a terrible state. She was not even sure that Linda was taking any of this in – there was never a response and the muttering continued. After just ten minutes, Anna felt totally drained and said her farewells. She felt guilty leaving Linda's neighbour to it, but had to get the truck back for her father in any case. She promised that Peter would visit the next day.

During the short journey to Cley, Anna remembered the happy meal they had all had together at Tern Cottage just a week previously. She couldn't believe how much had happened in the mean time; how people's lives had changed since then, including hers. Back at Marsh View she found Peter standing in the kitchen looking stormy.

'Hi, Dad.' She threw the truck keys on the kitchen table and kissed him on the cheek. 'What's up?'

'Sophie's smoking again,' he stated grimly.

'Oh, no. How do you know?'

'I went up to her room earlier to see if she wanted anything for lunch and I was sure I could smell smoke in there. Her window was wide open and I could see a lighter on the desk so it was pretty obvious. We had a bit of a shouting match after that and she hasn't come out since.'

'Oh, Dad. Look, I'll try and talk to her later, okay? I just need a coffee and to recover a bit first.'

'Everything all right with Harry?'

'Yes, fine, it's not that. I just dropped in on Linda on the way home and she's not doing well at all.'

'Oh?'

'She's just sitting, muttering, didn't even respond to me. Her neighbour's with her again now but I said you'd go and visit her tomorrow. The doctor said if there's no improvement soon they may have to take her to a mental health hospital.'

'What – section her, you mean?' Peter sounded shocked.

'I don't know, he didn't say that exactly. You don't mind going do you?'

'No, course not. I'll go tomorrow.' He picked up the bunch of keys from the table. 'I just need to get some bits from the chandlers in Blakeney now the truck's back. You'll keep an eye on Sophie won't you?'

'I'm here now.' Anna knew it would be difficult for her father visiting Linda, especially if she was still talking about Shuck. So much for a quiet half-term holiday. It felt like a long time until she was going to see Harry again. She wished he were here to lean on right now. Odd to think that he was only a couple of miles away; the journey by boat made it feel so much further.

After her coffee, Anna went upstairs and knocked on Sophie's bedroom door. She could hear music from within but there was no reply.

She listened at the door for a while before calling. 'Sophie? Sophie?'

'What?' came the grumpy reply after a pause.

'Can I come in and talk to you?'

'Get lost!'

Anna sighed heavily. She just didn't have the energy for a full-blown confrontation right now.

CHAPTER THIRTY-NINE

Having returned to the Watch House, Harry had locked himself in, and poured a large glass of whisky. It had been some days since he had had an alcoholic drink and he soon felt the effects. But the haziness this brought on served only to heighten his confusion about the encounter with the girl with the long black hair.

He built and lit a fire with the driftwood he had collected two days earlier – the day he had found the seal skull and bone – and sat in front of it eating a pork and stilton pie and drinking more whisky. There was just so much that didn't seem quite right about the girl: the slow delivery of her speech, the thin red dress on a cold and windy day, the lack of shoes, the strange name – *Trash*. Perhaps she had been a singer in a punk band and that was just a stage name that had stuck. She was certainly unusual, to say the least. She knew of Peter so he must certainly know her – maybe she was a well-known local eccentric.

Despite this analysing, Harry just couldn't get the vision-in-red out of his mind. As more whisky flowed through his veins he saw the red dress dancing in the flames of the fire. At one point, the situation – his whole adventure in Norfolk in fact – seemed so ridiculous that he burst out laughing. And then he couldn't stop, he lay on his back in front of the fire and laughed and laughed until tears streamed down his face. Then he thought of Anna – and stopped laughing. Not because she didn't bring him joy, but because he missed her so badly and felt uneasy about the intrusion of the girl-in-red. It wasn't that he wanted anything further to do with Trash and he would probably never see her again anyway, but the way she filled his head disturbed him.

It was fully dark now and getting late; he wanted to go to bed but needed a pee first. If only the house had had an inside toilet; the last thing he felt like doing was to go outside now. For the first time he truly regretted staying at the Watch House. All the spooky and weird things that had happened had just built up an increasingly sinister atmosphere about the place. He kept telling himself that it was just two more nights and then he could leave it all behind. It seemed ridiculous that despite being here on holiday he felt compelled to stay somewhere that unnerved him more and more each day. After all, he could pack his bags and leave right now if he wanted to: walk to Cley. Yes, it was dark, but as long as he kept the sea to his left he couldn't go wrong. By the time he reached the beach car park, the lights in the village houses would guide him. He could go to Marsh View, be with Anna tonight! Or even just go to a hotel: there was The George at Cley and they were bound to have a room at this time of year.

But something made him stay. Certainly the long walk to Cley in the dark was far from enticing, and he would feel rather sheepish admitting to Anna that he didn't feel up to staying at the Watch House any longer after all, but the real reason for staying was more indefinable. He just felt it was too soon to leave, as if there were unfinished business that must be dealt with first.

Harry shook himself out of these uncomfortable thoughts, told himself off for being so silly – that it was just the rambling mind of someone who had been on his own too long and had drunk too much whisky. He fetched his Maglite and left the house, locking the door despite the fact that he was going to be away for only a couple of minutes, before heading for the loo-with-a-view. As he stood, relieving himself, he again had that strange feeling of not being alone, of being watched. Leaving the tiny building he shone the torch all around, but there was nothing unusual to be seen, just endless shingle and stunted plants. In the far distance the lights of Blakeney twinkled. How he wished he were there, in a warm comfortable pub, surrounded by the chatter of relaxed local folk.

He quickly returned to the house and locked himself in again.

The sooner he was asleep the sooner his last full day here would come, so he undressed and slipped straight into bed, even though the fire was still burning.

Thanks to the excess of whisky, sleep came quickly. His dreams were confused and disjointed: waves and flames mixing together, boats tossed about on rough seas. At one point he was standing on the beach looking out to sea at a figure wading towards him. It was Anna. The jeans and blue top she was wearing were soaked through, her light brown hair hanging in bedraggled strands, but she was smiling and walked straight into his outstretched arms. She kissed him urgently with hot wet salty lips, filling his mouth with her tongue. It felt unbelievably wonderful but at the same time he couldn't breathe. Just at the point where he thought his lungs would burst he grasped her by the shoulders and pushed her back. But as he opened his eyes he saw the shoulders he was holding were clothed in red, and the long hair was jet-black. It was Trash. Shocked, Harry pushed her away roughly to see blood trickling from the side of her mouth.

CHAPTER FORTY

It was the shriek of a gull flying over the house that woke him. Harry sat bolt upright but immediately regretted it: his head was pounding, his mouth tasted rank. God, how much whisky had he drunk last night? Surely it was only three glasses at the most, not enough to produce this kind of reaction? He slowly stood up, feeling decidedly wobbly. Sun was streaming through the window. He peered through the dirty pane to see that the expected storm had not developed, although the sea looked strangely dark in the distance. He picked his watch up and squinted at the dial: it was just gone midday. He must have been sleeping for fourteen hours or more, the combination of sea air and whisky had certainly knocked him out.

Staggering into the main room he saw that the whisky bottle on the oak table was half empty. That couldn't be right, he definitely didn't remember drinking that much. But there was no sign of any spillage; he must have been too inebriated to recall later top-ups. Not like him at all. It explained why he felt so rough though.

Back in the bedroom he pulled on his jeans, then went outside and filled a bowl of water from the tank to wash his face. There was still a good breeze, low clouds scudding past, but no imminent rain by the looks of things. No Cleo either. He hoped Trash hadn't scared her off for good. The water was so cold it made him shout as he splashed his face – but it was invigorating.

The house smelt like a pub after a busy night, so he left the door wide open as he finished dressing. Then he checked his mobile in case Anna had left a message. There was a signal this time, but no calls or texts and he was dismayed to see the battery was almost used up – how could that be? It must be faulty. He had barely used it since being in the house; he would have to be really careful with it now. He switched it off quickly. He would phone Anna in the evening and arrange a time to meet her the next morning at Morston. There must be enough power left for one more call. That was all he needed.

He took a bottle of water and some pizza bread, and sat on the old fish crate outside the house, looking over the harbour towards Blakeney. Despite the strong breeze, the water was strangely calm. At least the conditions were good for taking the RIB for a spin.

Memories of the day before returned gradually, as they do to an alcohol-impaired mind: the brief visit from Anna; the bizarre meeting with the girl-in-red, Trash. Then he remembered his strange dream and his earlier feelings of wanting to get away from the Watch House, to leave this desolate place behind. Now, in the bright light of day, it didn't seem so bad. Perhaps he had overreacted and the whisky had just fuelled his paranoia. The food and water were making him feel better by the minute. He put the bottle on the ground and performed a few stretching exercises before taking several deep lungfuls of cold clean air. Yes, a trip round the harbour in the RIB was called for, he was looking forward to handling the boat on his own, without anyone more experienced looking over his shoulder. After that, he would decide whether to stay a final night in the Watch House, as originally planned, or admit defeat and head for civilisation. If he was to stay a final night he could always collect more firewood later – there wasn't much left now.

He could see the tide was nearly at its highest point, so now was the ideal time to set off in the RIB. He went back inside to collect a few essentials: jacket, keys, and only then realised he hadn't carried out his routine checking of every room in the house. It all felt a bit ridiculous now, but, having thought of it, he just had to do a quick inspection before leaving. All was normal. Even the skull had less of a presence. For a moment he considered taking it with him and dropping it in the middle of the harbour – laying the seal to rest in a watery grave. But his sensible side still told him to take the skull to show Peter: it might be a useful piece of evidence. He locked it in the house.

He was pleased Anna had left the RIB for him to play in. As he walked towards it he thought about how it felt only right to have your own boat at such a location. He stepped aboard, but, before untying the bowline, carried out a number of checks: spare fuel tank full to the brim; outboard tank nearly full; pressure in the tubes good – no sign of any air leaks. All seemed perfect. He switched the fuel tap on, untied the boat from the mooring post, and sat astride the seat. Keys in the ignition – engine starts first time. Using the trim switch he lowered the propeller into the water and put the boat into reverse. Slight pressure on the throttle was enough to pull the boat backwards into deeper water. Once there, he lowered the engine a little further, put it into forward gear, and headed for the middle of the harbour.

A selection of deserted vessels bobbed about gently, moored to buoys. Some were small cabin boats, probably used for hobby-fishing or family-fun in the summer, but others were larger. Harry headed towards an impressive catamaran and circled it slowly. It was shiny and clean, with tinted windows, all the latest navigational gadgets, and a tall mast. Who would own a boat like that? A sailing enthusiast who travelled the oceans? A businessman who wanted to impress clients? A playboy who needed a hideaway to entertain his girlfriends? It was the sort of boat Harry could imagine being draped with bikini-clad beauties in the summer.

A small wooden motorboat puttered past; the skipper at the helm looking the part with a navy-blue smock and cap, pipe puffing in his mouth. Perhaps he was off fishing, or had a few crab pots to check. Harry smiled and waved but the man just gazed at him blankly, a sour expression on his old face. Perhaps you wave only to those you know round here. Or perhaps the man recognised it was Peter's RIB and thought Harry was stealing it. But how many thieves smile and wave?

A low-flying cormorant distracted Harry's attention and

reminded him not only how little birdwatching he had done on this trip, but also how he had stupidly not thought to bring his binoculars on the boat with him. The bird, black neck outstretched like an arrow, flapped just inches from the water's surface as it headed silently out to sea.

A little further on, Harry noticed two seal-watching boats returning from the Point. Both had about a dozen punters on board, clad in brightly-coloured cagoules and anoraks. As he drew closer to them he could see the passengers smiling and chatting happily – they must have had good views of the seals today. Of course, the seals: Harry could take the RIB out to the Point and see them on the beach. There was a large number of buoys to weave around on the way: some were unused mooring buoys – their owners having taken their boats inland for the winter – and some were navigational markers.

Harry passed a sign indicating where the eight-knot speed limit ended as the harbour widened to meet the open sea. He pushed the throttle further open, enjoying the feeling of power as the RIB leapt forward, its bow rising in response. It was more choppy here and the boat skipped along, sending occasional sprays of salty water into Harry's face. He licked his lips, as if needing to confirm that it was indeed seawater.

As he approached the end of the shingle spit, where it grew broader at the Point, he noticed a dark round object floating in the water to his right. At first he thought it was another buoy, but when it vanished and reappeared again he realised it had been a seal. He slowed the boat right down and steered towards it. He expected the seal to swim away as the RIB drew close, but it stayed in the same position, staring at him with huge brown eyes. It was an adult grey seal with the characteristic long nose and it was clearly fascinated in the RIB. The seal looked right into Harry's eyes and appeared so curious and friendly that he couldn't resist saying hello to it. The seal bobbed and stared a few moments longer before plunging beneath the surface.

Harry gently opened up the throttle again and steered round the Point. From here he could see a great swirl of water where the tide flowing out from the harbour met the open sea. It looked hazardous, as if it could suck an unwary little boat under, but Harry was determined to take the RIB further out to see more seals. He headed to the west before turning north and meeting the larger waves. The buoyant RIB with its air-filled tubes coped perfectly well, despite the rough ride. Now Harry could see many shapes on the beach right at the end of the Point: a mixture of grey and common seals of different sizes. Some ignored his intrusion with this noisy machine, some turned their heads to gaze at him, and a few slipped into the water to surface just yards from the RIB and stare at him dolefully.

It felt very special to be looked in the eye by these huge peaceful creatures. Harry took the throttle down to an idle so that he could watch them for a while, but the waves soon pushed the boat too close to the shore and he had to rev up to take it further out again, so as not to be grounded or to disturb the seals too much.

Now, further out in the open sea, Harry felt an urge to see what the outboard could really do. He opened the throttle fully, holding tightly to the wheel to prevent himself being thrown backwards. It was exhilarating; he couldn't help but whoop as the boat bounced from wave to wave. At one point the bow rose so high he thought it might flip over. He tried a few turns – steering a figure of eight, tighter and tighter – and understood why there was a central seat for sitting astride: without it he would have been flung sideways out of the boat.

After playing for a while, he decided to head further east to view the Watch House from the sea – as it must have looked to smugglers many years ago. Sunlight twinkled on the crests of the waves; brilliant white seabirds dived like arrows in the water to catch fish. Harry felt alive, better than he had for some time. It was a fair distance to the Watch House and he was concerned about the petrol situation, so he turned the engine off for a moment to check the level in the tank. It was fine, still more than half-full, and he had the spare too. He would go a little further to see the house then turn round and come straight back. That would leave plenty of fuel for the final trip to Morston. He sat for a while as the boat bobbed, enjoying the peace with no engine noise. The sun disappeared behind a large cloud, enhancing the dark colour of the water. For a moment Harry was afraid that the engine wouldn't start again, that he would be helpless and adrift, but as he turned the key it burst back into life.

He continued until the Watch House came into view. It looked tiny and so isolated just beyond the low shingle ridge. Harry heard a familiar sound and looked up to see a pair of geese fly overhead. He couldn't be certain but was fairly sure they were Egyptian geese. As they flew over the Watch House, now just dark marks in the sky, one of them peeled off and disappeared from view behind the building. It must be Cleo! So she had a partner after all but still came to visit Harry. Obviously the lure of bread was strong, but she hadn't persuaded her partner to join her yet.

Harry motored a little further forward until he was level with the house, but still some distance out, and then turned the boat. The wind and the lack of sun were making him feel cold now. And what with the menacing colour of the sea and the knowledge that Cleo was waiting for him, he suddenly felt that the RIB adventure had gone on too long. He must get back.

He glanced at the house one last time, but what he saw this time caused a jolt of panic. Climbing into full view on the shingle ridge – just yards from the Watch House – came the unmistakeable profile of a large dog. It stopped at the top of the ridge and stood, gradually turning its huge head to look towards the RIB. Harry's mouth became totally dry; he couldn't take his eyes off the beast. It seemed to stay motionless for ages. There were no people in view at all. This must be the hound they had been searching for – the seal-killer – probably Frank's killer too. Despite the chill, which was now causing Harry to shake physically, he felt a trickle of sweat run down his collar.

The dog turned and slowly disappeared from view as it climbed down the other side of the shingle ridge to head towards the Watch House. Harry had to get back as soon as possible – to send a message to Peter. He fully opened the throttle and sped back towards the Point.

Chapter Forty-One

After a quick shower, Sophie crept quietly downstairs – unsure if she was the only one in the house. Her usual holiday lie-in meant she was rarely disturbed in the mornings, but a glance at the clock in the hall indicated that it was already lunchtime. She peered round the kitchen door to see a sheet of paper on the table. It told her that Peter had gone to the Point and Anna had gone shopping – would be back before tea. Perfect! She poured herself a glass of milk and put a slice of bread in the toaster before nipping back to her room to fetch her mobile. There were no messages, so she dialled Lara's home number.

'Yeah?' It was Digger's voice.

Sophie's face glowed at the mere sound of him. 'Hi, it's Sophie.'

'Oh, hi Sophie. You coming out with us today?'

'Yeah, course, need to escape.'

Digger chuckled. 'Do you want Lara?'

'Yes please.' There was the sound of the phone being put down on a table, Lara being shouted for, then hurried footsteps.

'Hey, Sophie.'

'Hey, Lara.'

'Are you still on for today?'

'Yes, when?'

'We're leaving in about half an hour, so get there as soon as you can.'

'Who's coming?'

'Digger, Alex and me. Tom can't make it.'

'Okay, see you there.' No need for further talk. They were on a mission.

Sophie finished her toast and skipped back upstairs to apply make-up. She didn't have time to straighten her hair so she tied it back in a ponytail. She was wearing tight faded jeans and a fluffy blue top, but decided to change this for her figure-hugging red one. A final check in the bathroom mirror – not too bad – how could Digger resist? She checked her bag contained the essentials: mobile, cigarettes, lighter, lip-gloss, house-keys, grabbed her coat and headed for the stairs.

She stopped halfway down as there was a sound at the front door; she was afraid her dad had returned and was about to catch her sneaking off. They hadn't spoken since the row about smoking the day before and she was sure he would ground her if he knew she was off to meet her 'bad-influence' friends. But it was just a number of letters emerging through the letterbox and falling to the floor. She waited a minute or two for the postman to disappear then opened the door: no sign of anyone around, good. She stepped over the post carefully – when Peter or Anna came back they would think she was still in her bedroom with any luck. If she were really careful she might even be able to slip back in later without being seen at all, then the whole expedition would remain a secret.

At the bottom of the drive she turned right to head away from the lane to the beach car park in case Peter were on his way back. Walking along the edge of the coast road she buttoned her coat up, feeling the chill wind. A couple of cars passed her, the second one so close that the wing mirror nearly brushed her sleeve. On her right appeared the Norfolk Wildlife Trust Information Centre, then, a little further on to the left, the track that led north to the shingle ridge.

In the field next to this track was a small herd of black cattle. Sophie stopped to look at the massive bull with a ring in its nose and laughed as she remembered her plan to have her nose pierced the next time she was in Norwich – whether her dad liked it or not. She hadn't raised the subject with him: what was the point? She knew what the answer would be. She just didn't get what was wrong with it. Lara had hers pierced already and

Digger even had an eyebrow stud. It looked cool. Her dad hadn't minded when she'd had her ears pierced when she was twelve – but then it was Mum who made decisions like that then. Parents just never seem to realise that the more they don't want you to do something, the more you want to do it. Dad was lucky she hadn't got a tattoo yet. She looked old enough to get one: sometimes. She was planning on a small dragon on her shoulder – for starters.

Further on from the cattle there were several geese nibbling at the short grass. Large brown geese with thick orange bills. She didn't know what sort they were – she didn't care. Her dad had always been disappointed with her lack of interest in wildlife; he would know what they were, and probably what sex they were and how old they were and where they came from. Why couldn't he see that she was just different, that's all? She had never wanted to live out here in the sticks in the first place but no one had asked her. As soon as she could she was going to get a flat with friends in Norwich, maybe with Lara if she was up for it. They had spoken about it a few times and Lara had sounded enthusiastic, but Sophie wasn't sure how serious she was. Well, if it wasn't Lara she would find someone else.

The track was now flanked by lagoons on either side with small flocks of waders and ducks milling around, probing the mud with their beaks. Up ahead, Sophie could see two men setting up scopes on tripods for a closer view. They were both dressed in heavy camouflage jackets, black woollen hats and gloves. To Sophie it just looked like a sad uniform – didn't they know how pathetic they looked? One of the men reached down, took a flask from his rucksack, and poured a cup of something steaming. He looked up at Sophie. It must have been odd for him to see a beautiful young girl, walking alone along the track; she was certainly not dressed for birdwatching or hiking. He couldn't take his eyes off her. She had no choice but to walk past the men, close by, as the track was so narrow. As she neared them, the staring one raised his cup to her and grinned.

'Hello, love. You all right?'

Sophie didn't like the look of his grin at all. She completely blanked him and carried on walking past.

'Be like that then,' he called after her, and laughed. A dirty-old-man's laugh, although he was probably only in his thirties or so. She pretended to be completely unconcerned but concentrated hard to hear if he was following her. She didn't want to appear uncool enough to look round, but as she reached the end of the track and turned right she managed a swift sideways glance which revealed that the two men were both fixed to their scopes again.

She decided to climb over to the other side of the shingle ridge so that the men couldn't see which way she was heading. As she half-ran down the ridge her shoes filled with small stones and grit. She sat down for a moment to shake them out, looking out at the vastness of the North Sea in front of her. Without the shingle ridge as a shield the breeze was stronger here and she started to wish she had worn warmer clothes. The sea, which she had swum in many times as a child, looked dark and threatening, cold and brooding. She suddenly felt lonely and stood up to head for the meeting point. Looking back along the beach towards Cley she could see a couple of fisherman standing at the water's edge, tiny in the distance. But in front there was nobody: exactly the way she wanted it.

She trudged along the beach for another ten minutes until she could just see the concrete roof of her destination. The pillbox was half buried in the shingle ridge and leaning at a slight angle. Built during World War Two to protect British beaches from a German invasion that never came, the hexagonal gun emplacements were named after the similarly-shaped medicinal pillboxes of the time. It was hardly a romantic hideaway – depressing grey concrete walls with rectangular slits in three of the sides. She climbed over the ridge to the entrance, which faced inland.

Sophie suspected the others hadn't arrived yet but called anyway. 'Hello?' No reply. She cautiously stepped into the dark interior and waited for her eyes to become accustomed to the lack of light. When they had started using the pillbox in the summer it had been in a sorry state: full of rubbish and stinking of fermenting piss. But they had cleared it out, buried the rubbish on the beach – not daring to burn it in case it drew attention. It had become a useful spot to meet and smoke, away from prying eyes. It still smelt damp and was cold, but at least it was out of the wind and rain.

Sophie sat down on one of the large rocks they had carried in to use as seats, and pulled out her phone. She selected Lara's mobile number and pressed the call button, but just as it started ringing she heard crunching on the pebbles outside. She quickly flipped the phone shut and held her breath. There were no voices – it couldn't be her friends. Her heartbeat increased in an instant. She was trapped. Maybe the leery birdwatcher had followed her after all. Or maybe it was a tramp looking for shelter for the night. She held the phone close to her chest. Where *were* they? She needed rescuing.

More crunching footsteps – really close now – then silence. A pause then suddenly a head popped into view causing her to jump.

'Oh! You're here already!' It was Digger. He disappeared from view and shouted. 'It's all right, she's here.'

'God, you made me jump.' Sophie said as Digger came back into the pillbox.

'Sorry. We figured you weren't here yet. I was starting to feel a right gooseberry.' He winked at Sophie and bent down towards her. For a moment she thought he was going to kiss her, but he was just lowering himself on to the rock next to hers. 'Shift up.'

She shifted, but only a tiny bit. 'A gooseberry? D'you think Lara and Alex are getting it on then?'

'Well I don't know about getting *it* on, but they're certainly getting on. Just listen.' Outside, Alex's deep voice combined with Lara's infectious giggle made Sophie smile. Then they too came into the pillbox, stooping under the low roof.

'Sophie!' squealed Lara, leaning to give her friend an enthusiastic hug.

'I'm glad you're here.' Sophie said. 'There are some right perves birdwatching on the track – thought they might be following me.'

'Don't worry mate, we'll protect you,' said Digger, patting Sophie on the knee.

The truth was that she felt totally safe with Digger and Alex around. They were both strong blokes and good-looking too. Alex was slightly taller and thinner, with cropped light brown hair and a huge smile, Digger was darker, with hair to his shoulders and stubble on his chin. He had the most amazing blue eyes that Sophie had ever seen.

Lara interrupted her thoughts. 'Come on then bro, get busy.'

'Desperate are we?' teased Digger, pulling a handful of equipment from his pocket: lighter, Rizlas, packet of Golden Virginia and a small lump wrapped in cling-film. He passed the lump and the lighter to Sophie. 'Hold these a minute'

He took three Rizla papers from the packet and licked the edges to stick them together to form the casing for the joint. After pulling some tobacco on to the papers he reached over and took the cling-film parcel from Sophie. As he unwrapped the small brown cube of cannabis resin and held it in his fingertips under the lighter to harden an edge for crumbling, Sophie looked at his face, a picture of concentration. It was always Digger that got the blow. Where he got it from she never knew – it seemed uncool to ask – she didn't want him thinking she was a pathetic youngster with no experience of the world. He was generous with it too: never asking for a contribution from the others for the smoke they shared.

Having crumbled part of the cube along the length of the tobacco he passed it back to Sophie before rolling the joint and licking the remaining adhesive edge to seal it. The last touch was a small torn-off piece of card from the Rizla packet, which he rolled into a tiny cylinder and inserted into the end of the joint.

While Digger had been busy, Lara and Alex had been chatting and giggling. Sophie noticed that the way they were sitting, their hands were touching: not obviously holding hands or anything –

just touching. Digger now lit the end of the joint and inhaled deeply as it flared and crackled. He held the smoke in for a while before breathing out a blue plume, filling the pillbox with that familiar smell.

Sophie noticed a dark shape on the skin of Digger's arm, peeping out from the sleeve of his leather jacket. 'Is that a new tattoo?'

'Yeah, only had it done about ten days ago.' He tried to push up his sleeve to reveal more but the jacket was too tight so he took it off. Rolling up the sleeve of his sweater uncovered an intricate Celtic design – all in black, vivid and new.

Sophie reached over and touched the slightly-raised surface where it had not finished healing. His skin was warm. 'I love it,' she found herself saying.

Lara spoke up. 'Well, Mum's not going to love it when she finds out.'

Digger just shrugged. He didn't care. He put his black leather jacket round Sophie's shoulders and took another long drag on the joint.

Sophie felt great: here she was with her best friends in a parent-free zone, holding the blow and wearing the jacket of the bloke she fancied most in all the world. Digger passed her the joint. She put it to her lips and pulled in the intoxicating smoke.

Chapter Forty-Two

Leaning on the massive rear wheel of the tractor, Peter surveyed the seal colony through his binoculars. From his vantage point he could see at least a hundred common seals and a smattering of grey – everything looked peaceful and normal. He had made the journey because of a phone call from a member of the public, that morning, who had reported that when she had been walking to the Point and back the day before she had found an injured seal bleeding on the beach. Why she had waited until the next day to phone Peter was a mystery. There was certainly no sign of an injured animal now and after two high tides any evidence of bloodstains had been washed away.

On his way out to the Point, Peter had stopped at the Watch House to check on Harry, but the building was locked up and there had been no sign of him. As the RIB was not at the mooring post, Peter assumed that Harry was out on the water somewhere; maybe he would catch him on the return journey.

A twinge of pain from his stomach ulcer caused Peter to move his hand to his belly. He wasn't surprised it had flared up again. The shock of losing Frank and the stress of having a seal-killing hound on the loose was bad enough, but the argument with Sophie had tipped it over the edge. A large glass of whisky in the evening was Peter's answer to stress, but that's the last thing you should feed an ulcer. He loved Sophie so much it hurt him to see her damaging her health by smoking, but it was a long time since they had had a decent conversation about anything. If only his wife were here, she'd know how to tackle the problem. He was trying so hard to be a good father, but it's tough when your daughter barely speaks to you. It was hard to tell how much of it was Sophie's own grief and depression, having lost her mother at such a critical age, and how much was just the usual teenage hormones. Thank God that Anna was here to take some of the load off his shoulders. But how long would it be before Sophie lightened up – became a normal human being again?

For a moment his eyes misted as he thought of his wife, sadness and anger mixed, but another wave of pain from his stomach brought him back to the present. He had to get home and drink some milk, or take one of his antacid tablets. That would soothe it. He could see he was going to have to start carrying his pills around with him again – he had hoped those days were over. The last thing he needed now was a spell in hospital. Or rather, it was the last thing his family and the seals needed. It was only at that point that he remembered that he had promised to visit Linda that day. Christ – he was not sure he had the strength for that, but he knew she was suffering. He would pop round after he'd gone home and eased his pain. It was just so hard to know what to say to her. It felt too early to reminisce about the good times with Frank – it didn't seem to help with the shock she still seemed to be in.

He climbed back aboard the tractor and started the engine. It seemed that at least he and Joe had managed a good repair between them. He drove north to the beach and then along the shingle just below the ridge towards Cley. All the time he was scanning around, hoping for a glimpse of the killer-dog, the shotgun with him in case. At least if he could despatch the hound it would put one of the hassles out of the way. The sky above was busy with fast-moving clouds, there was definitely some bad weather on the way.

Peter had already picked up a few items of rubbish on his way out: pieces of rope and a plastic drum. There were plenty of other bits of flotsam and jetsam around that would need clearing at some point, so he prioritised the things that might be a hazard to the seals. He'd lost count of the number of animals he had untangled from nets and ropes over the years.

Up ahead, he could now see something fairly large and bright red at the water's edge. Funny he hadn't seen it on the way out to the Point – it must have been only just washed up. He assumed it was a bundle of red fishing net, but as he drew nearer he wasn't so sure. It was about six or seven feet long and roughly torpedo-shaped. He could see that the surface was rough with bits of white showing through the red – and that's when the sickening realisation dawned on him.

He stopped the tractor, dismounted and walked towards the object. He was right – it was the carcass of a seal – a bull grey by the size of it. All of the skin and much of the flesh was gone, but this was not through days or weeks at sea, being nibbled away by fish and crabs – this was fresh, very fresh. There was no smell of decay. It looked as if the meat had been torn off the body in great chunks. Some of the remaining shreds were still oozing a little blood, and Peter could see part of the intestines beneath the ribcage. It was almost as if the animal had been peeled – flayed alive – before being devoured. Not a scrap of skin was visible anywhere: the nose and tongue had gone and the punctured eyes wept vitreous jelly.

There was no doubt about it: this was the work of the beast they had been hunting. But surely there hadn't been time for this carnage during Peter's brief visit to the Point? The carcass was on its back, so he rolled it over with his boot for a better look at the skull. The size of the teeth confirmed it was a bull grey indeed, but it was the gouges in the white shell of the cranium itself that demanded further inspection. Peter knelt down and ran his fingers across the grooves – they had been made by teeth, that was certain – and on the left side there was even a hole where the perpetrator's canine had pierced the skull completely. In God's name what sort of animal could do this? No ordinary dog, that was for sure.

Crouched down over the corpse, Peter had the sudden feeling that he wasn't alone, that he was being watched. He stood warily, looking all around, and walked slowly over to the tractor where he picked up the shotgun and loaded it with two cartridges from his pocket. He climbed aboard for a better view and scanned in all directions, but could see nothing unusual. It wasn't far to an area where small dunes and marram grass could be hiding anything. Peter climbed down again and walked towards the dunes, all senses on high alert, safety catch off the shotgun: just a pull on the trigger was all that was needed now.

Still feeling that eyes were upon him, he stepped into the waist-high grass growing from the sand. What did he think he was doing? The area was huge: there was no way he could search it all on his own. Reinforcements must be summoned. He retraced his steps, walking backwards slowly and silently to the tractor. He didn't want to abandon the seal carcass on the beach though – the marks on the skull in particular might help an expert identify the culprit. The tractor was fitted with a rear-end bucket loader which had been used on many sad occasions over the years to remove the bodies of seals. But these were usually animals that had died of disease or injury after being caught in a net or other discarded rubbish. Never for such a grisly lump of meat and bone.

Peter started the tractor, pulled forwards beyond the seal, and then reversed until the bucket was right next to it. Taking the shotgun, he laid it down on the sand next to the seal so that it could be grabbed at a moment's notice if need be. Scanning around did not reveal the owner of the eyes that still bored into him, so he reached down, grasped the mangled rear flippers of the seal and dragged it into the bucket. Bull grey seals are heavy animals and, although this one had lost most of its flesh, it took all his strength. He then lifted the front end of the carcass and twisted that until it was fully on board, his hands slipping on the greasy, bloody meat. Starting to feel nauseous, he stepped towards the water's edge, rinsed his hands in the sea and wiped them on his jacket.

Gun retrieved and back on the driving seat, he started the engine and used the loader controls to raise the bucket a little, before pulling forwards. He continued to scan all around as he drove, but another stronger twinge from his stomach reminded him of his need to get home quickly. Then, as the Watch House came into view, it occurred to him that Harry would probably have some milk. That would do the trick for a while – neutralise the acids that were eating him from the inside.

But as he walked over the shingle ridge, having parked the tractor opposite the house, he could see in the distance that the RIB was not back yet. Odd – he was sure Harry knew better than to take the boat into the open sea on his own – where else could he be? He realised that Harry might have quit the house altogether, but looking through the windows into the gloom he could just about make out some of his possessions scattered about. Maybe he had taken the boat to Morston: that had to be the only explanation. Peter wished he had taken the spare key for the Watch House with him – in his desperate state he would have gone in to help himself to Harry's milk. For a moment he even thought of breaking a window to get in as the pain gnawed at him, but then he considered that, as the Watch House had no fridge, there might not be any drinkable milk inside anyway. Perhaps that was why Harry had gone to Morston: to restock. Besides, it wasn't far to Cley now, he just needed to bear it a little longer. When he got home he could also try phoning Harry on his mobile, find out where he was.

Despite his love of the Point, and of the seals, it was with great relief that Peter pulled the tractor off the beach near the car park at Cley to head up the lane towards Marsh View. As he did so, he glanced over to the left, to see Mack loading up the back of his car with fishing gear. Mack stood up, waved, and shouted something that Peter couldn't make out above the noise of the tractor engine.

Mack came over towards him at a trot. 'Hello, boy. Anything at the Point?'

Peter indicated for him to look in the bucket loader. 'What do you make of that?'

'Jesus! What the hell?'

'Bull grey, freshly eaten.'

'The dog's still about then?'

Peter climbed down from the tractor. 'Yes, but look at this,

Mack,' he pointed to the grooves in the skull. 'What size of dog can do damage like that?'

'A big one, a sodding big one.' Mack glanced back to the car where his Alsatian, Prince, was waiting patiently for him. 'My Prince has been with me all day – you know it's not him don't you?'

Peter nodded. 'What we're looking for is a lot bigger than Prince.'

'So what's the plan now? Anything I can do to help?'

'Another sweep of the Point, I guess. I don't want to keep losing seals like this. It's not worth trying now: it'll be dark soon. Tomorrow though. Can you let some of the others know.'

'All right boy, you leave it with me.' Mack glanced up at the sky. 'There's something brewing, mind. What time shall we meet?'

'Let's say ten o'clock. Here.'

'I'll see what I can do.' He noticed Peter wince and clutch his stomach. 'Jesus, you're not having a heart attack are you, mate?'

'No, no, just an ulcer – an old war wound. Look, I've got to get home, I'll see you tomorrow.' Peter climbed on the tractor, pale and grim-faced, not realising that his troubles that day were only just beginning.

Chapter Forty-Three

Harry's phone didn't ring. It didn't ring because it was switched off. Anna was directed to voicemail.

'Hi, Harry. It's Anna. Just wanted to sort out meeting up tomorrow. I guess it will be about twelve before there's enough water for you to get the RIB into Morston so why don't we meet then? I'll get a lift to the quay then we can come back in your car. Unless I hear from you otherwise that is. Hope you're okay.'

It had been the first thing she had done on returning to Marsh View from her shopping trip, and now she turned her attention to the numerous supermarket bags dumped on the kitchen floor. Having hung her fleece on the back of a chair, she started unloading the bags of peas and sweetcorn, pushing them on to the top shelf of the freezer.

Her head had been full of Harry all day. She was excited about seeing him tomorrow and had been thinking about where they could go for their evening meal – The George was easy to walk to, and then they could both have a glass of wine or two, but there was always the chance that there might be someone she knew there, which could spoil the intimacy. No, it needed to be somewhere more romantic than that. It would be worth the drive to Holt, which was only about seven miles. There were a couple of nice places she had in mind where they could be more anonymous. She didn't dare think about the day following that, when Harry would be heading south, away from Norfolk, away from her. Half-term break over, she would then be back at work at the school in Blakeney; life would be back to normal. It would probably feel as if it had been a holiday romance. Maybe that's all it was to Harry, maybe she'd never see him again.

The sound of the front door opening interrupted the flow of

her thoughts. It must be her father back from the Point.

'Hi, Dad. How was it in seal-city?'

Peter came into the kitchen and, without answering, went straight to the fridge, took out a carton of milk and gulped a few mouthfuls down. 'God, I needed that.' His voice sounded rough.

Anna could immediately see from his grey complexion and pained face that something was hurting him. 'Dad, what's up? Not your ulcer again?'

'Afraid so.' He reached into a cupboard for his packet of antacids, popped two in his mouth, and pocketed the rest in case they were needed urgently later.

'What's brought that on, or is it a stupid question?'

'A combination of things I expect: including what I've just found at the Point.'

'Not more injured seals?'

'A big bull grey – not that you'd recognise it – almost all the flesh is eaten away, recently too.'

'Oh, God. Did you bring it back?'

'I did. It's in the tractor loader now. But I wouldn't look if I were you. It's not pretty. Enough to give you nightmares.'

'Are you going to get the vet to look at it?'

'For what it's worth. He wasn't a lot of help last time, but he may be able to suggest a specialist who could identify the culprit. There are teeth marks on the skull that might give them a better idea: huge they are.'

'Still think it's a dog?'

'What else can it be? But the size of it – from the marks and the amount of flesh that's gone. It just doesn't add up right.'

'Did you see Harry at the Watch House?' Anna was increasingly concerned about his safety with a killer beast in the area.

'No, the house was locked up. The RIB was gone so I reckon he must have gone to Morston.'

For a terrible moment, Anna considered the thought that Harry had gone home, had had enough of the house and the isolation and had just left.

Peter read her thoughts and put his hand on her arm. 'Don't worry, love. He's not gone for good, all his stuff's still in the house. He'll be back.'

Anna turned away, not wanting her father to see how weak she was feeling. 'I've left a message on his phone. Maybe I'll try again later. So, what are you going to do about this dog now?'

'Try another sweep of the Point. It's all I can think of right now. Mack's going to help get some men together. We'll do it tomorrow morning.'

'You won't need Harry for that, will you?' Killer-dog or not, the last thing Anna wanted was something else to shorten the amount of time she had with Harry on their last day together. She could feel herself flushing with frustration at the situation.

'Depends. We'll see who Mack comes up with.'

'Why don't you get the police involved? Surely they could send some men for a search.'

'I'd rather do it with men who understand the marshes. Besides, the police wouldn't like us carrying guns. But I guess if we have no luck tomorrow we should get them in. That's if I can persuade them that a dangerous dog's on the loose.'

'So, have they come to any conclusions about Frank's death?'

'Not that I've heard, yet.'

'That reminds me, I assume you haven't been to see Linda yet?'

Peter sighed; he had forgotten about that. 'No, not yet. I'll give her a call: see if it's a good time now – get it over with.' He picked up the phone. After seven or eight rings he put it down again. 'No answer. Maybe her neighbour's left her alone for a bit. I expect she's not up to answering right now. Look, I'll pop over in the truck: I won't be long, so why don't you get tea going and we'll eat when I get back? And get that sister of yours to help – it's no good her staying in her room all day.'

'Okay, Dad. Give Linda my love.' Anna followed her father to the front door and watched him drive off. She looked at the tractor, which was standing in the drive, and for a moment considered having a look at the corpse in the bucket loader, but then thought better of it and returned to the kitchen.

Having just done a major food shop she had plenty of choices for tea. Perhaps she would ask Sophie what she wanted to eat – that might even put her in a better mood.

She moved to bottom of the stairs. 'Sophie.'

No reply.

'Sophie!'

Still nothing.

Anna climbed the stairs, hoping she wasn't about to get another mouthful of teenage angst. She knocked on the bedroom door. 'Sophie. I'm only wondering what you want for tea.'

Silence.

'There's plenty to choose from.'

Further silence.

Anna opened the door, but Sophie was nowhere to be seen. 'Oh, God, what now?' she said out loud. A quick check on all the other rooms in the house confirmed that Sophie was not at home. Back in her bedroom, Anna could see that she had taken her bag and her mobile. Where was she? And why hadn't she left a note? She might have been away for hours.

Anna checked her own mobile but there were no messages from Sophie and, she was even more disappointed to discover, none from Harry either. She rang Sophie's number and was diverted to voicemail immediately.

'Sophie. It's Anna. Where are you? You should have left a message or something. Look, we're having tea soon so wherever you are please get back here. Dad's just gone to Linda's for a bit but he'll be mad if he comes home and finds you've been out all day without even mentioning it to anyone. I'll tell you what, if you get back before he does, I'll say nothing about it, okay? But phone me – when you get this – there's enough to worry about at the moment.'

The only place she could think of that Sophie might have gone to was her best friend Lara's. Sophie wasn't the sort to go for a walk for the sake of it. She looked up Diggory in the book –

there was only one and the code was right – that must be it. The phone was quickly answered.

'Hello.'

'Hello, is that Mrs Diggory?'

'Yes, who's this?'

'It's Anna Wild, Sophie's sister. I was just wondering if Sophie was there with Lara?'

'No, but then Lara's not here either. She went off with Ewan earlier today. To be honest I'm getting a bit concerned myself – it's starting to get dark now and I don't like the look of the sky.'

'Did they say they were going to meet Sophie?'

'No, but you know what these teenagers are like – don't want to tell you anything if they can help it.'

'Hmm. So they didn't say where they were going or anything?'

'Sorry, no. I'll try calling Lara and Ewan on their mobiles and call you straight back if I hear anything, okay?'

'Okay, thanks.' Anna put the phone down. Please let Sophie get home before Dad.

A little while later she was half-heartedly peeling potatoes – it was going to be shepherd's pie tonight whether Sophie liked it or not – when she heard the front door open and slam shut. It must be Sophie. Thank God.

But it was Peter who appeared at the kitchen door, looking even more tired than he had done earlier. 'She's gone,' was all he said.

'Who? Linda? What do you mean, gone?'

'Gone to hospital. They took her in this morning. There was no answer at Tern Cottage so I went to the neighbour's and she told me. Apparently Linda got worse overnight, couldn't stop talking about … Shuck.' He winced as he said the word. 'So they took her away.'

'Oh, God. Where've they taken her?'

'Hellesdon. And that's not all, what with Frank and everything, no one thought about Linda's old aunt Eileen – you know, the one that lives in Blakeney. The neighbour told me that yesterday when Linda didn't turn up for her weekly visit the old lady tried to use the bathroom on her own and had a fall – found this morning by the usual carer and carted off to hospital as well. Not Hellesdon, of course, but the Norfolk and Norwich.'

'Oh, poor thing. And poor Linda. We must go and visit her – maybe tomorrow.' As she said it, she realised that would be another potential reduction in her time with Harry. 'Or the day after.'

'We should, yes. We'll phone the hospital in the morning and see what the score is. I need to speak to the vet now and see what he wants done with that carcass.' He looked over her shoulder to see what was in the pan on the stove. 'Where's your sister? Is she refusing to help?'

'Well, that's the thing, Dad. She's … she's missing.'

CHAPTER FORTY-FOUR

As he tied the RIB to the mooring post, Harry looked around for a suitable weapon. It wasn't far to the Watch House, but the light was fading fast and the huge dog he had seen on the ridge couldn't be far away. Maybe it was watching him right now, waiting to pounce.

His aim was to lock himself inside the house as quickly as possible and call Peter on his mobile. Maybe a gang of men could be summoned straight away to sweep the Point – Harry could then join them when they reached the Watch House. There would be safety in numbers then, and the men would bring guns. For now, all he could find was a small piece of driftwood: not enough to beat off a massive hound, but at least he could ram it in the beast's mouth if he was attacked. This might buy him just enough time to make it to the house.

Door key in one hand, driftwood in the other, Harry stepped slowly towards the building. He scanned around constantly as he walked, ears straining to hear the slightest sound, taking care that his own footfalls on the shingle were as quiet as possible. The low-growing salt marsh shrubs around the house were being bullied by the growing wind; clouds above had become darker, angrier. When he was within dashing distance of the house, Harry ran for it. As he turned the key in the lock he could almost feel the cruel fangs sinking into his back, but no beast materialised. Inside, door locked again, he exhaled heavily.

His first thought was to climb up to the lookout room and survey the area for any sign of the dog. From there, despite the grimy pane, Harry was taken aback by the change in colour of the sky. Above the sea to the north the clouds had become purple in their rage. Edges were clearly defined, making them look solid and impenetrable. The lower clouds were moving faster than ever – heading towards the house like a charging army. Spotting a black dog in the dim light would not be easy, but Harry was sure he could see nothing unusual. Anyhow, his view was only of part of the beach leading down to the sea: there were plenty of other hiding places around the house.

Thinking how stupid he had been for not taking his mobile phone with him in the first place, he went down to his bedroom. Once it was fired up, Harry was just about to enter Peter's number when a message alert came up – he selected to listen to it.

'Hi, Harry. It's Anna. Just wanted to sort out meeting up tomorrow. I guess it will be about twelve before there's enough water for you to get the RIB into Morston – so why don't we meet then? I'll get a lift to the quay then we can come back in your car. Unless I …'

The screen went blank. Dead.

'No!' Harry shouted. He shook the phone and repeatedly pushed the button to switch it on, with no success. The battery was exhausted. But how could that be: he had barely used it since being in the house? He took the battery out and tried to warm it in his hands, but that had no effect either. He should have ignored the message and dialled Marsh View straight away. Even a few seconds might have been enough for him to tell Peter the dog was on the Point. And what had Anna been about to say when the phone cut off anyway?

'Fuck!' He threw the phone on to the oak table. It was so dark now that he could barely see, so he lit a couple of candles. As he did so, the marsh through the window was illuminated for an instant in a flash of bright blue-white followed a few seconds later by a low rumble.

Harry poured himself a whisky and sat down at the table. He had to collect his thoughts and come up with a plan. He realised he hadn't checked all the rooms in the house yet so that would be his first task, to reassure himself that he was safe enough locked in his prison. There was little wood left for a fire, just a few splinters of kindling and a couple of pieces of driftwood including the one he had carried as a weapon. Not that he felt like staying the night at the Watch House anyway. But leaving the house in the dark, in a storm, with a dark beast on the loose, was way down on his list of things he fancied doing. Then he would cook some food – something hot and comforting – before bedding down for the night. In the morning, as soon as the tide was high enough, he would leave in the RIB and get to Morston as planned.

He poured another glass of whisky – perhaps that would help him sleep as it had done the night before, despite the fear of what might be outside. Yes, he just had to get through this one last night then he could get this godforsaken place behind him. In a few days' time it would just feel like one of those bizarre memories – had he really been there? One more night. One last sleep.

He stood up from the table and swayed a little, feeling ridiculously tired all of a sudden. That whisky certainly seemed to have an unusually speedy effect. A dazzling bright light flashed twice through all windows of the house. The following thunder this time was louder and closer.

Harry fetched his Maglite and started his inspection, leaving the third bedroom until last as usual. The other rooms of the house had all been as he had left them and he really wasn't expecting anything unusual now from the remaining bedroom, just the skull staring at him from the corner as before. But what his torch illuminated sent a shock wave through his body.

The skull had disappeared altogether – the floor was now strewn with a handful of feathers.

'What the…' Harry said out loud. He stepped shakily into the room, shining the Maglite in all corners and under the bed. It was true: the skull was nowhere to be seen. He picked up one of the feathers for closer examination. It was a chestnut brown colour, the quill bloodied at the end where it had been ripped from its owner's flesh. The colour reminded him of … *oh God, not Cleo – please not Cleo*. He wiped the end of the feather on his hand;

it left a red trail – the blood was still fresh.

He now remembered he had seen a goose fly down to the house when he had been out at sea in the RIB, just before the dog had appeared on the ridge. But none of this made sense – the windows were intact, the door was locked – how could the skull have been taken, and how could the feathers have been put in? The only explanation had to be that someone else had a key to the house – someone who wanted him out of there, who was trying to scare him out. Well, they were succeeding. But why? He was doing no harm.

A rattle on the window made him jump and direct the torch up to the pane. It was the first wave of rain: large stormy drops followed by more lightning and thunder. At least he had got back to the house before this had started. He closed the bedroom door and carried the feather to the table. There was no point in looking for Cleo now; he would do that in the light of the morning. With luck she would be just injured, hiding from the storm somewhere near the house. Who would do such a thing anyway: tear feathers from a goose? And why? To put them in the house as a warning suggested it was someone who knew Harry had become fond of the goose, but surely Anna was the only one who was aware of this? Somebody else must have been watching him for some time. Harry was about to pour a third glass of whisky, but already regretted how fuzzy his head was feeling. The rain was slashing at the window now, the lightning revealing Blakeney in the distance, hazily surreal through sheets of falling water.

The single loud knock on the door had him on his feet so fast that the chair tipped over backwards with a clatter. 'What the hell …?'

Was it someone at the door or something hitting it, blown by the wind? But how could it be? The wind was coming from the other direction, from the sea. He quietly moved towards the window and looked at an angle to see if there was anyone, anything, in front of the door. But it was too dark. Shining the torch would give away the fact that he was home, but it seemed the only option.

Another loud bang on the door, followed by a flash of lightning in which he saw – he *thought* he saw – a brief glimpse of red. That was all that registered in his mind: the vaguest notion of something red, yet he immediately associated it as the colour of Trash's dress. But it couldn't be her – out alone on a dark stormy night. Unless maybe the storm had caught her out, and the dog was after her, and she was seeking sanctuary from both. Thunder rolled.

Two loud knocks this time. Harry moved to the other side of the door. 'Trash?'

No reply.

'Trash, is that you?' Louder this time; maybe she hadn't heard above the noise of the storm. Harry heard something in reply this time, but couldn't make it out. Was it her saying 'yes'? He picked up one of the wooden chairs, ready to use it to defend himself in case the visitor turned out to be malicious, holding it out as if to fend off a lion. Maglite in the other hand, he slowly turned the key in the lock, twisted the door handle and pulled it sharply.

Chapter Forty-Five

There, drenched, was Trash. Just standing. Another flash illuminated her briefly but brightly, enough to show that strange half-smile still on her face.

'Jesus, Trash, what are you doing out in this?' Harry reached forward to grasp her arm and pull her into the house.

After closing and locking the door he turned to face her. In the candlelight she looked even more unsettling, the wet dress clinging to her strange elongated figure, water dripping from the rats-tails of her hair. Despite the whisky, which now was making the room spin ever-so-slightly, Harry felt incredibly uneasy to be in the same room as her.

'You must be freezing. Look, sit here.' He guided her to sit on the wooden chair he had been holding. 'I'll get you a blanket and light a fire – there's not much wood but it'll be better than nothing.'

Having fetched one of the rough woollen blankets from the bedroom he draped it over her shoulders. She had said nothing yet. Harry wondered if this might be early signs of hypothermia. He had to warm her up quickly.

As he hurriedly built a fire of cardboard and kindling, he spoke over his shoulder. 'Did you get caught out by the storm?'

'No, I knew it was coming.' Again that slowly-paced, husky voice.

Harry struck a match and the paper flared up. 'You know there's a dangerous dog about – you shouldn't be out on your own, especially at night.'

She didn't say anything, so Harry turned to look at her. She stared into his eyes, gave a slight unconcerned shrug and smiled. Harry shivered, but the cold didn't seem to bother her at all, even in a thin wet dress. Little rivulets of water trickled from the bottom of the red material down her bare legs. She wore no shoes.

Harry put the last pieces of driftwood on the fire and then looked around for more fuel. He grabbed the other wooden chair, laid it on its back and wrenched the legs off.

'I'll just have to buy them a new chair.' He pushed the legs into the flames where they quickly caught fire. 'So, what on earth are you doing out here in the dark?'

'I came … for you.'

'For me?' This was making less and less sense. Harry stopped fiddling with the fire and looked at her. 'What do you mean?'

Trash slipped the blanket from her shoulders and knelt down on the floor, opposite Harry, their knees touching. The room seemed to lurch for a moment – if only he hadn't had that whisky. He had so many questions in his head but the way she held his gaze left him unable to talk. Her mesmerising brown eyes seem to be melting him from the inside – there was something teasing, something *naughty* about the expression on her face. Her smile was bizarre considering the circumstances, yet she seemed so relaxed, carefree, happy. Harry could feel panic rising in his chest.

The fire was kicking out some heat now and steam rose from her thighs where the red fabric stretched tight across them. Harry couldn't help but notice that she appeared to be wearing nothing under the dress, her bony ribcage clearly outlined under the thin wet material. He felt himself sinking, losing grip, as if slowly falling under the effect of an anaesthetic, yet never quite going fully under.

He opened his mouth to speak but it came out as a croak. 'Why … did you … come for me?'

'Because I want you.' Creamy, seductive voice.

'Why?' It was just a whisper.

'Shhh.' She held her finger to her lips.

Harry tried to speak further but nothing would come. His brain was whirling, dizzy, confused – thoughts of Anna flashing in and out, and a growing fear of the woman in front of him right now. He tried to rise from his knees but his body weighed so much he couldn't move at all, not even raise an arm – what the hell was in that whisky?

As he watched, she crossed her arms and took hold of the bottom of her dress, then with one smooth movement pulled it over her head. Her long, unnaturally bony torso, was like no other woman's body Harry had ever seen before. She threw the steaming material to one side and shook her head gently so that the long black hair tumbled down around her shoulders. Harry was frozen. This was all wrong – he had to get away from there but was paralysed. Somehow the woman – or whatever she was – had put some sort of spell on him; it couldn't have been the whisky after all.

Grinning now, eyes sparkling in the firelight, she reached forward with her left arm and hooked her hand around the back of Harry's neck – all movements slow and deliberate. She pulled him towards her: *such strength*, there was nothing he could do. As the room flashed bright with lightning, and thunder shook the house, her mouth approached his, in slow motion. He tried to raise his hands to push her off, tried to shout for her to stop, but his body no longer responded to any demand. As their lips met he could feel hers were wet and hard. Her tongue darted into his mouth, exploring, twirling around his, *so long*, strong and probing. Harry felt sick, repulsed by the intrusion and the strange bitter taste left in his mouth. He thought he would pass out from lack of oxygen, when she pushed him away with her other hand on his chest.

She reached down and pulled his shirt and fleece together over his head. Then, holding him by the neck pushed him down on to the floor, pulling his legs out straight so that he was lying flat on his back in front of the fire. As she undid the buckle of his belt, he again tried to stop her but could not move at all. The room rotated as more flashes lit up her exquisite body; he mustn't lose consciousness, must stay awake, must fight her off.

She pulled off his jeans and underpants in one go, leaving him also completely naked. Then she stood, placing her feet either side of his hips, tilted her head back and laughed. In the flickering light, Harry could see the wild look in her eyes, strings of spit hanging from her open mouth.

The panic Harry felt with his complete paralysis was overwhelming. What the hell was she going to do to him? He tried with all his might to move but to no avail. Then his vision started flickering. He had to keep a grip. *Think of Anna – think of Anna.* He closed his eyes. Somehow he had to summon his last ounce of energy to get away. But his body felt dead. Was this really happening? Was it some bizarre dream? He was slipping further. Perhaps the only solution was to lose consciousness after all – perhaps then she would leave him alone.

But an ear-spitting howl caused his eyes to snap open. And crouched above him he saw the massive hellhound, red eyes burning like hot coals, jaws open and pointed up to the ceiling as it bayed. Drool dripping from its dagger-like teeth on to his chest, jet-black shaggy fur steaming.

CHAPTER FORTY-SIX

Alex reached into his bag and pulled out a large packet of digestives. 'Munchies anyone?'

Digger leaned over and grabbed a handful, passing one to Sophie. 'Good man, Alex.'

After three joints, all four teenagers had lost track of time. It was pitch black outside the pillbox apart from the occasional flashes of lightning, which sent eerie bursts of blue light through the gun-slits. Sophie's head was buzzing; it felt as if it were swollen, under pressure, as if her brain were too big for the skull enclosing it. She was starting to have the vaguest feeling that she should be getting home, that people would be worried about her, but right now she could do nothing but sit and lean against Digger.

They could hear rain, heavy now, pounding the roof of the pillbox. 'Shit! We're gonna get soaked.' Alex said.

They all looked at each other for a moment then burst out laughing. And, once started, the giggling went on and on until tears were streaming down happy faces. Sophie had never been so stoned in all her life, yet felt truly alive. For once, she felt as if she was where she wanted to be and with the people she wanted to be with. Her sides ached from laughing. Digger's arm was around her shoulders, her hand on his knee. Lara had flashed her a few knowing smiles and winks as she had realised the two were seriously interested in each other, but in the main her attention was focussed on Alex. Now the giggling had subsided, Lara pulled Alex's face towards her and they resumed their snogging.

Sophie looked away, embarrassed. She looked up at Digger's face, hoping he might kiss her, but he was leaning his head back on the concrete wall, his eyes closed.

'Digger, will you walk me back to my house? I don't fancy it on my own in this storm,' she whispered.

'Sure thing, babe. Not yet though, I'm too shit-faced.' He didn't even open his eyes.

'I didn't mean now. But soon I guess. My dad's going to kill me.'

'No probs.'

As more blue light strobed into the pillbox, Digger slowly opened his eyes. He turned to Sophie and pushed his mouth on to hers, his hand sliding up her leg. Sophie's body tingled all over and her head seemed to fill with noise, until an extra loud clap of thunder made her jump. Digger pulled her closer. But as the rumble faded, Sophie realised there was another noise that demanded attention. It was hard to concentrate as Digger's tongue played with hers, but there it was again: movement on the shingle outside.

She pushed Digger away and hissed urgently. 'Listen.'

Lara and Alex also uncoupled their mouths as another sound of pebbles' being disturbed came from nearby.

'There's someone out there,' Sophie whispered.

'Fuck!' Lara said, and giggled.

'God, I hope it's not my dad.' Sophie flushed with anger. Was there nothing she could do on her own without being found out?

'Whoever it is, let's scare them off,' suggested Alex and started barking loudly like a dog. Lara snorted with laughter and clapped her hand to her mouth.

'Shut up, you prat!' Digger snapped at him. 'Listen.' Further noises suggested there was definitely someone, or something, prowling around the pillbox. The atmosphere inside suddenly became more serious. 'Alex, pass the torch.'

Alex picked up the large rubber-coated black torch and stood, stooping under the low concrete ceiling. 'It's all right, I'll go.' He stepped towards the entrance and then disappeared from view.

The three remaining teenagers sat perfectly still in the dark, straining to hear if Alex would speak to whoever was out there.

For a full minute there was no sound but the wind whistling around the concrete building. No voices. No footsteps. Maybe there was nothing out there that Alex could see after all. So why had he been gone so long?

'Alex,' Digger hissed.

He tried again louder. 'Alex!'

Nothing.

A blue flash illuminated the fact that Digger was now standing and making his way to the entrance.

'Don't leave us,' protested Lara.

'Well I've got to see what he's up to, haven't I? Besides we need the torch; we need to stick together.' Digger left the pillbox.

Lara moved over to where he had been sitting next to Sophie and hung on to her arm. 'I don't like this, Sophie, it's spooky.'

Now it was just the two of them, barely breathing, listening hard to make out anything above the wind.

'Digger, for fuck's sake, don't you leave us here!' Lara shouted out.

'It's all right, I'm here,' came Digger's voice from just outside the pillbox. He sounded wary, confused. He shouted Alex's name twice, loudly.

'Where is he?' No giggles from Lara now.

'He's … he's not here. He's nowhere.'

'What do you mean? He must be there.'

'Well, he's fucking not.' A beam of light shone through the entrance and Digger appeared holding the rubber torch. His shirt was soaked through. 'The torch was lying on the ground, just outside, but I can't see him anywhere. He's either playing a stupid trick on us or ... I don't know what.'

'He can't just disappear: let's all go and find him,' Lara urged.

'I guess we'll have to. It's fucking odd that's what it is – not the night for larking about. He'll get drenched. And this torch is all covered in grease or something.' Digger passed the torch into his left hand and shone it on his right. It was bright red. 'Oh, fuck!'

'That's not blood is it?' shrieked Lara, holding tightly on to Sophie.

Digger looked at his hand closely and sniffed at it. 'It must be. But what the fuck…?' He wiped the red hand on his jeans.

'Where's Alex, what's happened to him?' Lara was crying now, her voice shaking.

'I don't know, do I?' Digger snapped.

'What are we going to do?'

'We're all going to get out of here together, right?' Digger took the leader's role naturally but his voice was trembling. 'Gather the stuff up and we'll go – holding hands all the time – get back to the road then to Sophie's house, that's the nearest.'

He shone the torch to the floor as the girls hurriedly picked up the biscuits and smoking gear and shoved them into their bags.

'Right, ready? I'll go first, then Sophie.' He grabbed Sophie's hand and held it tight. 'Then you, Lara, right?'

'Right,' both girls said together.

They made their way to the entrance, Digger shining the torch in front. But just as he was about to step out of the pillbox, Sophie felt his hand grip more tightly as something made him start. 'Fucking hell!'

'What is it?' Lara squeaked, clutching Sophie's arm.

'Jesus! It's … it's … a fucking huge dog! Get back in. Get back in.'

They scrambled back into the pillbox and huddled together at the far end. 'It's like Black fucking Shuck!' Digger half-laughed but was shaking badly now. 'Get on your phones, girls, we're not going out there with that thing about. We need help.'

'You know there's been a dog about lately?' Sophie fumbled her mobile out of her bag and switched it on. 'It's been killing seals at the Point and Dad thinks it killed Frank Davies too – you know, the guy that died at Blakeney a week or two ago?'

'Yeah, we heard. Shit! Phone your Dad quick. Has he got a gun?'

'Yes, he's got a shotgun.'

'Well tell him to bring it.' Digger shone the torch on the two phones as the girls shakily selected their home numbers. Simultaneously they held the mobiles to their ears.

'But what about Alex?' Lara sobbed. 'The dog can't have got him. I want him back.'

'Maybe he's just been bitten or something. Hiding out there somewhere.' Digger looked questioningly at the girls: why weren't the phones being answered?

Both girls stared at their phones in disbelief, turned to each other and said in unison, 'Engaged!'

Then all three looked round as the sound of shifting shingle came from the pillbox entrance.

CHAPTER FORTY-SEVEN

'So, did you try ringing them?' Peter was speaking to Mrs Diggory on the phone.

'I did. As soon as Anna called me and several times since. But I just keep getting voicemail – their phones must be switched off. I did leave messages but they haven't replied yet.'

'Exactly the same with me when I tried Sophie's phone. And you've no idea where they might have gone?'

'Not really. But my husband's gone out in his car to look for them – you've met John haven't you? He's going to try the local pubs first. I can't imagine they're out in the open on a night like this. I'm sure my boy, Ewan, will look after them. He's nineteen now.'

'Hmm. Well, look, I'll go out in my truck and explore some of the smaller lanes. Be sure to call me the minute you hear anything, okay? You've got both my mobile and home numbers haven't you? Anna will stay here.'

'Yes, all right, Peter, and vice versa, let me know if you find them.'

Peter put the phone down on the table and turned to Anna, who was looking at him questioningly. 'They've heard nothing and have no idea where they are. I'm going out in the truck: I can't just sit here and do nothing.'

'Okay, Dad.' Anna helped her father into his jacket. 'Keep your mobile on and I'll ring if I hear from anyone. And careful in that weather: it's getting worse by the minute.' As she spoke a fresh roll of thunder shook the windowpanes of Marsh View.

Peter kissed his daughter on the cheek. 'Thanks, love. What would I do without you?' But just as he turned to leave, a shrill ring came from the phone on the kitchen table. He snatched it up and held it to his ear.

'Yes?' There was no reply but he could hear a lot of noise at the other end – crackles and shouts. 'Sophie? Sophie, is that you?'

Further noises, then Sophie's voice, hysterical. 'Dad! Dad, can you hear me?'

'Yes! Yes, tell me where you are, what's happening?'

'Dad!' She was sobbing. 'It's the dog! It's Black Shuck! He's got us!'

Peter felt as if he had been punched in the chest. 'What do you mean? Where are you?'

'Come quick! We're in the pillbox.'

'Pillbox? Which one?'

More shouts and scrabbling noises. Sophie's voice came through in bursts, punctuated with sobs and screams. 'Digger! Digger! It's dragging him! It's got him! We're in the one near Salt …'

The phone cut to silence.

'Sophie? Sophie?'

Peter quickly stabbed at the return-call button but there was no response at the other end. He turned to Anna, his face red, hands shaking.

She had her hand to her mouth, aghast with dread. 'What did she say?'

He spoke quickly. 'They're in trouble. The dog's after them. They're in a pillbox – I think it must be the one on the way to Salthouse – she was cut off. The truck should get me there in four-wheel-drive.' He took a handful of cartridges from the drawer and stuffed them in his pocket. 'You stay here, phone Mrs Diggory and tell her where I'm going, see if she can get her husband to meet me there. Then phone the police and tell them some kids have been attacked by a dog on the beach.' He headed for the door, picking up the shotgun that was leaning in the corner.

Chapter Forty-Eight

Something was dripping on his face.

Harry opened one eye, the other glued shut with some sort of mucus, but it was pitch black, wherever he was. He could make no sense of the way he felt – body aching and cold – so cold. One hand tentatively explored the floor around him: wooden floorboards; a stone platform – no, a hearth. That was it: he was lying on the floor of the main room in the Watch House. It was night. Maybe he had been having a nightmare, had fallen out of bed and crawled into the other room. Too much whisky.

But why was he stark naked, and what was that gunk in his eye and on his chest? He turned on to his side, every muscle in his body complaining. What the hell had happened to him? And what was that strange damp smell? He had to get the Maglite; had to get some clothes on and warm up. He started to crawl on hands and knees into the bedroom. That's when he remembered.

At first it was the red dress that filled his head. Then the way she had peeled it off over her head, revealing that bizarre body. But why had he not found the strength to push her off? And where was Trash now? So sickened was he by what he remembered he turned his head to one side and retched.

Shakily he got to his feet and, feeling with both hands, located the torch on the bed. He switched it on and by the light, which he was concerned to see was dimming as the batteries gave their last, looked for his clothes. That's right – he remembered now – she had pulled them off him in the main room. He grabbed his towel and wiped the sticky goo from his chest and face before staggering to the doorway and shining the torch around the room. There, indeed, were his jeans and fleece and shirt, inside-out – the way they had been left after being tugged from him. He hurriedly turned them the right way out and dressed, body shaking with cold all the time.

The candles on the oak table had burned down to nothing, pools of wax spreading across the table like miniature pyroclastic flows, so he went to the supply box near the cooker, took the last two candles from their carton and lit them. Looking around the main room in more detail he saw several large feathers scattered about the floor and more pools of mucus. He now had a vague memory of this gunk dripping on to him from … fangs! From the teeth of the massive hound that had stood over him. For a moment the hellish howl revisited his mind, his knees buckled and he crumpled to the floor.

That had been Black Shuck, no doubt, but what had happened to Trash? How much of it had been a dream, had been imagined in his inebriated and traumatised state? It couldn't all have been real, all have really happened – surely? He held his head in his hands, suddenly aware of a sharp headache, not sure what to believe or what to do. One thing was for sure: the sooner he got out of this place, the better.

'Get a grip! Get a grip!' he said aloud as he tried to formulate some sort of plan. Must call for help. He fetched his mobile but, just as he was switching it on, remembered the failing battery. As he feared, there was no spark of life in the gadget. He had to escape somehow: get back to Morston, to his car. Then he could drive to Marsh View – he might have to wake them up but this was an emergency.

Rain beat the window ferociously and the wind sounded stronger than ever. He wasn't sure whether there was enough tide, but surely it was worth a try in the RIB? If the worst came to the worst and he was grounded he could always wade the rest of the way.

Harry pulled on his jacket and went to unlock the front door. But wait a minute: he was locked in, key on the inside where he had left it – so that must mean that Trash and/or Black Shuck, whoever the hell had been with him last night, must still be in the building. He stood with his back to the wall, heart pounding.

The door to the second bedroom was already open and he could see from where he was, by directing the torch beam, that no one was in there. He cautiously stepped forward into the room and – heart pounding – took two steps up the iron ladder, just enough to stick his head through the hatchway to the lookout room. Completely empty. That left only the third bedroom. Always last. Standing outside the door he was sure he could hear movement from within: a strange kind of swishing and rustling. Again he found himself short of a weapon, fetched a heavy iron pan from the stove, and resumed his position outside the door.

CHAPTER FORTY-NINE

The driver's door of Peter's truck was nearly torn from its hinges as the wind whipped along the drive. Peter laid the shotgun across the passenger seat, started the engine, and headed east along the coast road. There were several World War Two pillboxes dotted along the coast, but the one he had in mind was on the shore about halfway between Cley and Salthouse. It made sense as the children's meeting place, as it was equidistant between Sophie and Lara's houses. He wondered how many times they had secretly met there before. Rain on the windscreen was so heavy now that even with the wipers at top speed it was hard to see ahead clearly. There were no other vehicles on the road. A lightning flash lit up the vast expanse of salt marsh to his left, reeds pushed neatly flat by the wind as if combed.

He reached the track that led to the shingle ridge and turned left. This was strictly a footpath, much used by birders on their way to Arnold's Marsh, but he was pretty sure it was just wide enough to get the truck along. He stopped for a moment and shifted the transfer lever forwards into the four-wheel-drive position. The truck inched forwards. Peter had to concentrate hard to keep it straight: straying too far to either side would send the vehicle into the deep ditches that lined the path.

What the hell were they doing in a pillbox anyway? Especially at night, in a storm. Smoking no doubt, maybe something worse. And how long had they been there? He prayed that this Ewan – the one they called Digger – would be able to keep the dog at bay until he got there. Perhaps this would be Peter's opportunity to finish the killer-hound off, once and for all.

The stony path scraped the underside of the truck on several occasions, but finally Peter reached the end and turned right to head along the shingle on the protected side of the ridge. Another flash of lightning revealed that spray from the sea was being blown right over the top of the defensive wall of pebbles. He tried to speed up a little but succeeded only in spinning the wheels, shooting pebbles out behind like a machine-gun. Glancing briefly at his mobile revealed that there was no signal. How could that be? It was so flat here, there was always a signal.

Up ahead, the outline of the pillbox came into view. Peter stopped the truck but left the engine running and the lights on full beam, illuminating the box and surrounding area. There was no one to be seen. Pray God this wasn't the wrong pillbox. He pulled up his hood, grabbed the shotgun, and climbed out of the truck. It was a struggle to walk straight, as the wind and rain pounded into his left side. God knew what he would find inside. Nothing? Bodies, God forbid? Black Shuck waiting for him?

A few yards from the entrance, he started calling. 'Sophie! Sophie, are you in there?' It was then that he heard the sobbing. Rushing into the pillbox, gun at the ready, he saw in torchlight two girls crouched over the body of a youth.

'Daddy!' Sophie screeched, running into his arms, tears streaming.

For a moment, all Peter could think was that this was the first time she had called him Daddy for several years.

His own eyes welled up now. 'Thank God you're safe. And Lara too.' Lara also ran to Peter and held on to him. He could now see that the long-haired young man lying on the floor was not dead, as he had first feared, but was holding his leg, grimacing in agony. 'What in God's name has happened here?'

Sophie spoke through sobs. 'It was the dog, Dad. Digger tried to fight it off but he got bitten. And Alex is missing.'

'Who's Alex?'

'A friend who was with us. He went to see what was making a noise outside and just disappeared. Then Digger went out to look for him and saw the dog.'

Peter shone the torch on the youth's leg. It was unmistakeable. A chunk of flesh was missing. Exactly like Frank's legs and exactly like the seals. It was the same beast all right.

Digger fell back, barely conscious, his ripped jeans dark with blood.

Peter knelt down for a closer look at the boy. 'We've got to get moving. He's losing blood fast. I'll carry him. Sophie you'll have to take the shotgun. If you see the dog – shoot.'

Sophie didn't have time to think as the gun was thrust into her hands. She had used it only once before when Peter had given her a go a couple of years previously, and she hadn't liked it then.

Peter struggled to pick Digger up, especially as he couldn't stand upright under the low ceiling. 'Lara, you'll have to help me. You take his feet.'

Staying close together they moved through the entrance and out into the full force of the storm. In the glare of the truck headlights, Peter scanned all around, looking for signs of the dog, but there was nothing to be seen.

'We'll have to put him on the back.' Peter yelled to be heard above the wind. 'Sophie, lower the tailgate.' Between them they managed to get Digger on to the back of the truck and under a tarpaulin. 'Lara, you get under there with him and make sure his head is cushioned as we go. Sophie, you get in the cab beside me.'

By now they were all soaked through and freezing. Sophie's teeth were chattering. 'I'm sorry, Dad.' It came out as a child-like sob.

'I'm just glad you're alive, love. But we've got to get that boy to hospital quick or he won't be. Have you got your mobile?'

'Yes.'

'Phone Anna and tell her what's happened, and get her to

try and have an ambulance meet us at the house.'

Sophie pulled her phone from her bag and stared at the screen. 'No signal.'

'Damn. What's going on with that? We'll just have to hope she's got them coming already.'

Peter turned on to the narrow track that led to the coast road. It was easier to see now as the rain was coming from behind them. Headlamps from another vehicle were visible on the coast road – parked just where the track turned off – but there were no blue flashing lights.

About fifty yards from the road, Sophie turned to make sure Lara and Digger were still under the tarpaulin in the back. Peter briefly glanced over his shoulder too. And that's when the truck pulled to the left, just enough to start slipping.

'Shit! I can't hold it.' Slamming on the brakes was enough to slow the descent, but within seconds they were nose-down in the ditch at forty-five degrees. Peter tried reverse, but it was useless. 'Damn! Why did I look round? Stupid!'

'What are we going to do, Dad?' Sophie cried.

'We'll just have to walk the rest. Maybe whoever it is in the car up ahead can help.'

Peter and Sophie climbed out of the cab and pulled up the tarpaulin in the back to find that Lara and Digger had slid toward the front of the truck. Lara was rubbing her head.

'How's he doing?' Peter shouted as rain slashed into his face. But Lara seemed unable to speak.

Just then a voice from behind called out.

They looked round to see the silhouette of a man walking towards them along the track from the parked car, waving his arms above his head.

Lara cried out. 'It's Dad! It's my dad! She scrambled off the truck and ran towards him. Peter now recognised it was indeed John Diggory. He had met him several times before when dropping Sophie off at their house.

Peter and Sophie pulled Digger towards the opened tailgate and heaved him on to the track just as Lara and her father arrived.

'Oh my God, what's happened?' John gasped.

'He's been bitten by a dog. Losing blood. Got to get him to hospital as soon as possible.' For a moment, Peter thought John might keel over himself. He grabbed his arm. 'If we carry him to your car, can you take him?'

'Of course. Oh my God!'

Peter took Digger's shoulders and John took his legs, while Lara and Sophie ran ahead, clinging on to each other, to open the car up. They slid Digger on to the back seat, his head resting on Lara's lap, his injured leg propped up high to try and reduce blood-loss.

John turned to Peter. 'What will you do? I haven't got room for everyone.'

'Don't worry about us – we'll walk from here – our house is only up the road. You get that boy to hospital as quick as you can. And there's another lad – Alex – missing. We're going to call the police to help look for him. Call us later.'

John waved his thanks, and pulled on to the road. Peter and Lara watched as the car sped off, wheels screeching, towards Salthouse. Then, holding on to each other tightly, they turned and set off in the other direction.

CHAPTER FIFTY

Harry hesitated outside the door to the third bedroom of the Watch House. A drop of sweat ran into his eye. He shakily wiped it away with his sleeve and, Maglite in one hand, pan in the other, turned the door handle slowly. He then raised the pan above his head and pushed the door open with his foot. The last thing he was expecting was the blast of air that made him step backwards. The window was smashed so that the full force of the storm from the north was streaming into the room. The feathers he had seen earlier were still there – now swirling in a vortex in the centre of the room. Was it just his imagination or were there more feathers than before? The skull was still missing, and that's when he realised how peculiar it was that the glass from the broken window was inside, on the floor. So, maybe it wasn't the case that Trash had broken the window to escape, but simply that the storm had blown it in. Maybe she had got out through the window *after* it had been blown in. Then again, maybe that's how Black Shuck had gained entrance while Trash had been paralysing him. The more he thought of possible explanations, the less sense any of it made.

None of this changed the fact that he had to get out of there. Back at the front door he turned the key and stepped out towards the mooring post, holding the hood of his jacket up against the wind and rain. But after a couple of steps he tripped over a bundle on the ground. Aiming the torch down, at first he couldn't make out what it was. Brown and white and red with a rough covering. He pushed at it with his foot. It was soft, yet fairly heavy. Then he recognised the feathers. Dropping to one knee for a closer look he could now see it was indeed the body of a battered goose: head, neck, wings and feet removed, bitten off.

The rest of its body torn and bashed, bloody rips showing where feathers had been wrenched away. The feathers were the same as those in the house, and this was not the result of any storm. He knew it was the dog that had done this. And he knew these were the sad remains of Cleo. He felt stupid as his eyes welled up – it was only a wild goose for Christ's sake.

He picked the pathetic bundle up, not being sure what he was going to do with it, but it certainly didn't feel right to leave it there. Tucking it under his arm he resumed the journey to the RIB, but as the mooring post came into view he could see something was not right. Rather than bobbing about on the surface, the boat appeared to have partly sunk. Maybe it was just full of water, or had flipped over in the wind. As long as the engine wasn't waterlogged there was still a chance he could get it going, but as he got near enough for the torch beam to illuminate it properly he could see that it had actually deflated. So that was it. The outboard was actually underwater. Useless. The inflatable must have snagged on the mooring post or something as it was buffeted in the gale.

He put Cleo's body down on the ground and pulled at the bowline. His first thought was to heave the engine out of the water so at least it could be draining, for Peter to retrieve at a later date, but then his attention was taken by dark stripes along one side of the grey plastic of the RIB. He pulled it out of the water just enough to see that they were long gashes, rips – four in a row – as if the boat had been slashed by the swipe of mighty claws.

He dropped the rope and stood back in alarm. So Shuck had prevented his escape. By boat anyway: at least he could still walk along the shore to Cley. It would be tough in the storm but better than waiting it out in the house. The house where anything could happen.

He picked the battered goose body up again and, leaning into the wind, marched back towards the Watch House. His aim was to leave the remains of Cleo in the house, find some sort of weapon to carry on his journey, and then desert this bedevilled place. If only he didn't feel so tired, so beaten up.

Reaching the house, just as the dying Maglite flickered feebly, he unlocked the door and pushed it open. Having stepped inside, he bent down to place the bloody bundle on the floor, when a gust of wind caught the door and slammed it into his head. Harry fell back, bashing his skull against the brick wall on the way down.

CHAPTER FIFTY-ONE

From her position at the large window overlooking the marshes, Anna could just make out the two figures battling against the wind. She had been desperately trying to phone Harry, Sophie and her father's mobiles both from her mobile and the landline. Her own mobile had shown no signal and the landline diverted her to voicemail for all three, suggesting that their phones were either switched off, or that none of them had any signal either. As she knew her father, at least, would have kept his switched on, this must mean that he had no signal. Maybe the transmitter had been taken out by lightning.

Now they were closer, Anna could see that it was her father with his arm around Sophie, struggling up the drive. She flew to the front door to let them in.

'Quick,' panted Peter. 'We've got to warm her up. She's on the edge of hypothermia.'

'Okay, let's put her in the lounge; I've kept the fire going.' Anna put her arm round Sophie's waist and helped to lead her through. Her feet were dragging and she looked awful despite no sign of obvious injuries. Anna pushed the armchair nearer the fireplace and they lowered Sophie into it. 'What on earth happened out there?'

'I'll tell you, but first we need to get her out of these wet clothes and warmed up. I'll find some blankets while you undress her.' Peter himself was shaking with cold and shock.

'And you need to get into dry clothes too.' Anna pulled Sophie's shoes and socks off and rubbed her bare feet briskly. They were ice-blocks. 'Sophie. Sophie, can you hear me?' She pushed the long hair back and looked into Sophie's eyes.

'Yes, I can hear you.' Sophie's tiny voice came through

chattering teeth. 'Just … so … cold.'

'All right, love, just stay with us. We'll soon get you warmed up.' Anna pulled off Sophie's jacket and started to unbuckle the belt of her jeans. 'Just stay awake now, okay.'

'But I'm so … tired.'

'You can sleep later, for now you need to stay awake and get warmer, okay?'

Peter appeared with a bundle of blankets. 'Wrap her up in these and make some hot tea will you, Anna? I'm going to get some dry trousers on.'

Anna finished undressing Sophie and tucked the blankets around her so that only her head was poking through the top. 'There you go. Feel a bit better?'

Sophie nodded her head and made proper eye contact for the first time – a good sign.

'Right, you stay here and get good and toasty while I make us all a hot drink.'

While Anna was filling the kettle in the kitchen, Peter came in and hung his dripping jacket on the back of a chair. He pulled out his antacid pills and dropped a couple into his mouth. He rubbed his hands together briskly. 'God, that's better. How's Sophie doing?'

'I think she'll be okay. A hot drink will help. Where's the truck though, and why did you walk back?'

'It's in a ditch, by the track to the beach between here and Salthouse. My own stupid fault – I looked back at the wrong moment and it slipped off the path. Did you call the police?'

'Yes.' Anna poured boiling water into three large mugs on the table. 'They said they'd try and get a patrol car out there as soon as possible, but apparently the storm has caused chaos all over the place: lightning strikes, a building on fire in Holt, car crashes.'

'Right, I'd better update them.' He grabbed the phone.

Anna pushed a mug of tea towards him and carried another through to Sophie. Cold hands appeared from the blanket-cocoon and circled the mug. Anna watched while Sophie took a few sips, then returned to the kitchen where Peter was talking.

'… All I know is that his name is Alex and he was last seen at the old pillbox between Cley and Salthouse on the beach. There's a big dog on the loose that attacked another of them so maybe he was running away from that. If I give you the Diggorys' number, they might have a better idea who Alex is.'

Anna frowned as she sipped her tea. She had heard of Alex before, as someone who hung out with Sophie and her friends.

Peter finished the call and looked up at her. 'They sound pretty stretched.'

'So, how are the others? Was anyone hurt?'

'Just the Diggorys' son, Ewan – you know, the one they call Digger. He was bitten badly on the leg. Same bite as I saw on Frank's body and on the seals. It's the same dog all right.'

'Oh my God! Where is he now?'

'On his way to hospital. We met John Diggory at the end of the track and he took his two off in his car.'

'Did you see the dog?'

'Nope. No sign of this Alex either.' Peter took a long sip of tea.

'Well, I hope the police find him. What the hell were they all doing in the pillbox in the first place?'

'God knows, but now's not the time for interrogations. Let's see how Sophie's doing.'

Anna stood up from the table. 'What are you going to do about the truck?'

'Pull it out with the tractor. Not until tomorrow though; we'll need daylight to see what we're doing and I'll need some help from Joe or someone.'

In the lounge, Sophie was sipping her tea and reaching her other hand out towards the flames. She looked up as Anna and her father entered. 'Any news on Alex?'

'No, love: the police are going to look for him though.' Peter placed a hand on Sophie's head. 'Are you feeling warmer now?'

'Yes, much better thanks.' She reached up and took her father's hand. 'And Dad …'

'Mmm?'

'Thanks – you know – for rescuing us.'

It was the first time Sophie had thanked her father for anything for some time. 'That's all right, love. We'll call the Diggorys in the morning and see how your friend is.'

'I'm sorry. For causing trouble.'

'We're not going to talk about that now. We're all exhausted. We'll see where things are up to in the morning.'

Anna could see that her father was flagging. His right hand, holding the mug of tea, was trembling slightly – something she had never seen before. 'Look, why don't you two head upstairs for bed? I'll bring you up hot-water bottles.'

Back in the kitchen and filling the kettle once again, Anna's thoughts turned to Harry. Now that the mobiles were useless there was no way she could contact him. She didn't even know if he had received her last message. She had no idea whether he was okay or not, nor even if he was still in Norfolk. Now that the truck was in a ditch, she couldn't drive to Morston to see if his car was there. Come to that, if the truck was too damaged when pulled from the ditch the next day, she wasn't even sure she was going to be able to get to Morston to meet him, as originally planned.

As the kettle came to the boil she started filling the rubber bottles: Sophie's childhood one with an Eeyore cover, complete with head and legs, her father's a plain tartan. Wind whistled round Marsh View. While she had been waiting for her father and Sophie, Anna had been listening to the weather forecast on Radio 4, and it wasn't sounding good. The electric storm was heading south and reducing in ferocity, but in its wake some exceptionally high winds were expected. The gale warnings for shipping had gone on for some time, including a forecast of storm force ten or eleven expected for Humber – the area of the North Sea to their immediate north. That wasn't far off a hurricane. If it were to be that bad she didn't fancy Harry's chances in the Watch House, if he were still there. But if the weather did turn out to be that bad then it would be highly risky for him to attempt to cross the harbour in the RIB anyway.

She carried the hot-water bottles upstairs. Sophie was already snuggled into bed, so Anna tucked Eeyore under the duvet near her feet.

'Thank you.' Sophie was still using the tiny voice reserved for when she was ill or afraid.

Anna leaned down and kissed her forehead. 'You sleep well now. We'll talk more about everything in the morning, okay?'

'Do you think he'll be all right?'

'Who, Alex?'

'No, Digger!'

'Digger? I don't know. How bad was he?'

'Looked awful. The dog bit a great chunk out of his leg. There was blood everywhere.' Sophie's eyes were brimming with tears.

'God, that must have been so scary. Did you see it – the dog?'

'Sort of. It was very dark. It just looked like a huge black shadow with big red eyes. I only saw it for a moment, before it dragged Digger out of the pillbox by the leg.'

It was a description Anna had heard many times before – but usually only in stories told late at night in front of a pub's blazing fire. 'You know what that sounds like, don't you?'

Sophie nodded, eyes wide. 'Black Shuck.'

'Mmm.' Anna's thoughts flew back to Harry. The killer-dog could reach the Watch House in no time. Pray God that Harry was safely locked inside – or indeed that he was away from Norfolk by now. But if he was, then why hadn't he called her? She blinked her own tears away.

Sophie reached up to hug her. 'Can you do me a favour?'

'What, love?'

'Can you call the Diggorys now and see if there's any news about Digger? My mobile's not working.'

'None of them are: there must be a problem with the transmitter in the storm. Okay, I'll give them a quick ring now.' Then the penny dropped. 'Are you keen on this Digger then?'

Sophie nodded slowly. 'I think I love him.' It came out in a half-whisper.

Anna sat up and looked at her not-so-little sister who turned away, embarrassed. So that was something they had in common: their men in danger from storms and dogs. 'Be right back.'

On her way to the stairs she carried Peter's hot-water bottle in and slipped it in his bed. He was in his pyjamas, standing at the bedroom window looking out into the blackness, as rain sprayed the glass in rhythmic waves.

'Dad?' As she said it, Anna realised she was using Sophie's tiny voice.

'Mmm?'

'I'm worried about Harry.'

'Harry! Oh God, I'd forgotten about Harry. Have you heard from him at all?'

'No, nothing. I was wondering if we can go out to the Watch House in the morning on the tractor and bring him back?'

Peter thought for a moment. 'I guess that's the only option. Best that I go alone though. You stay here and look after Sophie.'

Anna didn't like that idea. She wanted to be with Harry as soon as possible. She would work on her father about that in the morning. 'Thanks, Dad.'

Downstairs, she picked up the phone and entered the Diggorys' number. It was answered almost immediately.

'Yes?' Anna recognised Mrs Diggory's voice, sounding anxious.

'Hello Mrs Diggory. It's just Anna Wild again.'

'Hello, dear.' She paused and blew her nose. 'I was hoping it would be John from the hospital.'

'Oh, I'm sorry, it's just that Sophie was asking how Digger – Ewan – is. If there's any news.'

'Well they're all at the Norfolk and Norwich Hospital. John called about an hour ago after they'd arrived; he said they'd only just made it, the roads were so bad, floods and everything. Ewan's in surgery now.' A little sob followed.

'But he'll be okay won't he?'

'He's lost a lot of blood. Unconscious.' She trailed off, unable to force any more words out.

'Well, look, I'll get off the line in case they're trying to call. Just lots of love from us – to all of you.' Anna put the phone down. That didn't sound good. But before she went to tell Sophie she had one more call to try.

She entered the number of Harry's mobile. She knew there was no signal at the moment but at least she could leave him a voicemail message that could be picked up when it returned. Besides, if Harry had left the Watch House he might get a signal elsewhere.

The tone invited her to start speaking. 'Hi, Harry. It's Anna. I don't know if you'll get this message. In fact I don't even know where you are. But when you do, please, please call me. The storm is due to get even worse and I'm worried about you. Besides which, the dog is still about in the area – it attacked one of Sophie's friends tonight. If you have left the Watch House, maybe you're even back in Newmarket now, please let me know.' Anna welled up, struggling to keep her voice under control. 'But if you are still in the Watch House, for God's sake stay put and lock yourself in. Don't try and go to Morston in the boat – the weather's too bad, and whatever you do, don't try anything if you see the dog. Just stay there and we'll come and get you on the tractor tomorrow morning, okay?' She suddenly came to a halt. Even though it was a message that Harry might never get, it was the closest she could get to contact with him right now, and she found it hard to terminate the call. 'We're all okay here at Marsh View. Just need you here too.'

Chapter Fifty-Two

What on earth could be tapping on the bedroom window? Anna struggled out of bed and pulled back the curtains, but couldn't see anything unusual apart from the salt marsh reeds and grasses lying flat from the force of the wind. It was getting light already, low clouds over the North Sea seeming to rush towards her. Just as she turned to glance at the clock on her bedside table there was a sharp crack on the window right in front of her, so sudden it made her jump back. She looked up just in time to see that it was caused by a black cable that was swinging about, loose. There were also a few roof tiles on the ground below, at the front of the house. She quickly got dressed and washed and went downstairs to find that Peter was already up and making toast in the kitchen.

'Hi, Dad. You're up early.'

'Morning, love. Yes, I wanted to get the truck back as soon as possible – especially now that I've remembered I left the shotgun in the cab last night. I forgot it in all the panic of getting that boy into his father's car.'

'Have you seen we've got some storm damage?'

'I've not been outside yet, not been up long myself. What's the damage?'

'Come and look.' Anna went to the front door, Peter following. She wasn't prepared for the strength of the wind that tore the door from her hands once it was opened a little. It swung back and smacked into the wall, cracking the glass panel. 'Hell! Sorry, Dad. I wasn't ready for that.' She had to shout to be heard above the howling wind, which made an eerie whistling sound as it blew up the drive and around the garage. They struggled to the front of the house, holding on to each other for support.

'If this gets any stronger it'll be a hurricane all right: not far off it now,' Peter yelled. From there they could see that a tree, a few houses further down the road, had blown over and taken a telegraph pole with it. This had loosened the phone cables, which were now swinging against the front of Marsh View, occasionally slapping into Anna's bedroom window.

'It's that cable that woke me up,' she shouted.

'Well I hope it doesn't mean the phone's out of action – we've got calls to make. Let's go in and see, there's nothing we can do out here in this wind.'

Back in the house, Anna shivered and rubbed her arms. They had been outside for only a minute, but the cold wind had cut right through her.

Peter picked up the phone and listened a moment. 'Damn! There's no dial tone. God knows how long it'll take them to fix that, I'll bet there's lines down all over the county in this. I was just about to call Joe and see if he's free to help tow the truck out.'

'And we had to ring the Diggorys for an update.' Anna buttered slices of toast and passed one to her father who had switched on his mobile and was peering at the screen.

'Hmm. Still no signal. That's all our comms out.'

'So what are we going to do?' Anna asked, suddenly afraid that this might jeopardise the mission to fetch Harry from the Watch House. It also meant that there was now no way Harry could contact her even if he had received any of her messages.

'I guess I'll drive round to Joe's in the tractor and hope he's at home.'

'Dad, why can't *I* help you pull the truck out?'

'I need you here to look after Sophie. Besides I don't want you getting hurt: it's not going to be an easy job.'

Anna folded her arms crossly. 'You haven't forgotten you were going to go to the Watch House to bring Harry back, have you?'

'No, but first things first, I need to get the truck back. Besides, if I am going towards the Point, I want to take the gun with me in case I see that damned dog.'

Anna knew there was no benefit in arguing further. She pulled her father's coat off the back of the chair and held it up for him to put on. 'Okay, go and get Joe and come straight back when you've got the truck.'

'Will do.' Peter zipped up his jacket and checked he had all the right keys in his pockets. 'See you soon.'

As he left, Anna switched the radio on to catch the weather forecast, and sat down to eat her toast. After five minutes of news, which mentioned chaos across the country as the storm caused floods and power-cuts, the weatherman reinforced the warning that the wind strength was due to get worse. There were a number of hurricane warnings to the north and east of Scotland, but they were cautious about the strength over the mainland, leaving it at storm force eleven, possible twelve. That was bad enough. She made a mug of tea, but as she took her first sip, the front door opened and closed again with a bang.

It was Peter, looking angry, oil smudged across his chin and over his hands. 'Buggeration! Can't get the blasted tractor to start now!'

'Oh great, that's all we need. What's wrong with it?'

'Damned if I know. It's on its last legs anyway, so it could be anything. I just don't know enough; I'll have to get Joe.'

'How?'

'On foot.'

'But that'll take ages, and what if he's not there?'

'Well what else can I do?' Peter shouted it out in frustration and immediately regretted it as Anna stepped back, tears welling in her eyes. 'Sorry, love.' He stepped forward and hugged her. 'None of this is your fault. I know you're worried about Harry. Look, I really need to get the gun from the truck so I'll go and do that straight away, then I'll walk to Joe's, come back here with him, and then, when the tractor's fixed, I'll go straight to the Watch House. Maybe Harry can help me pull the truck later.'

'But what if Joe can't fix the tractor?'

Peter popped a couple of antacids into his mouth. 'Well, we'll just have to think of something else then.'

'Like what?' Anna was almost shouting now.

Peter had run out of answers and felt on the verge of raising his voice once more. He looked at Anna briefly then turned and stepped back out into the wind, fighting to close the door behind him.

'God!' Anna hissed between gritted teeth. For a few moments she didn't know what to do. The whole plan now had too many ifs for her to have any confidence in it: *if* Joe was at home; *if* he was available; *if*, and this was the biggest 'if' in her mind, he could get the tractor fixed; and *if* no other catastrophe had happened in the meantime. It all added up to a slim chance. Tears of anger flowed down her cheeks. She just *had* to know Harry was okay. It had all gone so wrong: this was supposed to be their special day together, a romantic meal in the evening – and instead she was stuck at home with no vehicle, no phone line, no mobile signal, no idea where or how Harry was, a killer-dog on the loose. Could it *get* any worse?

She reckoned it would take her father maybe an hour to get the gun, walk to Joe's and return with him. She was blowed if she was going to wait that long just on the off chance that the stupid tractor could be fixed. Why didn't she just walk to the Watch House herself? It was only a couple of miles. Yes, it would be tough in the wind: but at least then she and Harry would be together.

Suddenly invigorated by her idea, she ran up the stairs and quietly opened Sophie's bedroom door. The lump under the duvet was not moving. Anna tiptoed over and listened for a moment, relived to hear the peaceful breathing of her sister. No point in waking her. She'd be all right until their father returned. In her own bedroom, Anna pulled on her walking boots and a second jumper before heading downstairs.

At the kitchen table she wrote a note for Sophie on the pad used for shopping lists:

Sophie, I've gone to the Watch House. Dad's just gone to get Joe – he'll be back soon. STAY AT HOME. Make some toast etc.
Love, Anna.
P.S. The phone lines are down so no news from the Diggorys.

Anna tore the piece of paper from the pad, went upstairs and pushed it under Sophie's door. She then returned to the kitchen and wrote a further note for her dad:

Dad, I'm really sorry but I couldn't wait in case the tractor was fixed so I'm walking to the Watch House. Don't worry I'll be fine. Harry and I will walk back together or wait until the storm's blown out.
Lots of love, Anna. xxx
P.S. Don't be cross. I'm sorry but I have to go.

She knew full well that her father would be furious and would worry himself sick. She also realised that the note was rather vague about when she would be back, but she wasn't even sure she would find Harry there. For a moment she faltered. Was she being stupid? Was this dangerous? What would she do if he wasn't there – just turn around and walk back?

But the thought of staying put at home and waiting was even worse. She placed the note in the middle of the table, put on her waterproof jacket, and left the house.

For some reason Sophie's description of Black Shuck popped into her head just as she was closing the front door. Was she mad – setting off, alone and unarmed, to walk a storm-ravaged coastline patrolled by a savage beast? She nipped round the back of the house, slipping on more roof tiles scattered about the back garden, and fetched one of the long staffs from the shed. She wasn't sure what use it would be against a demon like Shuck, but it certainly gave her confidence to be holding some sort of weapon.

She set off down the road towards Cley village at a pace, but once she had turned north on to the lane that led to the beach car park, the headwind slowed her progress considerably.

Despite squinting, her eyes watered badly, made worse by the sand that was occasionally blasted into her face. She soon realised that she was badly unprepared: no food or drink, no torch, no first aid kit, just her and a staff. But there was no turning back now: she wanted to be out of sight before her father returned. He would try and stop her for sure.

She was shocked to find the car park flooded, as the storm flung seawater over the top of the shingle ridge. There were no other people around and just one car – a black VW Golf up to its wheel arches in water. She had a vague feeling she might have seen the car before but couldn't place its owner. No doubt they had abandoned the car and walked home. Turning left, she headed along the shingle spit towards the Watch House. Now she was walking on loose pebbles it was even harder going. She kept the ridge to her right, the full force of the storm now hitting her right side. Although there was no rain, she quickly became drenched as seawater sprayed over the ridge. It was as if the wind simply caught the waves, lifted them up into the air, and hurled them inland.

A mighty gust caught her on the wrong foot and flung her to the ground. She screamed out in frustration, her own salty tears mingling with the spray that continually lashed her now. She had to be careful not to be blown into the large harbour on her left: although it was partly enclosed, the surface was rougher than she had ever seen. Besides, the water was so cold, she wouldn't stand a chance. Several of the remaining moored boats had sunk, floating on their sides or with just a mast showing above the waves. She dug the staff into the shingle and stood up, pressing onwards, head down.

Please, God, let Harry be there. Let him be sitting in front of a crackling fire, ready to welcome her with warm strong arms. He would explain that he had not got her messages and had not known what to do about the RIB in the storm, but that he had been thinking of her every minute.

The thoughts of Harry spurred her on until she was blown off her feet again. This time, as she stood, she had the unnerving feeling that she was being followed, but looking all around could she see nothing. The feeling was enough to set her off thinking about Black Shuck again, though. Despite the legend – and despite both her own father and Linda having seen the beast before their spouses died – she had still refused to think that Frank's death and the seal killings had been caused by anything more than a real flesh-and-blood stray dog, albeit a huge and ferocious one. But there was something about the attack on Sophie and her friends the night before that was making her increasingly uneasy, increasingly unsure of long-held beliefs. If it was just a stray then why hadn't it been found yet? Maybe phantoms did exist. All the stories and experiences had to have some sort of basis. Even her own family were victims. And, above all, it was Sophie's description of the beast with big red eyes that had frightened the life out of her. Just like the stories. What real dog had huge blazing red eyes?

CHAPTER FIFTY-THREE

'Shuck, Galleytrot, Trash, Snarleyow, Shuck, Galleytrot, Trash, Snarleyow.' Anna spat the words out with venom as she struggled towards the Watch House. It was clearly in view now but there were no signs of habitation, no smoke from the chimney. She was using the staff as a prop-cum-walking stick – pushing it into the ground to her left to stop her being blown down again.

The more she thought about it, the more she began to believe that Black Shuck had it in for her: first it had been a portent of her own mother's death; then not only had it performed the same function for poor Frank but it had killed him as well; it had made her father ill by mutilating his beloved seals; attacked her sister's boyfriend; and now had scuppered her plans for getting together with Harry. If it wasn't for Shuck she would have had the truck to drive to Morston. Hatred was building inside and snarling out the names gave her strength to fight against the storm.

'Shuck, Galleytrot, Trash, Snarleyow ...'

Another airborne wave crashed into her, the freezing salt spray stinging her face. Nearly at the house now. Looking down to her left she could just about make out the mooring post, but was the RIB there? She could see something grey in the water – partly submerged – could that be it? If it was, it must mean Harry was still in the house. Unless Shuck had got him too. She thought about how Alex had just disappeared – maybe this had happened to Harry. All the time she had been assuming that he would either be in the Watch House or on his way to Newmarket. But what if he were simply never found? She would know soon enough if he were in the house.

'Shuck, Galleytrot, Trash, Snarleyow.' Still the feeling that she was being watched, being followed. Within yards of the house now, she walked around to the front, giving it a wide berth, not sure what to expect.

The door was open a few inches, blowing back and forth in the wind. There must be something just behind, preventing it from opening fully. She stepped forward, staff held out like a Samurai sword. Now that the house was between her and the sea, at least her face was no longer being sprayed with water. She glanced over her shoulders to the left and right – nothing behind. Nothing that she could see, anyhow.

'Harry!' she called.

'HARRY!'

Nothing. 'Shit!' He wasn't there.

Her lower lip trembled uncontrollably with fear and cold. Where the hell was he? She wasn't sure she could face the journey back on foot by herself again. She would have to rest a while in the house. Her father was going to be angry – so desperate had she been to be with Harry, she had barely considered that she might have to return home alone, admitting that it had been a foolish mission.

'Harry!' It came out as a sob this time.

She pushed at the door with her boot. Yes, there was something behind it. She pushed harder – it gave a little, but whatever was blocking it must be heavy. Leaning her shoulder on the door and shoving with all her might, she managed to move it far enough to push her head through the opening. To the right, she could see a body crumpled on the floor, partly leaning against the door.

'Harry! Oh Christ, Harry!' With extra effort she heaved at the door, just enough to slip through.

For a few seconds she just gazed down, paralysed. Harry's body was twisted to the right, his head resting on the wall, legs buckled against the door. There was a trail of dark blood down the wall, where his head had dragged down, and more blood, now a dried trail, from his left nostril, over his lips and down his chin. Next to him lay what looked like part of the body of a dead bird: a large one.

Of all the possibilities, finding Harry's body was not one Anna had considered. She just stood, shocked, her mind scrambled.

But then, wasn't that the tiniest movement of his chest? In an instant she fell to her knees, putting her ear to his mouth. 'Yes!' He was breathing! She touched his forehead and his hands – they were cold but not icy. Her brain now rattled through rusty first aid procedures learnt years ago. She knew she shouldn't move him too much in case his neck was damaged, or his skull fractured, but there was no way she could call for help or summon an ambulance. And if she didn't get him warm soon he would die of exposure anyway. She had to risk it.

Behind her, lying on the floor in a heap, was a rough blanket. She took this and laid it out next to Harry, gently lifting his legs on to one end. Then she carefully took his head in both her hands and moved it sideways so that it too was resting on the blanket. Gingerly she touched the area of his skull that had struck the wall. She could feel clotted blood in the hair and a raised bump, but nothing that suggested a major fracture. Now, feet either side of his torso, she took hold of his jacket and heaved the rest of his body over. Quickly, she took off her coat and slid this under his head. Now that he was fully lying on the blanket, she took hold of two of the corners at the head end and dragged him very slowly into the middle of the room.

Bending, her face close to his, she whispered, 'Harry. Harry can you hear me?'

No response.

Fire. She must light a fire. But there was no wood left, and any driftwood outside would be soaking. Besides, she wasn't going outside again while this blow was on. Poking in the grate she could see what looked like the remains of a chair leg. Looking behind, she saw only one chair at the oak table: she was sure there had been two before. That was it – she could burn the furniture – she just needed something to get it going.

In front of the stove, down the short corridor, she found the remains of a cardboard box with the rest of the food supplies in. She ripped the box into pieces and arranged them in the fireplace. On top of the cardboard she placed the few bits of charred chair leg that hadn't burnt up completely, hoping that they would be sufficient kindling. The matches lay on the oak table next to pools of hardened wax where candles had burned down. Having lit the cardboard with shaking hands, she started to break up the other chair, hitting it against the wall to loosen the legs. But although she now had a good supply of fuel, the charred wood was slow to catch, and she was afraid the cardboard would be used up too soon. She looked around for something else to get the fire going. Levering one of the lumps of candle wax off the table she broke it up in her hands and sprinkled the pieces on to the smouldering card. It worked well, the flames growing larger and bright orange. She laid the legs from the second chair on top of the growing fire, where they were soon engulfed.

Next, she fetched a bottle of water and one of Harry's t-shirts from the bedroom and began to wash the blood off his face. There had been something particularly macabre about the dark red trail from his nostril, enhancing the way he had looked like a corpse. She had no way of knowing how long he had been lying unconscious, but prayed that the warmth would bring him round. The fire was throwing out some heat now that the dry wood of the chair was burning fiercely. She sat across Harry's legs, her knees either side of his hips, and took his hands in hers, rubbing them briskly. Her long brown hair, salty and wet, hung down around her shoulders. Steam rose from her thighs as her sodden jeans warmed in the heat from the blaze.

CHAPTER FIFTY-FOUR

'Harry. Harry, come back to me.'

An eyelid flickered.

'Harry. Come back.'

Suddenly his eyes shot open, a look of horror spread across his face. 'Trash!' he shouted, flailing with his arms, catching Anna on the chin. She cried out and fell sideways as he continued yelling. 'Get off me! Get off me!'

'Harry! Harry! It's me, it's me, it's Anna.' She caught hold of his wrists. 'Harry, you're safe now. It's me.'

Gradually the strength drained out of his arms, but his expression of shock and fear remained.

'Trash.' he said again, sounding weak and confused now.

'No, darling, it's Anna.'

At last, recognition slowly softened his face, the tension in his body fading.

'Anna?' he said hoarsely.

'Yes, love, it's me.' She leaned forward and kissed him on the cheek.

'Oh, God. Oh, God.' He raised his hands to his face and lay back. 'Jesus, my head hurts. What's happened to me?'

'I don't know, love. I found you lying in the doorway. It looks like you hit your head on the wall and it knocked you out.'

Harry groaned.

Anna took his hand in hers. 'How do you feel? Do you think anything's broken?'

Harry felt around the back of his head with his free hand and winced. 'No, just a bloody big lump. Hang on, how did you get here?'

'Look, I'll go and make us a hot drink and then we'll talk about everything, okay?'

Anna went down the corridor to heat some water on the stove. The range of emotions she had experienced in the last hour left her totally drained. Yet now that she and Harry were together, and alive, she felt mentally strong and warm inside. But why had he called her *Trash*? What on earth had the man been through?

She carried two mugs of steaming tea back into the main room and sat in front of the fire next to Harry. He was now raised up, leaning on his elbows, a better colour in his cheeks. She passed him a mug. 'Black I'm afraid. No milk.'

'That's okay. Thanks.' He took a sip then sighed heavily. 'God, that's better.'

Anna pushed the rest of the broken chair into the fire and looked at Harry, unsure where to start. 'So, you saw Trash then?'

Harry looked at her, surprised. 'Yes. You know her?'

'*Her*?' Anna frowned.

'Yes. She said she knew Peter.'

'But … but I thought you meant Black Shuck: the dog.'

Harry looked even more confused. Anna continued, '*Trash* is another name for him used in some villages in Norfolk. There are other names too – Galleytrot, Snarleyow and more. You cried out *Trash* when you came to: I thought you must have seen him, must have known that was another name for him.'

As memories and realisations filled Harry's head he lay back again, covering his face with his hands and groaning.

Over the next two hours, the pair cuddled in front of the fire, exchanging fears and theories, catching up on the succession of crises. Harry told of his meetings with Trash, how she had somehow overpowered him and then had turned into the huge howling black dog, but how he had been in such a state at the time he hadn't known what to believe – how much of it had really happened. Then he explained how he had tried to get away from the house, discovering Cleo's body and then the RIB slashed. He could vaguely remember bringing the body back to the house, but nothing after that. He still had no idea how he had been knocked unconscious.

In turn, Anna told him about Linda's decline and Sophie's traumatic evening, Digger's injury and the missing Alex, the lack of tractor, truck and phones. It was all so much to take in, they both felt dazed.

CHAPTER FIFTY-FIVE

'I still don't understand. Are you sure the girl wasn't just in a dream or something?' Anna called over her shoulder as she opened a tin of soup.

'No, I saw her several times, on the beach at first. She was … seemed … real.' Harry stood at the window above the oak table looking across the storm-torn harbour towards Blakeney. Wind howled around the outside of the house and through the broken window of the third bedroom, where they had temporarily put Cleo's broken body, out of view, for it was a pitiful and macabre sight. The bedroom door rattled as the storm threatened to break through. Spray from the sea lashed at the windows, adding to the unnerving soundscape.

Harry still felt wobbly, but mentally so much better for having been reunited with Anna. The throbbing of his head where it had smacked into the wall was starting to subside a little. 'I mean, there was definitely something very odd about her: the way she spoke; her name; not feeling the cold or wearing shoes; always wearing the same red dress.'

Red dress. The vivid colour was still bright in Harry's mind. He wanted to erase the image but it stayed, and everything about that redness now signified danger.

Anna appeared carrying two bowls of steaming soup, with a packet of chocolate biscuits tucked under her arm. As there were no longer any chairs in the house they both sat on the floor to eat. 'Why did you let her in the house in the first place?' Anna was fighting back the needle of jealousy that was nagging at her.

'Because it was dark and raining and she was soaked. I thought she was lost or something – needed refuge from the weather.'

'And then she overpowered you, just like that?'

'Well, yes. But not with physical strength – it was more … mental. Oh, I don't know, I can't explain. I just couldn't fight her off, as if I was paralysed.'

'Hmm.' Anna sounded suspicious.

'Anna.' Harry put his spoon down and reached for her hand. 'You know it's you that I want.'

She held his gaze for a moment, struggling to find the right words. Harry leaned forward and kissed her on the mouth, tasting the salt on her skin, the sweetness of the soup on her tongue. When he finally pulled back he could see that there were tears in her eyes.

'I just don't know what to think any more, Harry.' Her voice was quavering. 'Black Shuck has been around for hundreds of years as a legend, but has always been just a big black dog – never a … a *fucking* girl in a red dress.' She spat the words out.

'I don't know either. I guess I was drifting in and out of consciousness after she ... he ... it – whatever – attacked me. Then I saw the dog on top of me, howling, and then I passed out again. I didn't know what had happened or what to think – whether the dog had come in and chased her away or what. Now you're suggesting that Trash *was* Black Shuck – in another form – how is my brain supposed to process that? In the light of day it all just sounds such nonsense.' He paused. 'I thought you didn't believe in Black Shuck anyway.'

Anna considered this for a while. 'Well, I guess I do now. Too much weird stuff has happened. I suppose you must too, now ... believe, I mean?'

'I just take things as they come. But the way they've come recently … I can't ignore what I've seen. I guess it was a mistake coming here: to the Watch House. The isolation was starting to drive me mad.'

Anna put her arms round Harry's neck, burying her face in his shoulder. 'God, Harry, I was so worried about you here, and with good reason as it turns out.'

'Well, whether Shuck is just a big stray killer-dog or a phantom or whatever, it sure doesn't mean us any good. The sooner we get away from here the better.'

'So, what shall we do?'

'I think we should just go for it.' He paused to listen to the noise of the wind. 'The storm doesn't sound like it's about to die down soon. Let's just go: walk to Cley.'

'Are you sure you're feeling strong enough – it was pretty tough getting here, you know?'

'I think so. Besides, we can support each other now. It's only a couple of miles, surely we can manage that?'

'Okay let's do it.'

Harry finished his last spoonful of soup, pushed a biscuit into his mouth, then stood up and looked out of the window again. Such was the force of the wind coming from the north that small salt marsh shrubs were ripped from their roots and sent sailing into the harbour, larger ones rolling across the shingle like tumbleweed in a desert. There was not a single moored boat left floating upright now – it looked like a watery graveyard of masts and partly submerged hulls: a war scene. Blakeney, in the far distance, appeared deserted.

'No time like the present.' Harry pulled his jacket on and passed Anna hers. 'There's no point in taking any of my stuff; we can come back for it after the storm's passed.'

He headed for the door, but Anna caught his arm. 'Harry, I have to tell you that on my way here I felt ... like I was being followed. I think Shuck's still out there.'

Harry frowned. 'Well, that wouldn't surprise me,' he said gravely. 'That dog's got it in for us. We'll take your staff. Come on.' Harry grabbed Anna's hand and opened the front door. As the wind surged around and past the house it formed a part-vacuum in the lee of the building, which almost sucked them out. Immediately they were practically on their knees, gripping each other's jackets, leaning on the staff for support.

'Just don't let go of me!' Harry yelled.

'Never again.' Anna words were whipped away from her and sent screaming towards Blakeney. Harry didn't even hear them.

They trudged forward, painfully slowly, bent double. With

hooded heads down as seawater constantly sprayed over them, they could barely see more than a few paces in front. Anna knew they were not alone but it was just impossible to keep looking around. Harry felt it too.

The two miles would take hours at this pace. Their jeans were already thoroughly drenched. The wind kept blowing their hoods off and after a while Harry gave up pulling his back, cursing the cold water that coursed down his neck and filled his ears. There was no point in trying to shout at each other; all their energy was needed to keep going. A small airborne shrub, yellow horned-poppy, tumbled up over the ridge and hit Harry on the side of his face, stinging his cheek. He swore and dropped to his knees as his legs buckled. Anna bent to help him up, but as she did so, the staff she was leaning on slipped sideways and she fell on to her side, rolling towards the harbour.

Harry thought the wind was going to keep rolling her right into the water – he yelled out and got to his feet, only to be blown straight down again. Crawling on hands and knees and then diving towards her he managed to get close enough to grip her boot just before she reached the edge of the water.

Anna grabbed his jacket with frantic hands, pulling his head close to hers so that she could yell in his ear. 'I can't do it! We've got to head back!'

Harry shook his head. 'No! We must be nearly halfway there now. We can make it!' He took the staff and levered himself up, pulling Anna with him. But just as he did so a huge wave crashed into the other side of the shingle ridge, powerful enough to push right through it, sending frothing water and pebbles hurtling into their legs. Anna cried out in pain as the stones pummelled her shins.

Harry held her tight, struggling to balance. They must stay on their feet: if they fell now they were sure to be washed into the harbour. But looking ahead he saw, in disbelief, that the waves had breached the ridge in several places further on, washing the entire sea-defence towards the harbour, flattening out the shingle spit as it did so. Up ahead the flood could be feet deep and the situation was getting worse by the moment. The power of the storm was changing the shape of the coastline before their very eyes.

'Shit!' He looked at Anna, who was holding on for dear life, gasping for breath, eyes wide with shock. 'It's no good. We're cut off!'

She said nothing, but understood and nodded. Exhausted. They turned and headed back towards the Watch House, their progress hampered even further by the now-ankle-deep freezing seawater. Heads down, teeth gritted, they struggled on, spray stinging their faces, pebbles bruising their legs. Feet numb in water-filled boots, white knuckles on hands almost too cold to grip. Harry occasionally glanced round, to see that the shingle ridge was collapsing further behind them. At that point the sea and harbour became one, making the Point an island, waves surging across centuries-old reed beds, tearing them apart.

The house was up ahead. It was all about survival now. Anna's energy seemed to be flagging, and she cried out with the effort of every step. Harry's head was pounding; he felt near to collapse but forced himself on, pulling Anna by her jacket. He tried to shout words of encouragement but the roar of the storm was so loud now that he couldn't hear even his own voice. Step by step they drew closer, the Watch House the only shelter for miles around. The seals would be safe enough in the water, but surely nothing else could survive in this maelstrom. Unless it, too, took asylum in the house.

CHAPTER FIFTY-SIX

'Are you all right, old friend?' Joe looked anxiously at Peter who was wincing and rubbing his stomach. 'Shall we stop for a rest?'

'No, it's not that.' Peter raised his voice to be heard above the wind. 'It's this ruddy ulcer. I've been taking antacids but they're not having the effect they used to.'

'That'll be stress – making it worse.'

'Tell me about it. I just need to get home and take a good slug of milk.'

'Have you seen the doc about it?'

'No – I don't want them pushing tubes and cameras inside me. I'll beat it.'

'Well, just make sure it doesn't beat you first.'

The two men continued traipsing through Cley village on the way to Marsh View, Peter with the shotgun he had collected earlier over one arm, Joe with a canvas bag of tools slung over his shoulder. When Peter had reached the truck, before collecting Joe, he had found the water in the ditch was halfway up the bonnet. Turning the key produced no result. They were going to use the tractor to tow the truck all the way back to Marsh View, dry the engine out, and then see what the damage was. That's if Joe could get the tractor going.

Joe lived in a quaint old cottage between Cley and Blakeney, about half a mile inland. Peter was shocked to find that the storm damage here was far worse than on the coast, partly due to the larger number of trees, many of which had been blown down. Joe's old van was unusable, as an old Bramley apple tree in his front garden had smashed through the windscreen. Many telephone and electricity cables had been brought down; on the way Peter even had to walk cautiously around a cable that was still sparking in the road.

Joe had been glad of the excuse to get out of the house and go on a rescue mission. He didn't like being stuck indoors, under his wife's feet, even when there was a storm blowing. Besides, he liked to feel needed, happily pulling on his dirty blue overalls, telling his other half he would be back 'at some point in the future ...'

Their plans for a major dog-hunt that morning were in ruins. Joe explained that he had heard from Mack, just before the phones went dead, that he had had no luck in getting support from the others: they were either involved in clearing up their own storm-damage or couldn't get there because of blocked roads. And he was still under the impression that his own son, Wayne, was away visiting friends in Norwich. Away from danger. Little did he realise that the bedraggled remains of the young man's body, torn and unrecognisable as human apart from the shreds of clothing, were starting to stink and about to be washed away, never to be found.

As the two men passed the windmill at the far end of Cley they noticed that two of the huge white sails had been ripped to splinters, debris spread along the street. While walking, Peter had given Joe a blow-by-blow account of recent goings-on, mostly shouted in his ear owing to Joe's loss of hearing as well as to the noise of the storm. On several occasions they had dodged shrapnel as tiles were torn off roofs and sent spinning towards them.

So it was with relief that they finally reached Marsh View. 'Let's go in and warm up before you get started,' Peter shouted. Joe gave him a thumbs-up.

Inside the house, Peter made a beeline for the fridge, pulled out the milk carton and took several large gulps. 'I needed that. God, I needed that.'

'Looks like you've got a note.' Joe nodded towards the piece of paper on the kitchen table.

Peter picked it up and read it, his complexion turning visibly whiter as he did so. 'She's gone to the Watch House! She's going to bloody walk it!'

'Who?'

'Anna. The stupid, stupid girl!' He looked through the window, across the marsh towards the car park, but there was no sign of anyone. 'God knows how long she's been gone. I told her to wait here. Damn! As if things weren't bad enough already!'

'Look, Peter, before you do anything, please just sit down for five minutes, or you're going to blow a gasket an' all.'

Peter didn't even register Joe's words. 'She'd better not have taken her sister with her.' At that, he made for the kitchen door and ran up the stairs. To his relief, Sophie was standing in her bedroom doorway, still in her nightdress, hair tousled, reading the note Anna had slipped under her door.

'Hi, Dad. Anna left this.' Sophie handed the note to her father. 'Why's she gone to the Watch House?'

'Thank God you're still here.' Peter quickly read the note. 'She's gone to get Harry, the stupid girl. The tractor wouldn't start so I went to get Joe. She just couldn't wait, could she?'

'What are you going to do?'

'I'm going to have to go and get her, aren't I?'

'Are the phones still down? Is there any news about Digger?'

'They'll be down for some time I'm afraid, love. No news from the Diggorys. If we get the tractor fixed I can maybe drive over to Salthouse tomorrow and see where they're up to. Assuming they know.'

'What do you mean?'

'With phone lines down and roads blocked it's possible that Mrs Diggory hasn't even heard from the hospital herself. We're pretty well cut off from the outside world at the moment. In any case, the priority at the moment is to get Anna back.'

'What shall I do then?'

'Just stay here.' He looked at Sophie sternly. 'Get up, have a bath, do whatever you want, but for God's sake stay in the house: I seem to be spending all my time looking for missing daughters at the moment.'

'Sorry, Dad.' The tiny voice was back.

'I'll leave Joe working on the tractor, so you won't be alone. I'll tell him to stay here 'til I get back.' He turned and went down the stairs.

In the kitchen, Joe had made some coffee and was holding out a mug for Peter.

'No time, Joe, I've got to find Anna.'

Joe took hold of Peter's arm with a strong hand and spoke in a calm but commanding voice. 'Peter. Sit down and drink this before you do anything. A couple of minutes won't make any difference.' Normally light-hearted, Joe's serious demeanour gave him a fatherly presence despite his being only ten years Peter's senior.

Peter sighed, took the mug, sat at the table and put his head in his hands. 'Thanks, Joe. I don't know what the silly girl thought she was doing. In a wind like this she could get blown off her feet into the harbour.'

'So could you, for that matter.'

'I know what I'm doing. I'll take some rope – then we can tie each other together for the return journey.'

'And take the gun too, in case you meet Trash.' Joe had grown up in a nearby village where the phantom hound was known more commonly as *Trash* than as Black Shuck.

Peter knew who he meant. 'Thanks for being here, Joe. I've told Sophie to stay in the house and that you'll be here working on the tractor while I'm gone – okay?'

'You sure you don't want me to come with you?' Joe already knew the answer to that question.

'No. Thanks, mate. But please stay with Sophie until I get back.'

Peter drained his mug and stood up. 'I'll just find some rope then I'll be off. Have you got everything you need for the tractor?'

'Hope so.' Joe patted his tool bag.

'Well, help yourself to the tools in the garage if there's anything of use in there.' He picked up the shotgun and headed for the door. 'Oh, and Joe?'

'Yes?'

'If I'm not back in, say, four hours …'

'Mmm?'

But Peter struggled to come up with a back-up plan. With no phone to call the police or coastguard, what could be done anyway?

Joe helped out. 'If you're not back in four hours I'm coming to get you on the tractor.'

Peter considered this for a moment but could think of no better solution. The situation wouldn't arise anyway. Fours hours should be plenty. 'Thanks, Joe.'

Ten minutes later he was fighting his way down the lane that led to the car park, gun in right hand, coil of rope over left shoulder. As he headed north, the full force of the wind was in his face, every step was an effort. It was far harder than he had expected, the storm even worse than when he and Joe had walked back to Marsh View.

He kept the grass bank, which ran along the edge of the lane, to his left, as it deflected a little of the wind. So it wasn't until he reached the car park and climbed up the shingle incline to turn left towards the Point that he saw the staggering rearrangement of the coastline. He leaned into the wind and stared open-mouthed for several minutes. Just a few hundred yards in front of him, the shingle ridge simply disappeared into water, and for a good half-mile or so, instead of beach, it was a raging sea. The Point, including the Watch House, was now entirely cut off: an island. The water in the harbour was higher than it had ever been, as the storm drove bigger and bigger waves towards Blakeney.

'ANNA!' he screamed into the wind. A wave crashed on to the shore to his right, sending a spray of stinging seawater into his face. He took a step forward, as if he were about to march straight into the water, but stopped. What the hell could he do now? And where was Anna? Did she make it to the Watch House, or was she drowned in the harbour somewhere?

A powerful gust forced him to his hands and knees. He had to think clearly. Had to come up with a plan. If he tried to reach the Watch House he would drown for sure. He was a good swimmer but knew from experience that being tossed about in a stormy sea can leave you exhausted within a minute. He had to assume that Anna had made it to the Watch House and was there, marooned, and, he hoped, with Harry to look after her. They had no way of contacting the outside world so it was up to Peter to organise some sort of rescue mission. But he could think of no way of getting word to the coastguard. Even if he and Joe got a vehicle going, they couldn't drive to the lifeboat station in Wells, owing to the number of cables lying across the roads. And even if they could summon a helicopter it was far too windy to attempt an air-rescue.

So, what was left? He had to think.

Peter got to his feet and, bent almost double, ran back towards the car park. He probably would have recognised Wayne's car had it not been tumbled by the storm behind the old coastguard lookout, out of view. The journey to Marsh View was much quicker now that the wind was behind him. The whole time he was racking his brain to try and think of solutions, but nothing realistic presented itself. Perhaps Joe would have an idea. Maybe the water level at low tide would actually sink enough to get the tractor across the stretch of water after all, especially if the wind dropped too. That could be their only chance.

He walked up the drive to find Joe lying on his back under the tractor. The old engineer looked up at Peter, surprised to see him back so soon, and raised his eyebrows in question.

'I can't get through. The shingle ridge has washed away. The Point's completely cut off.'

Joe whistled through his teeth, not that Peter could hear above the noise of the wind. 'What are we going to do now?'

'Maybe the tractor can get across when the tide's lower in an hour or two.'

'Sorry, old friend.' Joe crawled out from under the engine and stood to face Peter. 'She's not going anywhere. The shaft's buggered. It's a big job and we don't have the parts.'

Chapter Fifty-Seven

Harry and Anna lay on their backs on the floor of the Watch House for some time. Both were exhausted and shocked at their predicament and at the ferocity of the storm.

Eventually, Harry turned his head to look towards Anna and reached out his hand to hers. 'You okay?'

'Just about. But what the hell are we going to do now?'

Harry sat up, shakily. 'I suppose we've just got to wait out the storm. What else can we do?'

'I don't know. Maybe Dad will organise some sort of rescue. Oh, God, he's going to be so mad at me!'

'Well, whatever we do, we must get dry and warm. I don't know about you but I'm bloody freezing.'

'Me too. But there's nothing left we can burn.'

'I'm sure we can find something.' Harry stood up and disappeared into his bedroom for a while. He returned with his bird book. 'Here, rip out the pages of this and put them in the fireplace while I try and find some wood.

'But Harry – your book – are you sure?'

'Of course. I can buy another book.' He went through to the corridor leading to the stove. 'I can pull the doors off this cupboard and smash them up for start.'

As he did so, Anna opened the book to tear out a handful of pages. Written on the first page in blue ink was the message:

For Harry
Happy Christmas darling
and lots of happy birdwatching in the future
All my love
Louise xxx

Anna frowned at this. 'Oh, well, you can burn, bitch!' she said quietly to herself, tearing the page out and ripping it into tiny pieces. She scattered these on to the pile of ashes in the fireplace, which were still smouldering from the fire Harry had made earlier. The paper caught light with a pop and burnt quickly. Anna tore up further pages and added them to keep the flames going.

Harry appeared with an armful of broken pieces of wood. 'These will get it going – they're bone dry – but we need something bigger to make it last.'

Anna looked around. 'The only things left that are wooden in the house are the bedroom doors. And the table I suppose but that looks too big to break up.'

'I think the doors should be a last resort.' Harry nearly added that they might need to use them to barricade themselves in a bedroom. He heaved the table on to its edge and had a look at its underside. 'The top's too big, but I reckon I can work these legs loose: they should burn for ages.' He grabbed hold of one of the legs, now sticking out horizontally at waist height, and leaned his weight on it until it pushed down a little. He then pulled upwards and repeated the process until there was a loud crack and the joint broke apart. 'Success!' He laid the end of the leg in the fire. 'Now feed these smaller pieces from the door around it until it catches light.' Anna did this while Harry worked to free the other table legs.

Twenty minutes later they were both stripped to their underwear, huddled under a blanket, in front of a good blaze. Their boots steamed on the hearth, the rest of their clothes also dried in the heat, draped over the table top, now propped up close to the fireplace. Harry kissed Anna on the cheek. 'Warmer?'

'Yeah, much. Just fretting about my dad.'

'I don't suppose he'd see the smoke from the chimney – and know we're all right?'

'I doubt it. You can't see the Watch House from home or from the car park, and now the ridge has washed away he won't be able to get close enough. You can just about see it from Blakeney, but you wouldn't notice smoke, not in this wind. I'm not sure why he'd go there anyway.'

'Well, if the storm dies down overnight we might be able to get out of here tomorrow.'

'Tonight was going to be our posh dinner together,' Anna said sadly.

'And I was supposed to be driving back to Newmarket tomorrow.'

'I don't want you to go ...' She kissed him on the lips and ran her fingers through his hair, forgetting about the bump on his head. He winced.

'Oh, shit, sorry! I forgot.'

'That's okay.' Harry touched the lump gingerly. 'Just a bit sore still.'

Anna noticed a feather in the corner of the room. 'It's sad about Cleo isn't it?'

'Yeah. At least I assume it's her. Can't be sure, but I reckon it is.'

'What are you going to do with the body?'

Harry looked up to the door of the third bedroom where he had placed the bloodied bundle earlier. 'I guess I'll bury it outside when the storm's over.' As if to demonstrate that it had a long way to go yet, the storm rattled the door even louder than before. 'It's got to blow out soon, surely?'

'The forecast wasn't good. Dad says it's not far off a hurricane. The worst in Norfolk for – well, I don't know how long. Got to be worse than '87.'

'I was abroad then. Were you in Norfolk at the time?'

'Yes, I was still at school. We were hit pretty bad. The highest wind speed was recorded near Yarmouth I think – over a hundred knots.'

'Wow!'

'And loads of caravans all along the coast were smashed to pieces. Most of the boats at Blakeney were sunk or wrecked, and of course loads of trees were knocked down and buildings damaged. We had to have our house roof re-laid after that.'

'Anybody hurt – locally I mean?'

'Quite a few hurt and some killed, mainly by trees falling on cars, that sort of thing. Nobody we knew, though.'

'I suppose people weren't really talking about climate change at the time.'

'Not that I can remember. But they sure are now.' She cuddled closer to Harry. 'I wouldn't have let you come out here if I'd known this was coming.'

Harry kissed her on the top of the head. 'It didn't help that I didn't get your messages, or I could have got out in time. I guess I need a new battery for my phone: that one just doesn't seem to be able to hold the charge.'

'Mmm.' Anna looked pensive. Daylight was fading. 'Do you think Shuck's still out there?'

'I don't know. Did you still feel … watched, when we were out there earlier?'

Anna nodded.

'Well maybe he's trapped on the Point with us then. Can he get *trapped*? I mean can he cross water? It all sounds so ridiculous.'

'How much do you know about him already?'

'Very little really. Frank told me about him being a portent of death and described him as a huge black shaggy dog with burning eyes. But it upset Peter so much when I asked him about it, that I didn't dare mention it after that.'

'He's very touchy about it. Even more so now.'

'Because of Frank?'

Anna nodded.

'I'm not surprised.'

'So when you saw the dog on you yesterday, did you think it was Shuck, or just a dog, or what?'

'I don't know. I was barely conscious. I didn't even know if I was dreaming or not. It did feel real, but it certainly didn't look like any dog I've seen before.' Harry reached over and felt their jeans hanging from the table top. 'These are pretty well dry now, shall we put them on?'

'Okay.' Anna stood up and stepped into hers.

Harry couldn't help but admire her slim legs as she did so. He pulled his jeans on as well and turned the boots round to warm on the other side. 'What more can you tell me about Shuck?'

Anna sat back down again and pulled Harry's arm around her shoulders. 'Well, it's mainly stories about people coming across him on a deserted marsh path or somewhere and then someone they love dying soon after. There are hundreds of stories like that and that's how the legend grew. And as you've heard for yourself, it's happened to Dad and now Linda too.'

'Does your dad believe in it?'

'I don't really know. He won't talk about it.'

'When we went hunting for the dog with the men on the Point he was angry when Wayne called it a 'Shuck-hunt' – said it was just a killer-dog.'

'Yes, that sounds like Dad.'

'Have there been any other stories of Shuck actually attacking people?'

'Some, yes. The most famous one actually happened in Suffolk in the sixteenth century.'

'What happened?'

'There was a big storm, thunder and lightning, on a Sunday when all the local people were in church. Anyway, as one congregation were in a church in Blythburgh, which is a little village near Southwold, this huge black dog ran through the church killing two people, and scorching others.'

'*Scorching*?'

'Yes. That's what's led some people to think it was just a type of lightning or something – *ball* lightning they call it. Especially as the spire and bells also crashed down in the storm.'

'Jesus! But odd to mistake a big dog for lightning.'

'I know, but there are even scorch marks on the door of the church that you can see today: they say they were caused by Shuck's claws. I've seen them myself, on a school trip about twenty years ago. We did a school project on East Anglian legends, that's how I know about it'

'What do they look like: the scorch marks?'

'Just black stains on the door. But it doesn't end there. At the same time in another church – this time in Bungay – Shuck appeared again and ran through the congregation killing two more people and leaving another – and this is the bit I always remember – described as *shrivelled like a drawn purse.*'

'Oh, my God!'

'I had such nightmares about that. I could just image this burnt and shrivelled little man – lips all puckered like leather.' Anna shuddered and leaned closer into Harry.

'I can see why that gave you nightmares.' Harry pushed the burning table leg further into the flames.

'And then there was some other story about the sound of howling coming from the shrivelled man's house every night after that.'

'But that was all in Suffolk?'

'That's right. But most Shuck sightings have been along the Norfolk coast.'

'Any theories why?'

'Well, there is a story that Shuck is the ghost of a dog who belonged to a trader who sank his boat and drowned, in yet another storm. And that Shuck has been haunting the area ever since, looking for his master.'

'Hmm. Whereabouts did the boat go down?'

'Well, some say, just off the coast here, just off the Point.'

The two were silent for a while, their faces illuminated in the flickering orange of the flames as darkness slowly engulfed the house. But the thump on the third bedroom door was so loud and unexpected that both Harry and Anna leaped back in alarm.

CHAPTER FIFTY-EIGHT

'What the hell was that?' Anna hissed as she and Harry scrambled to their feet.

'No idea.' Harry picked up one of the heavy table legs and held it before him as a weapon, facing the bedroom door. 'Sounds like something's in there.'

A second thump made Anna instinctively jump behind Harry. 'What shall we do?'

'I guess I need to go in and look.'

'But it might be *him*.' Anna was whispering now, despite the continued rattling of the door in the wind. 'It might be Shuck!'

'Well, we can't just ignore it. Look, you go into my bedroom and shut yourself in. Barricade the door or something and only let me in.'

'No way! I'm not letting you out of my sight!'

Harry figured there was no point in arguing about it. He had not taken his eyes from the bedroom door, which was visibly vibrating as the storm poured through the broken window. Was that just his imagination or did he see a vague shadow through the narrow gap under the door? No, not a shadow, for night had fully fallen now and it was dark inside the room. But there was something moving inside: he could feel it. Whatever it was had to be dealt with somehow. They couldn't run away – not in the dark and the storm. He stepped forward and reached for the door handle.

Anna gripped his arm. 'Stop! Where's the torch?'

'In my bedroom – but I think it's out of juice.'

'Wait there.' She nipped into the other room and returned with Harry's Maglite. The light it produced was dim and flickering, but better than nothing. 'Any candles?'

'Nope. I used the last two last night.'

'I should have bought a torch, I'm so stupid. I never thought we'd still be here after dark.'

'We'll just have to make do. You shine the torch inside when I open the door, I need both hands to hold this.' He readied the table leg. 'Okay?'

'Ready.'

'Turn the door-handle, slowly now.'

Anna reached past Harry and gently turned it until the door clicked open. She then stepped back behind Harry and shone the torch over his shoulder. He hesitated for just a moment, his mouth dry, feeling the sweat of fear starting to accumulate. Using the end of the table leg he nudged the door open a few inches but it immediately slammed shut with a bang, causing them both to leap backwards. Was that the force of the wind slamming the door – or something inside? Something that didn't want to be disturbed.

Harry remembered Cleo's body. So the dog, Black Shuck, or whatever it was, had returned, climbed through the broken window, and was now feasting on the goose remains. Perhaps this was the perfect chance: to club it to death with the heavy oak table leg while it was occupied. Harry didn't even stop to consider whether, if it was indeed Black Shuck, phantom hounds *could* be clubbed to death. It was now or never.

'I don't like this, Harry.' Anna's voice trembled badly. 'What shall we do?'

'Turn the handle again.' It came out as a stern command.

Once more, Anna reached forward and did as she was told. This time, Harry pushed with much more force, causing the door to swing fully open and back on its hinges with a bang. They were hit with a surge of damp salty air. Anna shone the torch into the room, its weak beam wobbling as her hand shook.

'Shine in the corners,' Harry barked.

She did. But there was nothing to see but a few remaining feathers skittering across the floor.

'Under the bed.'

Again she complied, but there was nothing there.

Harry relaxed his shoulders. 'It's gone.'

'What has?'

'Cleo's body.'

'Oh, God! Of course. What could have taken it?'

'Must be the dog. Come back to finish what it started.' Harry took the Maglite from Anna, stepped over to the window and shone it through, bracing himself against the blast of air screaming through the opening. 'Can't see a thing: torch is too weak.' The Maglite flickered its last and went out. Harry shook it and switched it on and off a few times, but to no avail. 'Shit! Let's go back.'

They returned to the main room, Harry closing the bedroom door after them. 'We can't even barricade the door as it opens into the room. We'll just have to hope he doesn't come back.' He leaned the table leg against the wall. 'I guess we should leave one of these unburnt, in case we need it.'

Anna let out a sigh and put her arms around Harry's neck, holding him close and tight. 'What now?'

'I suppose we just keep warm and keep waiting.'

Anna was so spooked now that she had to keep Harry within touching distance, a hand constantly on his arm or holding the material of his fleece, seeking comfort. She couldn't imagine how he had stayed so long in the Watch House by himself. Nor could he, now.

She nuzzled his neck. 'This is a nightmare, Harry. I can't believe any of it. I just want to be home.'

'I know. Me too.' Then, without thinking what he was saying, he blurted out, 'Same thing happened to the skull.'

'Skull! What skull?'

Harry winced, wishing he hadn't mentioned it, not wanting to freak Anna out any further. But it was too late now. 'I found a skull on the beach. A seal's skull. A bone as well, actually: I put them in the same room to show Peter later, but they disappeared.'

'When?'

'Well, I found them a few days ago, then the bone went missing …' Harry calculated in his mind. And realised. '… went missing after I'd seen the girl on the beach. And then the skull went missing …' Again he had to think – he was losing track of which day was which. '… yesterday – my God, was it only yesterday? The day that she … attacked me.'

Anna shuddered. 'But why did you bring the skull into the house, why did you want to show it to Peter?'

'Because there were tooth marks on it, big ones. I thought they might help identify whatever was doing the biting.'

'Why didn't you tell me about it before?'

'I was going to when you came before, but forgot. We had so little time together.'

Harry pushing a second table leg into the flames; it now provided their only light as well as heat.

Despite the continuing storm, with the warmth from the fire, exhaustion caught up with them. After a while, Anna started to doze, cuddled in Harry's arms and wrapped in the blanket. Hypnotised by the crackling of the fire, Harry dropped his head, visions of dogs, red dresses and long black hair swirling in his mind. He had intended to stay fully awake and alert – ready if action was required – but the efforts of the last few days had taken their toll, and he fell into a fitful sleep.

Confused dreams ebbed and flowed. He saw Louise, in a red dress – *Trash's red dress* – flirting with a stranger right in front of him, throwing her head back and laughing as she saw Harry's pain, *enjoyed his pain*. They were in some dark pub or somewhere, the tall man leaning against the bar with a pint of beer in his hand. Harry tried to tell Louise it was hurting him to see her like this with someone else, tried to pull her back by the arm, but she snatched it away, went up to the other man and kissed him full on the mouth, occasionally breaking away to laugh at Harry, only to return and suck at the man's face even more lustily, pushing her body into his. Although he was dreaming, Harry could feel the pain this caused physically throughout his whole body. He felt like doubling up from the agony, but just stood, watching. It was as if his heart were being wrung like a sponge, all his love dripping out of it, wasted, her sharp red fingernails cutting into the organ. As Harry watched the couple intertwine, he could feel himself rocking from side to side. Then it became more violent, more jerky, as if someone unseen were pushing him aggressively.

The movement slewed him into a wakeful state. For a few seconds his mind had to catch up – reload the recent real-life events and ditch the painful dream. But the jerky pushing continued. It was Anna. She was convulsing somehow, her shoulders banging into Harry's ribs, legs kicking out at nothing. Yet before Harry could compute that she was having her own nightmare and he simply had to wake her up, she gasped loudly and sat up suddenly.

'What's happening?' She sounded greatly distressed. But before Harry could console her, she shouted out. 'Wet! I'm wet! What's happening?'

And that's when Harry, too, realised that the underside of his legs and backside were freezing cold despite the fire, and not just because of the cold floor, but because of the icy water they were now sitting in.

Anna was on her feet in seconds. 'Shit! Shit! We're flooding!'

Harry also stood hurriedly now that he was finally awake enough to grasp what was going on. 'Fuck! Where's it coming from?'

'Look!' Anna pointed to the door to the third bedroom where, in the flickering light from the fire, water was visibly pulsating under the door, flowing into the main room in little waves, almost as if it were being pumped in.

Harry stepped forward: for a moment he was about to open the door, but thought better of it. 'The storm must be pushing waves through the window.'

Just as he finished speaking there was a loud crash from the other side of the house, which sent Anna diving into his arms.

'Harry!' was all she could say. He could feel her body shaking.

'Damn! I think the window's gone in my bedroom now.' He

stepped towards the door, the blast of air confirming his suspicion. 'My stuff's going to get soaked.' He leaned forwards, feeling in the dark for his rucksack.

'But what broke the window?' Anna sounded desperate.

'A wave, it must have been a wave.' As if the storm were waiting to demonstrate its growing power at the perfect moment, another gigantic surge hit the north side of the house, sending cold seawater and fragments of broken glass all over Harry.

'Damn!' he cried again.

Anna pulled him back by the fleece. 'Leave the stuff, you'll get hurt.'

Suddenly the house was plunged into complete darkness as the water flowed from the two flooded bedrooms into the main room, over the hearth, and extinguished the fire with much hissing.

Anna gripped Harry's arm. 'Oh, God, Harry, I can't see a thing. Don't let go of me.'

CHAPTER FIFTY-NINE

Peter and Joe sat opposite each other at the kitchen table in Marsh View, listening to the weather forecast on the radio. Joe had been a wise and calming influence, forcing Peter to slow his panic while they came up with a plan. Without his presence, Peter was in a state to try anything – even to swim to the Watch House – such was his desperation to rescue Anna. Joe managed to convince him that as long as she was in the house with Harry then they would be safe for a little while longer. Now that they had no vehicle they simply had to come up with an alternative way of reaching them.

Sophie had come downstairs to join them for a while. She was beside herself with worry about Digger, and now Anna too, and was furious with her father for not letting her walk to Salthouse to call in at the Diggorys' house in person. She was not surprised, however, as it was dark now and the storm continued to rage, but still cross nonetheless. She stomped up stairs to her bedroom again and switched the music on: loud.

The national forecast on Radio 4 was grim: further high winds expected over much of the country overnight, possibly calming the next day. Already they were pronouncing this the worst storm since 1953, when hurricane-strength winds had caused a sea-surge, which flooded much of the Norfolk coast, drowning many people. After the forecast, Peter tuned to the local station – North Norfolk Radio – and caught the tail-end of the news, which included numerous warnings of sea-defences broken, flooding, and roads blocked by trees, cables and abandoned vehicles.

His intake of antacids had increased to a couple of tablets every hour or so. They had already discussed whether anyone else had a tractor suitable for crossing the flood to the Watch House, but even if they had, there was no way of knowing how deep the water cutting off the Point was. Even at low tide it might be deep enough to swamp a tractor engine.

Joe sucked his teeth. 'You know, Peter, the more I think of it, the more it seems the only way of reaching the Watch House is going to be by boat.'

'I agree, but no small boat is going to survive in this weather. Besides the RIB is at the house already: Harry was using it there.'

'No, I wasn't thinking of the RIB. You need something bigger if the rescue's going to happen before the storm's fully blown out. Preferably a lifeboat.'

'I know, but Wells and Sheringham are both a long walk away and the chances are the lifeboats are out already in this.'

The two fell silent for a while. Then Peter's grey expression brightened. 'What about Constance?'

'Constance?' Joe looked puzzled.

'Yes, you know, the old lifeboat that's now used by the training school.'

'But she's moored out in the harbour isn't she?'

'Usually yes, but a couple of days ago I saw her tied up at the quay.'

'Blakeney?'

'Yes!' Peter was getting excited now. 'And Mack's one of the tutors at the school, isn't he?'

'That's right, but it's a training boat: he wouldn't be allowed to take it out on a rescue.'

'Allowed! Allowed! This is an emergency, man! Lives are at stake!' Peter stood up from the table and started pacing around the kitchen.

'I know, but what if Mack's not there? What if the boat isn't serviceable? What if there's not enough water to get it out of the quay?'

'It's got to be worth a try, surely? I bet there will be enough water, the way the wind's pushing it south.'

'Okay, so how about we walk to Blakeney in the morning and see if Mack's about?'

'No! Let's go now. The sooner we go the better. I can't sleep in this state anyway.'

Joe nodded towards the window, opaque with wind-smeared rain. 'You sure you want to walk to Blakeney in this?'

'I'll bet we can do it in an hour or less. If we follow the coast road the hedge will keep some of the weather off us.'

Joe could tell that there would be no stopping him now. 'What about young Sophie?'

'She'll just have to stay here' As Peter started pulling his coat on, the lights in Marsh View flickered for a moment and then all was dark. Looking through the windows, Peter could see there were no lights on in any houses or buildings in either direction. He wasn't surprised: it was odd the power had stayed on for so long considering the number of cables down. It would be off for some time now: maybe days.

Feeling his way, he found his powerful torch in a kitchen cupboard. As he made for the stairs, he jumped back in alarm when the torch beam illuminated a ghostly figure standing motionless at the top.

'Dad, I'm scared.' It was Sophie, back in tiny-voice mode.

'Oh, love, you made me jump. Don't worry, we've just lost power, that's all. Now listen, Joe and I and going to Blakeney to see if we can get the old lifeboat out to fetch Anna.' Peter tried to make this sound a simple, everyday operation.'

'How will you get there?'

'We're walking.'

'Can I come?'

'No, love. It's dark and stormy out there.'

'Pleeeease …'

'I'm sorry, love. I need to know you're safe here. We'll be back as soon as we can. If you get too scared or have a problem go round to a neighbour's okay?'

Sophie humphed loudly 'You're just going to leave me in the dark?'

'Sorry love, but we've got to try and get Anna. Here, take this.' He handed her the torch and she disappeared into her bedroom.

Back in the kitchen, Peter found a second torch and a lightweight rucksack. 'Right, Joe, what shall we take?'

'I'll take me tools in case the boat engine needs tinkering with. Ammo for your shotgun – I assume you're taking that?'

'Definitely.' Peter pulled a number of red cartridges from the drawer and pushed them in a side pocket of the rucksack.

CHAPTER SIXTY

An hour later, Peter and Joe were only halfway to Blakeney. The hedge along the side of the coast road did indeed offer them some protection from the screaming wind, but even so it was harder going than Peter had expected. On several occasions they had to manoeuvre carefully around obstacles on the road including several trees and deserted vehicles. If it was like this all over Norfolk the clean-up operation would take weeks, if not months. Had Peter's tractor not needed serious repair, it would have been in demand to help clear the roads: dragging fallen trees and other debris out of the way. Further along, as they approached Blakeney village, they had to break through a hedge and walk along a field for a while, to avoid a large fallen ash tree which would have been impossible to climb over in the dark.

They stuck to the coast road through the village as it offered more shielding from the northerly wind, then turned right down Westgate Street towards Mack's cottage. Although it was late by now, and the majority of people would be tucked up in their beds, there was clearly no power here either: Peter and Joe's torches were the only lights to be seen. Finally they reached Mack's home, Anchor Cottage, and Joe knocked lightly on the door. As there was no response, Peter rapped a good deal harder on the ship-shaped knocker. When there was still no sign of life, Peter could feel the acid rising in his stomach. He had no contingency plan. What next? He certainly couldn't face the walk back to Cley, knowing, or at least hoping, that Anna was still out there in a tiny deserted building, ravaged by the storm.

He was just about to knock a third time when the two men saw a tiny flickering light appear through the glass panel in the door. As it approached it was clearly a candle flame, and Peter breathed a huge sigh of relief when Mack opened the door. He stood in pyjamas and dressing gown, the candle blowing out the instant the wind got to it.

He looked at the two men in confusion. 'Blimey, what are you two buggers doing out in this?'

'Let us in and we'll explain.' Peter answered bluntly.

'Of course boy, of course, get you in the warm.' Mack ushered them through to the kitchen where more candles were lit.

Peter had much to tell Mack about: Sophie and the other teenagers' experience in the pillbox and the reappearance of the massive black dog; Ewan Diggory's injury; the loss of the truck; Anna heading for the Watch House; the shingle ridge collapsing; the lack of parts to fix the tractor. Mack looked increasingly shocked as the story went on, but sucked his teeth loudly when Peter finally announced the plan to rescue Anna and Harry using Constance, the former lifeboat.

'You know we brought her to the quay a few days ago for refitting some of the interior woodwork, I'm not sure she's in a seaworthy state. Besides, there'd be hell to pay if we took her out and got into trouble – she doesn't belong to me you know.'

'I know, Mack, but this is an emergency. She was designed to save lives and that's what we need her to do now, what we need you to do, as skipper.' Peter could tell from Mack's expression that, despite his misgivings and doubts, he was already rising to the notion of being a lifesaver again.

In his youth, Mack had served in the Royal Navy, followed by many years of running his own fishing trawler before he inherited some money from a wealthy uncle. He was ready to give up the fishing by then, especially as quotas and restrictions made it increasingly hard to make a living from the game. But he kept his hand in as a lifeboatman operating from Sheringham where he and his wife had lived until they moved to Blakeney a few years ago. That was supposed to be full retirement for Mack, but he couldn't resist acting as part-time tutor on Constance when he heard the school were looking for experienced skippers.

'But I've got no crew, and it's years since I've handled a boat in seas this rough – if ever!'

'You've got me and Joe.' Peter urged him on. 'We both know what we're doing around boats and you know Joe's great with engines. Yes, the sea's rough, but the Watch House isn't far, we don't even need to leave the harbour.'

'It's a big risk.' Mack stroked his chin.

'Leaving them there is an even bigger one.'

'Hmm.'

That was all Peter needed to hear to know that Mack was truly hooked. 'I'll never forget this, mate.'

The feeling of being so desperately wanted, *needed*, to save lives, filled Mack's heart with a pride he had not felt for years. He looked at Peter's pleading face. 'When are you thinking of going, boy?'

'Now! Let's go now. She's got lights hasn't she?'

'Aye, she's got the full works. But it'll be a challenge in the dark in this weather.' He paused, but there was no going back now. There was nothing further Peter needed to say and they both knew it. 'Give me a minute and I'll explain to the wife what's going on.' He headed for the stairs. 'She won't like it.' He added, but with a grin that told Peter that he cared not a jot: he was now fully on board.

Within an hour the three men were aboard Constance, fully kitted up in yellow waterproof jackets, trousers and boots. The road along the side of the quay was knee-deep in water which had made climbing on board the lifeboat highly treacherous: it was impossible to see the edge of the quay and a step too far would have plunged them into deep water. Waves pounded against the Blakeney Hotel and other buildings along the quay-front.

The forty-two foot Constance, with her Royal National Lifeboat Institution livery of dark blue hull and orange upper decks, looked ready for the job at first sight. But before they could set off there was a good deal of work to do, for the interior of the boat was full of tools and pieces of timber that would fly around if left loose. All these had to be gathered up and stowed in cabins and lockers. There was also the problem that the engines, a pair of fifty-five horsepower Gardner diesels, were partway through a service, and Joe had to do a certain amount of re-assembling of components before they were ready.

After much grunting and dropping of torches, Joe finally gave Mack the thumbs-up to start the engines. But turning the key produced only a tiny click.

Chapter Sixty-One

Harry and Anna had taken refuge in the lookout room above the second bedroom. When they had climbed up there, feeling for the iron ladder in the dark, the water in the Watch House was already ankle-deep and rising. For the last couple of hours they had sat in the tiny empty room in the pitch-black, Anna shivering in Harry's arms. At least they were out of the wind and water for now.

In their haste they had taken nothing with them; in any case the torch no longer worked and there were no candles left. As they waited for the storm to subside, they listened to the soundscape of waves crashing against the north side of the house, spray lashing at the small window of the lookout room, and the eerie sound of water flowing around the rooms below them. They couldn't tell how much water there was, but had the uncomfortable feeling that it was gradually getting deeper all the time.

Having not spoken for many minutes, Anna reached up and touched Harry's face. 'You don't think the water's going to come up this far do you?'

'I can't see how it could; the sea-level would have to rise much more to cover the house.'

'But it sounds like it's rising all the time. I'm scared and I'm cold.' She was struggling to hold back the tears. After all they'd been through already she couldn't believe the predicament they were in now. 'I don't want to drown.' It was a simple statement, spoken with a quiet desperation.

'You're not going to.' He kissed the top of her head as she snuggled into his chest. 'I think the problem we've got is that as the waves are being pushed through the broken windows at the seaward side of the house, there's nowhere for the water to go – it's just filling the place up.'

'There's nothing we can do about that, is there?'

'Well, perhaps if I went down and …'

'No! You're not going down there!' Anna interrupted in horror at the idea.

'Wait, hear me out. I'm just suggesting that I go down and open the front door: that way any water entering from the north side can flow out to the south through the door, so the house won't keep filling and filling.'

'Please don't, Harry. Anything could happen.' She held on to his fleece tightly.

'I'll just open the door, nothing more, it'll take one minute.' He paused. 'The problem's not just the depth of the water itself – but if it rises above the level of the lower windows then we shall be in an airlock, we might run out of oxygen.'

'What about the window here?' Anna reached out blindly towards the small window in the lookout room.

'It doesn't open – it's sealed shut.'

'Couldn't we break it?'

'Yes, but then water will come in there too. And wind. We're cold enough as it is.'

Anna fell silent for a while, her stomach churning. She knew everything Harry was saying made sense. She just couldn't bear to have him out of touching distance, for anything else to go wrong.

Harry stroked her hair. 'Look the sooner I do this, the less wet I'm going to get. I'll just be one minute, okay?'

Anna sighed. 'Okay, but promise you'll keep talking to me the whole time?'

'Promise.' Harry lowered himself through the hatchway, reaching for the ladder with his feet. 'Okay, I'm going down the ladder now … my feet are in the water now … it's a bit deeper than I thought … cold too … shit, that's cold … okay, it's up to my waist but I'm now standing on the floor … feeling round the door … okay, I'm in the main room now … feeling my way round … nearly at the door … you okay, love?'

'Yes, keep calling.'

'I'm at the front door now … still waist-deep … feeling for the handle … got it … Jesus! I'm pulling but it won't open … the pressure of the water's too great … hang on … okay, I've got my feet up on the wall to pull harder … whoa!'

As he had been pulling with all his might, the biggest sea-surge yet flowed right around the house, temporarily causing the water lever to be higher outside the door than inside. At this point the door burst open towards Harry as water crashed over him into the house. It was all could do to hold on to the handle as the door swung to and fro, buffeted by the swirling water.

'Harry!' Anna screamed. 'What's happening?'

But he couldn't hear. His head was underwater.

Then as the surge receded to the south, draining towards the harbour, the level outside fell and water started pouring out of the house. As the torrent caught the door it tried to swing it shut, flinging Harry, like a rag doll, through the doorway, trapping him between the door and the frame. He cried out as his head broke surface, retching seawater from his lungs.

'Harry!' Anna screamed again, desperate.

Water flowed past and around him: the pressure of the door squeezing his chest made it difficult to talk. 'The door … stuck …'

'Hang on, I'm coming!' Anna felt along the floor of the lookout room with her hands, trying to find the hatchway.

'No!' As the water levels inside and outside the house gradually started to equalise, the pressure trapping Harry began to reduce. 'It's okay! Stay there … I'm nearly free.' He was gasping for breath.

Suddenly, as the water in the house drained out until it was only knee-deep, the door swung free, enabling Harry to push it back fully open against the wall.

By now Anna was at the foot of the ladder, also up to her knees in the freezing seawater. 'Harry! Where are you?'

'I'm here. It's okay, I've done it. Where are you?'

'I'm at the bottom of the ladder.'

'Okay.' Still panting. 'Get back up there, I'm coming to join you.'

Anna climbed back up with shaking legs. Harry waded towards the second bedroom but something made him stop and turn round to look through the now-open front door. Although the clouds were still hurtling inland, there were occasional gaps where the moon peeped through, highlighting the tops of the waves with a weird blue-white light. Blakeney in the distance was now swathed in blackness, not a light to be seen: all Harry could make out was the vague impression of endless water. It was almost as if the house had been rotated a hundred and eighty degrees, and that he was now looking out on the open ocean.

But that wasn't what had made him turn round.

'Harry. Are you coming?'

'Yeah.' He sounded distant, confused. 'Just coming.'

But he stayed, watching. It was two red lights that had caught his attention. They were fairly far off at first – over the harbour maybe – but getting closer. What could this mean? A boat maybe: a rescue boat with red navigation lights? But Harry knew enough about the rules of the sea to know that vessels at night should carry a red and green light, on port and starboard, and then one or two white ones. The red lights he was looking at now were close together, bobbing about in the water, and definitely getting closer. Harry stared, mystified, unable to tear himself away.

And then he realised why. He had seen them before. The sickening realisation of what was now heading straight for him hit home.

Chapter Sixty-Two

'Harry – what's happening – why aren't you coming?' Anna shouted, not realising that Harry was just beneath her, near the foot of the ladder.

Her words spurred him into action. He rushed forwards, splashing through the water, and pushed the front door closed again, turning the key which was still in the lock. He then waded back to the ladder and climbed hastily into the lookout room, stretching out his hands to feel for Anna.

She, too, reached out for him, feeling his sodden clothes as he sat down next to her, breathing heavily. 'God, you're soaked, Harry. What happened? It sounded like you just closed the door again.'

'I did.'

'Why?'

'We've got a new problem.' It was spoken in a stunned monotone.

'What! What now?' Anna's voice clearly expressed that she could take no more.

'We've got company.'

'Company? What do you mean?'

'Black Shuck.'

'What! Where?' She sounded increasingly frantic, gripping Harry by the fleece, unintentionally wringing seawater from it as she did so.

Harry leaned his head back momentarily on the wood-panelled wall of the room, exhausted. 'Outside. In the water. Coming this way.'

'What – swimming?'

'I guess.'

'What did you see exactly?'

Harry held his head in his hands: it was starting to throb again. 'The eyes. I just saw the eyes: two red lights, getting closer.' Just as he spoke there was a loud thump on the front door, a thump they felt as well as heard, causing Anna to shriek and pull Harry closer.

'Oh, God! He's here, he's here! What do we do?' Her voice shook.

'Shit! We've got no weapon or anything. Wait a minute: where's the staff?'

'I left it downstairs, leaning in the corner.'

'Which corner?'

'In the main room – to the right of the window.'

'I've got to go and get it. If the water hasn't washed it away.'

'No way, Harry!

'Without it we have nothing.' He pulled himself free of Anna's grasp and wearily stepped down the ladder once more.

Standing at the doorway to the main room he then heard a slow scratch on the outside of the front door. It was the same sound he had heard at night shortly after arriving at the Watch House; a slow dragging sound as if a large spike were being gradually raked across the wooden panel of the door, and with great pressure. The sound of the wind and waves outside had eerily diminished as the beast had reached the house, intensifying the effect of the gouging claws. Still knee-deep in water, Harry started wading as quietly as possible towards the far corner.

'Harry, what's happening? Come back!' Anna shouted from above.

'Shhh!' he hissed. The closer he got to the staff, the louder the claw-sounds on the door became – as soon as one drag ended, another began.

Finally he reached the corner, but his heart sank when he could feel no staff. It must have washed away after all. He felt underwater with his feet, all along the side-wall towards his bedroom, but nothing.

The scratching on the door started getting faster.

Harry stepped a pace further forward and again felt with his feet along the floor toward the front wall. And just as he reached the wall there was something against the skirting. He reached down and felt with his hands in the water. Yes! It was the staff. He pulled it up just as the clawing at the door intensified further: now more rapid, one stroke after another, two paws clearly being used – raking the wood faster and faster – frantic even.

Harry strode back into the second bedroom. 'Here take this.' He passed the staff up to Anna then quickly climbed up to join her.

Just as he grabbed hold of her shaking hand there was a loud crack, as the panelling of the front door split open.

CHAPTER SIXTY-THREE

Harry and Anna held each other tight, not daring to move a muscle or make a sound. Below, they could hear further splintering of wood as Black Shuck tore his way into the house. Then all was silent. Even the storm seemed to have suddenly subsided.

Anna pulled Harry's head close to her mouth and spoke in a barely audible whisper directly into his ear. 'Is he inside?' Her voice was almost unrecognisable: child-like and trembling.

But before Harry could answer, there came from below the sound of something wading through the water in the house – the swishing sound eerily echoing around the bare walls. It was searching the rooms, looking for them. Harry slowly moved his finger to Anna's lips, urging her not to speak again. She nodded slightly, understanding.

The splashes from below increased in both volume and intensity as if the beast were becoming angry at his inability to find his prey. Harry strained to interpret the dog's location, following its imagined progress from room to room. He was struggling to keep his breathing steady and quiet so as not to give away their hiding spot. As Shuck was no mortal dog, a million possibilities screamed through Harry's brain. Would the beast be able to smell them up there in the lookout? Would he simply *know* that they were up there? Would he able to get up there even if he did?

And then they heard the growl.

It started as a breath – a slow exhalation – then metamorphosed into the deepest throaty snarl. The noise went on and on – as if the hellhound never needed to stop to draw a lungful in – increasing in intensity all the time. Anna's shaking became more and more violent in Harry's arms. He held her as tight as he could, despite the arrows of ice shooting down his spine. The growling grew and grew until every wall in the house was shaking too: vibrating in resonance with the storm-demon's frustration.

Then, just as Harry thought the snarl was dying down, it climaxed in a deafening bark. A gut-wrenching deep outburst of anger that seemed to have the power to blow the very house apart. Anna jumped in Harry's arms at this discharge and let out the tiniest squeak, clapping her hand to her own mouth as she did so.

Then all was quiet again. Shuck was listening.

Harry was sure the dog knew where they were now. The low growling started again. The tension was so tangible that Harry thought it would be only moments before both he and Anna started screaming uncontrollably – unable to hold it in any longer. Then the game would surely be up. But next – the strangest thing – Harry gradually realised that the deep rumble was now coming from *outside* the house. From the north. It grew stronger. Could it be that the dog had moved outside to look for them? But no – as the rumble became louder and louder and developed into a roar, it was clearly not the dog at all this time.

Splashing noises that sounded as if they were coming from the main room confirmed that Black Shuck was actually still in the house, below them. But the roar continued to grow and the house started shaking.

Harry understood, too late, that the reason the wind and the waves had dramatically died down was that the Watch House had been in the eye of the storm. And now that the eye had passed over, it was bringing with it a wave mightier than ever before: a thirty-foot swell that powered into the entire north side of the house, almost demolishing the building in one explosion of power.

Just as Harry was about to shout to Anna to get her head down, the wall of water struck. All the remaining windows in the house burst inwards. Shards of glass and gallons of water powered into the lookout room, sweeping Anna and Harry towards the far end – the end where the hatchway lay gaping. The building shook, shuddered.

Anna's scream became a bubbling gurgle as water covered her head. Harry, arms flailing to try and grab her, failed to make contact. He was aware of her body disappearing through the hatchway along with huge quantities of water – pouring through into the room below – just as he managed to brace his legs against the frame of the hatch and prevent himself going the same way.

Then the rocking of the house calmed as the wave passed and continued towards the harbour.

'ANNA!' he screamed, as water continued to drain through the hatchway. He had to get down and protect her somehow; Shuck must still be in the house. Blood ran down his arms where glass had cut his shoulders and neck, but he felt nothing.

Rapidly descending the iron ladder, he found himself waist-deep in water. It would have been far worse if it were not now draining out of the huge hole Black Shuck had smashed through the front door. But where was Anna? And where was Shuck?

Harry started to wade forward, but something bumped into his legs making him jump. He reached down into the blackness. It was something large and soft, floating on the surface. It was Anna.

He quickly pulled her head out of the water, for she had been floating face down. 'Oh, Jesus! Breathe, Anna! Please, breathe!' He urgently needed to try and resuscitate her, but where could he lie her down to do this? He doubted he had the strength to carry her up the ladder back into the lookout room, and it would be especially hard in the dark.

Then something else drifted into his shin. Something hard. Holding her up with one arm he reached down with the other to find it was the camp bed that had been in the second bedroom, now drifting towards the door as water continued to drain out. In fact the level had already sunk to his knees, and as he heaved Anna's limp body on to the camp bed he was relieved to feel its legs making contact with the floor. Now she was lying on her back, her face just above the surface of the water, he pinched her nose and blew into her mouth, just as he had done with Mike only months previously. He couldn't let another loved one slip from his grasp. Not now. Her chest rose and then fell as he pulled back, but there were no signs of life. Tears of desperation, of disbelief, sprang to Harry's eyes. He tried again, but all the time aware that he was being watched, feeling a great presence in the house. A dark, evil presence that was just biding its time.

On the fifth inflation, Anna's body convulsed. She retched out a little water and took in a great gasp of air. But then the deep growl started again. And this time it was from right behind Harry.

Chapter Sixty-Four

Harry turned slowly. And there, in the middle of the main room, just feet away, the two red eyes stared at him, except this time they were as large as saucers. As he stared back, eyes locked with the beast's, the first rays of dawn lit the scene in a dim orange glow. Just enough for him to make out the shaggy outline of the huge creature.

The growl rose in volume. Anna choked and cried behind him, but as long as he could hear her at least Harry knew she was alive. What now? He had no weapon: the staff must have washed down through the lookout room hatchway along with Anna. Just as before, the growl intensified until the whole house shook, then ended with a mighty bark that caused Harry to jump backwards involuntarily.

And that's when Black Shuck attacked.

Harry instinctively held his arms up before his face. The dog leaped forwards and took one of Harry's forearms in his great jaws. It clamped down but did not shake – that would surely have torn Harry's arm from its socket. Pain barely registered, there was so much adrenaline surging through Harry's veins. As he staggered back he felt something brush against his leg – reaching down he could feel that it was the staff. He picked it up quickly and with a brutal yell rammed the end into one of the dog's eyes. It released its grip on Harry's arm and recoiled into the main room, yelping in surprise and anger. Although Harry could feel his arm was punctured in several places there was still no pain – yet. He quickly repositioned the staff so that he was holding it before him in both hands.

With the physical battering Harry had taken over the last day or two his strength was flagging badly. He stepped forward into the doorway of the bedroom so that Shuck could not get through to Anna. It was getting lighter by the moment and he could now see more detail of the infamous Black Shuck: as big as a calf with broad hunched shoulders, thick shaggy coat and fearsome-looking fangs glistening with blood. Harry's blood.

The terrible growling started again, but this time the dog flew at Harry before the sound developed into a bark. Harry was ready this time and brought the point of the staff up beneath the animal to strike it in the chest. The dog landed on the staff with all its weight and force. As Harry had wedged the other end of the staff against his foot on the floor, there was nowhere else for the staff to go other than into Shuck's chest cavity. It entered several inches, causing the dog to scream an ear-splitting hysterical wail. Harry braced his full weight against the staff and then pushed upwards against the hellhound, forcing the spike deeper. And then he was charging forward; the dog squirming and screaming on the end of the staff until it crashed into the far wall of the main room. At this point Harry slipped but managed to keep hold of the staff with both hands. By now the salty flood had drained to ankle-depth, enabling Harry to keep his face above water and see what he was doing. Shuck was directly above him, pierced through the heart by the staff, massive body convulsing as it slipped down the shaft towards Harry.

Then it all changed.

As Harry watched, exhausted and in shock, the shaggy fur of the beast, bathed in the orange light of the rising sun, became red and grew smoother. The high-pitched screaming continued; Harry was desperate to clamp his hands over his ears, sure that his eardrums would burst, but had to keep hold of the staff. Then the dog from hell seemed to grow smaller, the flailing limbs longer but thinner and the shining red eyes smaller and darker.

It was now bright red material that was swirling about as the creature writhed, long black hair tossed about, but only from the head. It was *Trash*, impaled and screeching, eyes bulging as she slipped down the staff closer and closer to Harry. The shock of seeing her figure again, which Harry now saw as the repulsive vision it was, nearly caused him to lose grip of the staff. Her mouth, with its ruby lips gaping in agony and fury, dripped blood as it approached Harry's – the Devil's final attempt to breathe death into his body. Harry desperately tried to turn his face away but his neck muscles seized. And as Trash finally made contact, his world blackened and fell away.

Chapter Sixty-Five

It had taken Joe a further twenty minutes to locate the loose connection that prevented the twin diesels from starting. Little did they realise, as the engines burst into life with a reassuring throb, that if he had taken much longer their entire rescue-mission would have been brought to a dramatic halt.

Initially, Peter had taken the sudden calming of the storm as a good omen that this was the perfect time to launch. Now that the engines were running, all the lifeboat's lights and electrics were switched on, including the bright searchlight that Peter played around the quay. It was a scene of some devastation. The majority of the other boats, which had been tied at the wharf, all smaller and less substantial than Constance, were smashed to pieces. Some floated on their sides, others had sunk with just a bow visible – taut lines still attached to the heavy stanchions along the quayside. The caravans, which normally supplied crab sandwiches and pots of cockles to tourists, had been demolished: just a few broken panels visible above the water that flooded the car park.

The three men had now donned lifejackets and harnesses as well as their full waterproof gear. Joe was sent to release the lines holding the boat to the quay – a job made far easier now that the water was eerily becalmed. Back on board, all three clipped their harnesses to the guard-rail. Peter shone the torchlight ahead to help Mack navigate through the wreckage. The water level was so much higher than usual that it was impossible to detect the edges of the creek that led out to the natural harbour. To anyone else it would have looked like the open ocean ahead, but Mack knew there was a patchwork of mud flats and sandbanks that now lay under the surface of the water. He slipped both engines into forward gear and applied just enough throttle to move the boat away from the quayside. He had to take it extremely slowly to avoid the submerged boats and the banks where he could so easily run aground. Peter thanked God that Mack was at the helm, for he knew that Mack had taken boats from Blakeney quay to the harbour hundreds of times and instinctively knew the twists and turns even though they were no longer visible.

Every now and again they would hear a grating sound as some piece of flotsam scraped the hull. But a remote roaring was initially drowned by the throb of the diesels. It was Peter who heard it first – initially thinking it was distant thunder, but then the sound continued, amplified. He signalled to Mack to reduce the engine speed so that they could hear better, and directed the searchlight to the north: the source of the sound. And then they saw it: a huge wave, as wide as they could see, heading straight for them. If it hadn't been for the four-mile long shingle spit, the wave would have been far higher – the bank and the harbour, a mile wide, robbing it of much of its energy. Even so it was still fifteen feet high as it bore down on the boat. If she had still been tied to the harbour, Constance would have been smashed for sure, but now Mack knew that the only way to tackle this was to hit it head on at full power.

'Hang on tight!' he yelled, ramming both throttles fully forward. Constance had been built to cope with heavy seas, but the wall of brown water, illuminated by the searchlight, seemed to tower over her as she motored towards it. Joe, not the slightest bit religious, made the sign of the cross on his chest. At the last moment the three men ducked low, holding the rails tightly.

There was no way the three-and-a-half thousand ton vessel was going to rise over the top of this wave – instead she punched through the middle of it like a heavy torpedo. Peter took a lungful of air and closed his mouth and eyes as the water crashed over the boat. It felt as if the they were fully submerged for too long, and for a moment he feared the weight of water had simply pushed them deep – never to resurface. He started reaching blindly for the safety line tethering him to the railing – with the thought that his only chance was to release himself and swim to the surface – when the boat burst out of the other side of the water-wall. The decks were fully awash, but the boat was designed for this and the water quickly washed away over the sides and stern. Peter and Mack simultaneously got to their feet and gasped for air, but Joe was nowhere to be seen.

Looking around frantically, Peter spotted the clip to Joe's safety line hanging taut from the starboard guard-rail. He rushed over and found Joe swinging from his line, holding on for dear life as his body banged against the hull.

'Hold on, Joe! I've got you!' Peter yelled, heaving on the line. He managed to pull Joe just high enough for him to grip the guard-rail and pull himself back on board. For a few moments he lay on his back on the deck, panting.

'You okay? You hurt?' Peter shouted.

'I'm okay,' Joe managed, then slowly pulled himself to his feet and joined Mack at the helm.

Peter took hold of the searchlight again and directed it behind them, just in time to illuminate the mighty wave striking Blakeney quay. They all watched as the hotel and other buildings along the front took the full force of the surge – many windows imploding, the spray from the impact reaching fifty feet into the air.

Their attention then turned back to the north. The Watch House was a good mile from the quay, as the crow flies, but Mack still had a few obstacles to navigate around, and as the wind was hitting them head-on, progress was slow. Despite their waterproof clothing all three men, having been fully submerged, were now drenched to the skin.

Peter looked up – he could now make out the shape of the cloud formation, heading south, and understood they had passed through the eye of the storm. Over to his right, the horizon had grown orange as the sun made its first appearance for several days. Peter's heart knotted tight as he thought about what that wave might have done to the Watch House. He knew the wall of water would have been much higher and more powerful when it had hit the shingle ridge; the chances were that the Watch House would have been completely demolished. As it was, he didn't even know for sure whether Anna had made it there, or whether Harry had still been there.

Constance had now cleared the creek and was in the open harbour, Mack able to steer directly north towards the house. It was still too far away for the searchlight to pick up, but as the sun continued to rise, Peter strained for any sign of the tiny building on the skyline. Despite the protection of the Point, the water was rough in the harbour, sending spray over the bow and salty water into his eyes. And then he saw it – bathed in an otherworldly red light – a small square shape, all alone on the horizon. From this distance it appeared to be floating on the water like a tiny ark, nothing of the Point visible above the surface.

Peter turned to Mack. 'I can see it: the Watch House!' He pointed forwards and Mack nodded enthusiastically.

Joe laid a hand on Peter's shoulder. 'Not long now.'

But what would they find when they got there? The house would be wrecked certainly. Peter didn't dare to contemplate what he would do if it were empty.

When they were within a few hundred yards of the house, Peter swung the searchlight to the west. As far as he could see, no land broke the surface – it seemed that the entire Point had been washed away. In any other situation he might have thought about the fate of the seals; they should be safe enough in the water, but would have nowhere to haul out now. Not to mention his job: how could he warden the Point if it no longer existed? But for now, his mind was focussed on his daughter.

Mack eased up on the throttles as they approached the area where the mooring post used to be. It was hard to tell the depth here and his plan was to edge the lifeboat slowly forwards until the bow hit the muddy bottom. They would then be able to go no closer in the boat.

The searchlight, shining directly on the house, showed the

window at the front to be blown out. The door was also smashed – just a few jagged pieces of wood now hanging from the frame. The acid in Peter's stomach burned, as he fought the realisation that the house must be deserted. There were certainly no signs of life: no faces at the window, eagerly awaiting rescue.

Something scraped along the underside of the hull – possibly the mooring post – and forward motion rapidly ceased as the bow ploughed into the submerged muddy edge of the harbour.

Mack reduced the power but kept the engines in forward gear. 'I'll have to stay with the boat to keep her from drifting,' he shouted to Peter and Joe. 'Lower yourselves from the bow – it shouldn't be deep there – but keep hold of the bowline.'

The wind was reducing by the minute as dawn bathed the whole scene in red. Peter and Joe unclipped their safety lines and climbed to Constance's bow. Here, Peter unfurled the bowline, throwing it out in the direction of the house. He ducked under the guard-rail and lowered himself down the rope, relieved to find that the water came up to his thighs only. Joe followed, and the two men started wading towards the Watch House, hand over hand along the line.

The water grew shallower as they struggled forward; it was clear now that the tide was pretty much level with the ground floor of the house. With luck that would mean any occupants had escaped drowning at least – if they had managed to stay in the house.

And then the sight that Peter had been longing for: a figure appeared in the doorway. He lifted his hand and was about to shout to Harry that rescue had arrived, but stopped in his tracks, open-mouthed. For the man that the searchlight illuminated was not Harry. He was much older-looking, with long straggly hair and a rough weather-beaten face. But the strangest thing of all was the clothes he wore: a leather waistcoat over a cream shirt with hanging sleeves, dark breeches to his knees, then stockings and heavy boots.

Peter turned to Joe, who had also stopped beside him. 'Who the hell is that?'

Joe shrugged. Peter had considered only that the house would be empty, or that it would be harbouring Harry and Anna. It hadn't occurred to him that anyone else would be there. And it was only then that he thought about the dog they had never found. 'The shotgun – I left it at Mack's cottage, damn it!'

The strange figure had receded into the shadows, and it was Joe, now, who walked forwards towards the doorway. Exhaustion and confusion rooted Peter to the spot for a moment but then he quickly caught up with his old friend and followed him into the building. However, as their eyes became accustomed to the dimness inside, it was not the Elizabethan-looking character they found.

Lying on the floor, in just an inch or two of water, lay a body. Kneeling next to it was a young woman, soaked to the skin, her hair falling about her shoulders. She looked up at the two yellow-clad men, her face etched with shock and weariness.

'Anna! Oh, Anna!' Peter cried, falling to his knees next to her. For a moment she looked into his face, her pained eyes seeing but not recognising.

Peter pulled his hood back. 'It's me, love. It's Dad. Everything's going to be all right now.'

Anna slowly reached her hand up and touched her father's cheek, as if afraid he might be a ghost. And then her face softened and crumpled as reality dawned. She threw herself into Peter's arms sobbing, 'Oh, Dad. Oh, Dad. Oh, Dad …'

As they held each other tight, days of tension flowed out of Peter's body. He felt drained of all energy and unable to speak. Looking sideways at the body on the floor he could see that it was Harry, his head now resting in Joe's lap.

Harry turned his head to one side and let out a cough and a groan. Joe glanced up, grinning.

'Thank God,' Peter breathed, as his daughter shook in his arms.

Chapter Sixty-Six

Ten days later, Harry and Anna were sitting opposite each other, holding hands over the kitchen table at Marsh View. Harry's bags were packed and waiting by the front door, the doctor having given him the all-clear to drive, the day before, when the stitches in his arm had been removed.

Sophie ran down the stairs and came into the room waving her phone. 'Mobiles are working again.' She opened the fridge and, grinning, took out the milk.

Anna couldn't help but notice that Sophie was struggling to contain something. 'And what are you looking so pleased about, young lady?'

'Oh, nothing.' The beaming continued as Sophie busied herself reaching for a glass.

'Come on!'

She turned to them. 'Well … I've just had a text from Digger …'

'And?'

'And he's coming out of hospital tomorrow. And he wants me to go over to their house and see him.'

'That's good news.' Anna smiled at her. 'You can go and play Florence Nightingale for a bit.'

'And all the wounded soldiers fell in love with Florence Nightingale,' Harry added, winking at her. Sophie turned away, blushing, and carried her milk upstairs.

Harry was just about to stand up and say the goodbyes he had been putting off for the last half hour when the front door opened, and Peter came in.

Anna looked up, relieved to see the expression on her father's face. 'Hi, Dad. Fancy a coffee?'

'Ooh, yes please, love.' He hung his coat over a chair and sat down next to Harry. 'Still here then, Harry?'

Harry laughed. 'Yes, still here. But leaving any minute. Besides, I wanted to say goodbye to you, too, before I went. And hear how you got on.'

'Yes, Dad, how did it go?' Anna asked.

'Pretty well, actually. Mack's new RIB is a corker – more powerful than my old one and bigger too. We went all round the Point and although most of the dunes have been washed flat there's more of it above sea-level than I was expecting – at the far end anyway.'

'Any seals?' Harry asked.

'Plenty: hauled out on the sand as if nothing had happened.'

'So, what's going to happen – to the Point I mean – now that it's cut off?'

'Well we need to have a proper meeting with the Trust, but from what we could see today, the water where the ridge was is pretty shallow, so we should be able to bulldoze a new spit into shape at low tides.'

'Dad, that's great news!' Anna passed him a steaming mug.

'And it's not the only good news I've got. On the way home I called at Linda's neighbours to see if they knew how she was, and she was there!'

'Linda was there?'

'Yes! Not quite herself yet, and on a cocktail of drugs of course, but out of hospital at least.'

'Did she recognise you?' Anna asked.

'Oh, yes. We had a good chat. She sends her love, and to you, Harry.'

'Bless her.' Harry said. 'Perhaps I'll pop in and say goodbye on my way home.' He hadn't really meant to say the word *home*, it just came out. It certainly didn't feel as if he were going home – it felt more like *leaving* home. He noticed that Anna was also looking unhappy that he had mentioned it, and decided that the time had come.

He stood up and offered Peter his hand. 'Well, Peter, there's so much to thank you for, but above all, once again, thank you for rescuing us.'

Peter shook his hand warmly, then pulled him closer and hugged him briefly. 'Don't mention it. You know you're always welcome here.'

There was much more Harry wanted to say but felt unable to. It would come, in time. He turned and headed out of the kitchen, followed by Anna. As he bent to pick up his heavy rucksack he winced at the pain in his arm.

Exactly ten days earlier, on the morning the storm finally subsided, Harry had been carried by Peter and Joe from the former-lifeboat, Constance; Mack following and supporting Anna. They had gone straight to Mack's cottage, where a large fire was lit in the living room. Mack's wife had busied herself fetching dry clothes for all five of them, making numerous hot drinks and bowls of soup. When Mack was dry and warm again he had left to fetch Doc Kelly, returning half an hour later with the tired young man who had been busy all night treating storm-victims. Under normal circumstances both Harry and Anna would have been sent to hospital; Anna had a nasty gash on her head where she had struck it on the side of the hatchway as she had been washed from the lookout room of the Watch House; Harry's main injuries had been the large puncture wounds on his left forearm where Black Shuck had grabbed him. Both had been suffering from shock and exhaustion.

The doctor had sewn up the larger of Harry's wounds, but decided Anna's gash did not warrant stitches. Both had been sedated, and soon had fallen asleep in the guest bedroom of Anchor Cottage, where Mack's wife checked on them frequently over the next twenty-four hours.

During this time, local fishermen, farmers and other folk, had set to work clearing up the storm damage. Trees and vehicles blocking roads were removed, windows boarded up, debris collected and neighbours visited. Joe had found the parts he needed to fix Peter's tractor at the local garage, and so, a further day later, Peter had been able to join the clear-up operation. His truck had been retrieved and repaired by Joe, who was now in huge demand, as were all local mechanics, such were the number of vehicles that had been swamped by the great wave. Harry's Freelander, which had been left at Morston all this time, had been carried several yards by the wave but luckily had remained upright and suffered little damage. Joe, now an expert at drying and fixing flooded engines, had quickly got it going again and returned it to Marsh View where it now stood ready in the drive.

The whole country had been ravaged by the storm, but nowhere quite as badly as North Norfolk. It took weeks for all the repairs to be finished and normal communications to be fully restored. Although it was known nationally as The Great Storm, and all agreed it to be certainly the worst since 1953, people along the Norfolk coast simply referred to it as The Big Wave.

Searches for the missing teenager, Alex, grew in size and scope as no clues to his whereabouts were found. Police were soon joined by hoards of local people keen to help the frantic parents.

Harry threw the last of his bags into the back of the Freelander, slammed the door and turned to Anna. She put her arms around his neck and buried her face in his shoulder.

Harry stroked her hair. 'I'll see you soon, okay?'

She looked up, eyes awash with tears, and nodded, her throat too tight to say anything more. One last kiss and then, unable to watch him drive away, she turned and walked back to Marsh View.

Little had been said about the strange man that Peter and Joe had glimpsed in the doorway of the Watch House on the morning of the rescue. Despite apparently being in the same room, Anna had sworn she hadn't seen anyone else there. But weeks later, as the Watch House was repaired, an ancient skeleton was found beneath the floor of the third bedroom. Archaeologists moved in temporarily and the bones were identified as a middle-aged male and dated to around the mid-sixteenth century.

Little, too, was said about the killer-dog that had attacked seals and people on the days that led up to the storm. Local people assumed the dog had drowned in The Big Wave, for no seals were savaged from that point on.

Eileen, Linda's elderly aunt, never made it back to her bungalow. After a spell in hospital, recovering from her fall, she then moved into a residential care home near Blakeney where Linda could still pay her the odd visit. Alex was never found, despite months of searching. It seemed the boy had simply vanished. Sophie and her friends regularly go back to the pillbox and lay flowers in his memory, but since that day have never used it as a meeting place.

Joe and his wife eventually discovered that their son, Wayne, had never made it to his friends in Norwich. A further week later his car was discovered, upside down and almost totally submerged in mud, in the middle of a stretch of marsh. There was no trace of Wayne himself and he was assumed to have perished in the storm; one of the number of fatalities from the North Norfolk coast.

And what of the future of Black Shuck? Of course the name *Black Shuck* was just that given by East Anglian folk to any large black dog glimpsed on a lonely country path or salt marsh. On many occasions it had indeed been Grimes's dog, as large as a calf, with burning red eyes, but not always. And now that the original hellhound was where he belonged, and finally reunited with his master, the way was open for further Shucks. In some ways the people of East Anglia need a Black Shuck. They will certainly never be without him.